18 Things

JAMIE AYRES

A Division of **Whampa, LLC**
P.O. Box 2540
Dulles, VA 20101
Tel/Fax: 800-998-2509
http://curiosityquills.com

© 2013 Jamie Ayres
http://jamieayres.com

ISBN: 978-1-62007-150-2 (ebook)
ISBN: 978-1-62007-151-9 (paperback)
ISBN: 978-1-62007-152-6 (hardcover)

Table of Contents

To all the teachers out there,
you show me every single day that there
is such a thing as immortality
because you go with us on our journeys
in our hearts and minds, touching lives forever.

This book is for you because all the thanks
in the world will never be enough.

Prologue

"The Universe is but one vast symbol of God."
—*Thomas Carlyle*

The best sight on the lake was Conner after he slid out of his shirt. I hid behind my *Seventeen* magazine, an effort to conceal my ogling. His sandy colored hair swept low over his forehead, just a gleam of sweat under his eyelids. *His lashes are obnoxiously long*, I thought, before I noticed his quizzical stare. He leaned in close to me, lips parted. The scent of his energy drink still lingered on his breath, drawing me closer. I licked my lips, dreaming of our first kiss.

He strained, like he was trying to look around me. "What smut are you reading, Olga?"

Typically, I'm not a *Seventeen* reader, but the magazine was an impulse buy at the bookstore where I worked. *Better study your enemy, since half the girls at school are in love with Conner too.*

The breeze blew around us, my hair flying in all directions. After placing the magazine on my lap, I took the hair tie off my wrist and secured my curls in a ponytail before answering. "I just flipped to this month's featured friendship quiz; it's about honesty."

He yanked the pages from between my thighs. "Okay. Number one: Tell me honestly, do you remember how we met?"

Looking upward, I took a deep breath of fresh air, thinking back through all my memories of Conner. "In kindergarten; I hid under the slide every day at recess because some boy would call me Olga Ugly. One day you stopped him. Just like magic, I found my guardian angel to protect me through harsh years of pre-adolescent angst."

I placed one hand over my heart and pretended to wipe a tear with the other.

He beat his chest. "That's me, Defender of Justice. Number two: What song reminds you of me?"

At first, I thought about answering with a quip remark; the choices were endless, and I was scared of giving away too much about how I really felt. Then, I remembered the quiz title.

"Easy. *Home* by Edward Sharpe and the Magnetic Zeroes." The song spoke of home being *wherever I'm with you*, one of Conner's favorites.

"Interesting." He looked down at the magazine, blushing.

Is my honesty making him nervous?

"Next one. Oh, this ought to be good. What do you hate about me?"

That I've been in love with you for almost a dozen years now, and you still haven't asked me out! "You date too many cheerleaders."

We both laughed until I gestured with my hand for him to continue.

"Give me a nickname and explain your reason."

I scratched my head. "Forrest. Because you run fast and act slightly retarded sometimes."

Crossing his arms over his abs, he laughed deeply. "Not bad, not bad at all. I've taught sarcasm to you so well that I think my nickname should be Master Yoda."

"I'm not calling you anything that involves Master."

Leaning forward, he delivered the last question with a devilish grin. "Have you ever wanted to tell me anything, but couldn't?"

I shoved him backward in the boat. "It does not say that!"

He flung the magazine at me. "See for yourself."

I glanced at the page. "Well, seeing this is the fifth question, I think I'll plead the fifth."

He waggled his finger. "Nuh-uh. Give me the whole truth, and nothing but the truth."

"You can't handle the truth!" I yelled in my best Jack Nicholson impression.

"Try me."

It was my idea to go sailing today. We always took our first spring sail together when the weather got warm enough. Now I curled my arms around my knees as a shiver ran through me, wishing I'd just gone home to study instead. My heart sped up to a million beats per second, telling me I so wasn't ready to finally tell Conner I was in love with him.

A smile flitted across his face as the sound of thunder rolled across the dark clouds coming in from the north, and a flash lit up the sky. "Guess you're saved by the bell. We better head back."

"Wait." I closed my eyes and felt the cool air whipping across my shoulders and neck, urging me on. "I'll tell you on prom night." That gave me one week to gather my courage. I couldn't hold back forever if I wanted next year, our senior year, to be the best ever.

"Can't wait." Conner covered his bare chest with his long-sleeved flannel, buttoning it up all the way. Studying the sky for a moment, he rubbed the wispy soul-patch on his chin and handed me an extra flannel. "It feels like another cold front moving in already."

"You're always prepared, aren't you?"

"It's the Boy Scout way of life." Conner held up three fingers.

I nodded toward the threatening clouds. "We probably only have a half-hour before the bad weather hits, don't ya think?"

Before he answered, the storm descended upon us, raining down ferociously, leaving us nowhere to hide. I searched frantically for the lifejackets, but the rain was blinding. "Conner, where are the—?"

Boom! A sharp, loud crack pierced the sky like a gunshot.

My mouth hung open. Conner gripped the stern; his hair stood on end, and a strong smell I didn't recognize entered the atmosphere. The sailboat mast made this weird crinkling noise, and a trembling hand flew to my chest, breathing heavily but silently.

"Conner!" My voice was shrill, but before I could properly warn him, lightning struck.

Literally.

Struck.

Conner.

Time moved in slow motion. His hair caught fire, and the force of the bolt sent him flying off the boat. My heart stopped, my eyes burned from the pelting rain. I didn't even notice my sobbing until I tasted the salty tears.

I couldn't see him anywhere. The realization made my heart restart, pounding faster and harder than ever.

"*Conner!*" I threw a floatation device overboard, took a deep breath, then dove into the freezing water. Once, I dove to the bottom of an almost frozen swimming pool to look for a ring I lost. The cold sucked *really* bad but didn't have anything on what I suffered through now. Cold worse than the dead of winter. Titanic cold. But I knew I had only twenty seconds to rescue him before he'd be floating face up, twenty seconds before I'd never see him again, twenty seconds before he *died*.

CPR training covered that.

I found him drifting away from the boat. Unconscious. A feeling of despair swelled in my belly. I reached under his armpits and hooked my hands together around his chest. Leaning back, I kicked toward the surface, but he bogged me down. *Kick, kick, kick,* I chanted in my head over and over while struggling to hold onto his body. Under any other circumstance, my efforts would've been futile. I'd have an easier time hauling a sack of bricks. But pure adrenaline pumped through my veins, my legs propelling me like a motorboat. With each kick, my body wavered between burning and feeling numb, but I gritted my teeth and stayed focused on my task.

His shirt buttons dug into my hands, but I didn't dare loosen my grip. The pain became distant as a part of my mind played the *what if* game: what if Conner died? What if I died? What if we both died?

The black void of the storm eclipsed my senses of time and space, but I knew the surface couldn't be much farther now. I kept my eyes on the red blur floating just above my head and gripped him tighter, reaching. In a frenzy of gasping, splashing, and screaming, I scrambled to pull him up. Draping Conner over the lifebuoy, I pushed and swam.

The wind cut steadily at my arms and face. The blue-gray froth lapped at my head, constantly covering Conner's body. My throat grew thick from trying not to cry. Tears streamed in my vision as I lost the battle, and I gripped Conner tighter around the lifebuoy. The realization this might be the last time I ever held Conner threatened to drown us both, but the task of saving him was mine alone. I would save Conner.

I had to.

Nothing but darkness stretched across the horizon as my numb limbs moved through the water toward our boat. I wasn't just fighting the current now but myself too. My arms were so stiff they wouldn't move. The lake was a black hole into which every sound, every sight, every feeling had been sucked.

Only two kicks away, I kept telling myself, until it was finally true. I reached out and placed a hand against the smooth wood of our sailboat, an anchor in this storm.

I climbed aboard, clutching the string attached to the buoy so Conner wouldn't float away. The wind howled like a pack of wolves, and I turned my back to it. I retrieved his phone out of his backpack, then punched 9-1-1. The call took three attempts, my fingers fumbling as my body rocked violently with shivers. Cold so intense I wished I was the one knocked unconscious.

Barely able to form words, I forced myself to shout to the operator over the pounding rain. My teeth chattered uncontrollably, and my hearing was muffled as though I was still underwater. I tried deciphering the woman's response over the line and dug in the backpack for my inhaler, coughing and wheezing. When I couldn't find it, I laughed deliriously, imagining the stupid headline. "Girl Survives Lightning Strike and Near Drowning but Dies From Asthma Attack."

I glanced at Conner and noticed he wasn't breathing.

At all.

I dropped the phone inside the backpack and risked flipping the boat by pulling him up. The fourteen-footer tilted and swayed and almost dumped me. Breath floated around me as I panted from exertion. My mind flashed to when Conner and I were kids, obsessed with seeing our own air in winter. We'd down hot chocolate and run outside, blowing 'smoke' out of our mouths. Now, I couldn't believe I had any warmth left in me to cause this phenomenon. One arm clung to the boat, the other to Conner as I hauled him up, falling backwards. His body collapsed on top of me. His face was chalk colored as if he was dead.

I flipped him over. His flannel shredded, I briskly rubbed my knuckles over his chest, trying to wake him as my heart pounded.

No response.

I checked for a pulse on his neck... faint but there. I opened his airway, tilted his head, and put my ear to his mouth.

No airflow.

No chest movement.

I pinched his nose and administered a rescue breath—big enough to make his chest rise. Watched his chest fall. Repeated.

His lips were blue. Each breath of my own was agony. I couldn't feel a good portion of my body as I repositioned his head and repeated. The rain stopped as suddenly as it came. The only sound was water lapping against the boat. I knew this sound would haunt me the rest of my life.

Despite my shortness of breath, I repeatedly blew into his mouth. I heard voices. Maybe I was hallucinating from lack of oxygen. I struggled again to draw in breath, but I valued his life more than mine. So I repeated. Every five seconds, like clockwork.

This is not how I imagined our lips touching for the first time. Something knocked me hard in the back of the head, and I faded away into darkness as horizon gave way to light. I didn't know if it was Heaven or our rescue.

My mother helped me into the wheelchair. The ambulance ride and my time at the hospital blurred together. Had minutes passed? Hours?

"You're going to be okay, Olga," a nurse reassured me. "We've taken care of your hypothermia, but you need an MRI and—"

Someone screamed, loud and bloodcurdling.

I glanced into the trauma room across the hall and spotted Loria on her knees. Robert fell next to her and held his arms around her shaking frame.

Conner was lying still on a table.

Too still. His body, except for his head, covered by a sheet.

"No, no, no!" I tried to stand, but the nurse restrained me, instructing me to stay calm. "But that's my best friend!" My arms flailed. "*Conner!*"

I wailed until his parents looked at me, and their sneers shocked me into silence.

Conner's death was my fault.

I should've realized he wasn't breathing sooner. I replayed the accident in my mind. Should I have called 9-1-1 first, or gotten him out of the water and started CPR right away? Was it the lightning that killed him, or did he have hypothermia like me?

The doctor in the trauma room closed the door.

Mom and Dad wrapped their arms around me.

"What happened?" I pleaded. "I don't understand."

"I'm sorry, sweetie." Dad touched a finger to my forehead and swept a piece of hair behind my ear.

I hit his hand away, and he shuffled back a step or two.

The nurse wheeled me toward a row of chairs against a wall, out of the way from other nurses and doctors rushing around the ER.

"We didn't want to tell you until we knew you'd be okay," Dad explained. "Conner was already in cardiac arrest when they brought him here. They've been working on him for the past hour, but the doctor just came out and said there's nothing more they can do. A respirator is keeping him breathing for now, but he's brain dead."

I placed a hand over my heart, checking to see if it was still beating. It was, but how could I be alive when Conner wasn't?

"You wanted to wait until you knew I'd be okay?" I echoed his words back to him, sobbing. "I'll never be okay again. Conner's my best friend!"

I buried my face in my hands, and my body rocked again. From grief this time, not cold.

"We know, honey. We know." Mom rubbed my arm, crying with me.

"You *don't* know. I wanted him to see me as more than his nerdy best friend. And it might've been working. He flirted with me on our sail earlier. I had my chance to tell him how I really feel. But I didn't. I was gonna tell him I love him at prom next week instead. How can this be happening? How can this be God's plan?"

Dad frowned and took my hands in his. I yanked my hands away, then put them on the wheels of my chair and pushed myself toward the trauma room.

"Olga!" Nicole ran through the ER's front entrance with Sean and Kyle behind her. "Thank God you're okay. We heard a news report that a seventeen-year-old was killed after being struck by lightning while sailing on Lake Michigan, so we drove to the hospital, worried it was—" She stopped short. "Is Conner okay?"

The question felt like a punch to the face and I gripped the sides of my head, squeezing my eyes shut as the tears fell.

"Oh God," Nicole whispered, pulling me into a hug.

"Jesus!" Sean shouted. "No!" Kyle screamed, his eyes bulging, looking from me to Conner's parents.

The words of our friends exploded around the room like bombs. Loria and Robert stood and staggered toward us.

But my mission was the same. "Can I go in and see him?"

Loria's breathing was uneven. She pulled a hand through her hair in the same manner Conner often did and then silently slumped into a plastic chair against the wall.

Robert tugged his horn-rimmed glasses to the edge of his nose and peered down at me.

"What—?" He broke down in tears, unable to finish his sentence.

I knew he wanted to ask what happened. But there'd be time for that later.

He nodded a slight yes before joining Loria, dropping his head on her tiny shoulder. Her face was a mixture of sadness, anger, confusion, and hatred. Hatred directed toward me, but I wheeled my chair into their son's room anyway.

Nicole tried to push me from behind.

"No." My voice was firm. "I want to go in alone."

I slowly approached the bed; the smell of disinfectant in the air made me nauseous. The sounds of the monitors weren't loud, but they were impossible to ignore. Tears formed in my eyes. A thousand conversations whirled in my head, made me dizzier. Discussions of our future, studying for and taking the SAT's, searching the web for the colleges we might attend, talking about how cool it'd be for his band to score a record deal and for me to land a scholarship. All these words seemed bittersweet now. I grabbed his hand. It was already cold to the touch even though those must've been third degree burns, and I wondered what his internal body temperature was compared to mine.

Did I kill him? Why did I pick today to go sailing? I knew the answer. I was jealous Conner asked Tammy, the head cheerleader, to prom today. I wanted to make her jealous in return by proving I could go on a 'date' with him whenever I wanted.

I stared down at his lifeless hand; a couple fingernails were missing. Maybe they were blown off by the impact, but I couldn't focus on that or I'd puke again. I stood and placed my other hand on top of the sheet, where I thought his heart would be, and closed my eyes.

"Jesus, please bring Conner back. Please, don't take him. I need him more than I need life. I refuse to accept this. You said we can ask anything in your name and it will be given. I'm asking you this now—no, begging. Please, God, please." When I opened my eyes, Conner's vacant expression stared back at me, his usual easy smile gone. I shook him, pounded on his chest. "Wake up, wake up, wake up!"

Little red dots littered his pale face. I had them, too. The nurse said they were from capillaries bursting underneath the skin. I wondered how his tan could've disappeared so quickly. His eyebrows were singed. A bald spot stretched across the top of his head, a red circle resembling a giant hickey taking the place where hair used to be. I guessed this was where the lightning struck him and remembered the flash of flames before the electricity flung him off our boat.

It was probably too late for this to be a Lazarus and Jesus situation, but I still couldn't let Conner go. I decided to bargain with God.

"Okay, can we make a trade? Him for me? This is my fault. Please, do anything to me, but don't take him. I understand if you need another soul or something, but why not me? Or maybe this is my wakeup call? I promise to do better, God. I'll only think good thoughts. I'll help the poor, the orphans, and the widows. Please forgive me, but don't punish Conner. And, please, help me to be mindful of your presence from this day forward. I beg for your presence now. Jesus, please raise Conner from the dead." I counted to thirty in my head, tears streaming down my face.

Nothing.

"Please, God! I'll become a nun after graduation or a missionary in Africa. Anything you want, God."

I whispered those last four words over and over again until Dad's hands gently squeezed my shoulders. "Other people need to say goodbye."

There was nothing left for me to do, except... I leaned down and whispered in his ear. "I love you. I've always loved you. I'll spend the rest of my life loving you. I wish I would've told you sooner. I wish I could take your place right now. I'm so sorry I couldn't save you."

"The realization this might be the last time I ever held Conner threatened to drown us both, but the task of saving him was mine alone."

Chapter One

"How we remember, and what we remember, and why we remember form the most personal map of our individuality."
—Christina Baldwin

Once I smashed my hand in the car door. The thought of returning to school today felt worse than that. I shoved my book bag into the backseat of Nicole's idling silver Honda Civic.

"Hey, Olga. How are you holding up?" she asked, hunched over her steering wheel. As her best friend, I could tell when her smile was a patent fake, plus, no amount of cucumber slices could cure the dark circles under her eyes.

I took two puffs from my asthma inhaler. "Just drive."

She snapped her fingers. "I know just what you need. Some Espresso To Go."

What I need is Conner.

We laid him to rest yesterday. I was so not ready for this, but Mom made me. Thought she knows best. I knew Mom wasn't trying to be cruel, although at times, I wouldn't put it past her. But she's the kind of person who thought in practicalities. To her, going back to school seemed like the logical next step in moving on. If she let me stay home, then we were making Conner's death even bigger, since as the probable valedictorian, I *never* missed school.

She and Dad returned to work today too, always setting the 'good' example, even though they knew Conner well and grieved with me. Going back to normal was their way of coping with things. Usually I'd agree with being practical, but I was beyond that now. Conner's death couldn't be any bigger; I was the one responsible for not saving him.

That's the biggest truth that'll ever affect my life.

Nothing will ever be important to me again.

Nic pulled up to the drive-thru coffee shop on the corner and ordered me a Snickers-flavored latte topped with whipped cream. I set the Styrofoam cup in the drink console without a sip, then flipped down the visor mirror.

My glasses making me look like a female version of Harry Potter were all smudged, and I hadn't even noticed.

Odd. Though I hadn't been aware of much this past week, aside from the gaping hole inside my chest where my heart used to be.

I cleaned the lenses on my baggy sweater, then slid my glasses over my bloodshot eyes. They were so red I could barely see the blue pupils, but I tried to pat my frizzy red curls down through the blur. I hadn't washed my hair the last three days, so I washed it three times this morning.

Just to waste my time.

I hoped I wouldn't be ready when Nic picked me up and Mom would say I could stay home after all. No such luck.

Sighing, I flipped the mirror back up and gazed out my window. Every perfect Victorian home mocked me. To everybody else, our town was the American Dream achieved. Lemonade stands and Dad-built tree houses in the backyard were standard.

At the stoplight right before the school entrance, I took a swig of coffee to stop myself from crying, thinking about how Conner would never get to build his kids—*our* kids—a tree house someday.

The light turned green and Nic whipped into the parking lot, brown liquid sloshing down the front of my black sweater.

"Olga! Oh my gosh! I'm so sorry."

I opened her glove box to find some napkins.

"No difference. Today hated me from the start. I don't know what I'm doing here. Why don't we just skip?"

Nic parked, then leaned closer. The air was thick with flowery perfume, and her long straight hair the color of mourning tickled my skin. "Listen, I know this day is gonna suck. But you're not alone. You have me, Sean, and Kyle to help you get through it. You've been my rock through so many things. Now it's my turn."

She reached out, then held my hand. My nails were a disaster, bitten down to the quick with worry. Another pair of hands slamming on glass made me jump.

Reporters shouted through my window.

"Olga, sweetie, how have you been since the accident?"

"Olga, do you have any words of encouragement for your fellow classmates today?"

"Olga, is there something you wish you would've done differently on that night?"

"Olga, what's the last thing you remember before being knocked unconscious?"

I guess they figured I'd had enough time to grieve, and now, they wanted their exclusive interview. Grand Haven was a small town, so someone dying from a lightning strike was big news... even a week later. Fortunately, our friends Sean and Kyle were already in the parking lot. I opened the door and heaved my overstuffed bag onto my shoulder, clutching my extra textbooks to my chest to conceal the coffee stain, and my friends blocked the cameras shoved in my face.

Staring straight ahead through glassy eyes, I made my way to the front entrance. I'd never been drunk, but I probably looked like I was with my wobbly, uncertain steps. In fact, my whole body shook. My mind couldn't even process what was happening. I knew today would be tough, but I never expected reporters.

None of us said a word to each other. We wouldn't have been able to hear if we tried. Nic just kept holding my hand and led the way as the parking lot became more like a frenzied mob at a boxing arena.

Once we got inside, my gaze flickered to Conner's locker, which was in the same hallway as mine. People wrote messages with markers on his actual locker. Flowers, cards, and pictures littered the floor around it. Notes were stuffed inside, pieces of paper overflowing out of the tiny slots. People shoved notes inside mine, too. Which I thought was weird because mostly everybody wrinkled their nose at me. Then again, maybe they weren't making faces. Maybe my imagination was running wild with guilt.

"Okay, I should get to my class," Nic said as I spun the dial to my tiny compartment, wishing it were bigger so I could hide inside. "You gonna be okay, or do you want me to walk you?"

The boys were in the office, telling the administrators about the reporters so they could get rid of them.

"Go ahead. I'm fine." Which couldn't be more of a lie, but I hugged her and then trudged to my first period class anyway.

Walking through halls and corridors seemed too surreal. Conner did the same thing just last week, with thousands of students who knew him or knew of him so well. Would any of them ask me how I was doing today? Would they want the low down on the accident? Or maybe they'd yell at me?

"Yeah, everyone is totally blaming that girl Olga for his death. Because like, who dies from a lightning strike? I hear she was jealous he asked another girl named Tammy to prom, so she pushed him off the boat, and he actually drowned."

My stomach tightened, and I wished I would've taken Nic up on her offer to walk me to class.

Don't cry, don't cry, don't cry.

I wasn't sure if they knew I walked behind them or not... it's probable they didn't even have a clue what I looked like. I wasn't popular.

Keep walking. You can cry later. I promise.

I made it to my first period class without a tear, but now I was rooted to a spot outside the door, unsure if I could go through with this. Hiding out in the bathroom for the next forty-five minutes sounded better. I turned, thinking that was the best plan—

"So let me get this straight." Toe-touch Tammy, AKA head cheerleader bully and prettiest girl at school, stepped in front of me.

The whole hallway seemed frozen. I had no doubt the crowd watched for Tammy's response to my presence so they could copy her appropriately—like they did with everything else.

"First, we have to tolerate you attending Conner's funeral yesterday, when it was clear you *killed* him." Her perfect posture was stiff, her stare fevered. "And now, we have to deal with you at school, too? Haven't you ever heard of homeschooling, geek? Better yet, do us all a favor and find yourself a new town to live in so we never have to see your loser face again."

Someone lightly placed their hand on my shoulder. "That's quite enough, Ms. Fitzgerald. Why don't you all get to class. Now."

Tammy dropped her gaze to the ground in front of her, then walked away.

I turned and found myself face to face with Mrs. Cleveland, my AP English and Journalism teacher. The onlookers shuffled through the hall, still staring at me and whispering to each other.

"I'm glad you came to school today, Olga. If you need anything, *anything*, you know where my room is." She squeezed my shoulder.

"Thanks, but I better get to class or I'm gonna be late." Suddenly class sounded so much better than having a heart-to-heart with a teacher, even if she was my favorite.

Unfortunately, my homeroom teacher, Mrs. Davis, kept encouraging everyone to voice their thoughts and feelings during class. She meant well, putting out some punch and cookies, wanting my return to school to be 'a positive experience.'

All of it made things ten times worse. I would've preferred a confrontation with Tammy over this. Mrs. Davis set up the desks in a semicircle, and the students took turns talking about Conner. The discussion caused me only more anger that he died, and not punching a hole in the wall took everything I had. When the bell rang, I headed straight to the office and called Dad to pick me up.

At least he couldn't say I didn't try.

Dad dropped me off at home a half-hour later and lingered for a bit.

"Don't tell Mom," he said, running a wrinkled hand through his gray hair before leaving to head back to work.

When I heard his car start, I spread the notes on my bed to read. They weren't the condolence kind of letters; they were full of the things I suspected my fellow classmates felt all week long. The boy they loved was gone, and the one they viewed as responsible still walked among them. Notes detailed the steps of treating hypothermia so I wouldn't kill anybody else, asking how a genius girl could be so dumb. Notes telling me my ashes should be spread over Lake Michigan, not Conner's, so why didn't I just kill myself?

I didn't hold hard feelings toward my anonymous writers, as their thoughts echoed mine. One note wasn't really a note at all but Conner's obituary cut from a newspaper. I never even thought to look at the newspaper headlines through all my grief during the past week.

Conner Anderson was granted his angel wings on April 1, 2012. His life would seem too short to many, and although this may be true, those who were touched by him understand the quality of existence far exceeds the quantity of time in which one lives.

His sense of humor, his kind smile, and his giving heart brought much joy to family and friends. He enjoyed music and was the lead singer of a local teen indie band titled the Cantankerous Monkey Squad. He was also captain of the Grand Haven High School competitive sailing team.

Conner is survived by his loving parents, Robert and Loria Anderson of Grand Haven, MI; sister Megan Anderson; paternal grandparents Bob and Arletta Anderson; and maternal grandparents John and Maxine Bergeron.

A memorial service will be held at the Christian Reformed Church off Lakeshore Drive at 11:00 a.m. on Monday, April 8th.

My heart beat so fast it hurt, the claws of grief threatening to rip it out of my chest. If I looked up the news reports, would they blame me? Would I discover all the threats of my classmates were warranted? I hadn't looked before, but I had to now.

OTTAWA COUNTY LIGHTNING STRIKE
TEEN KILLED, GIRL SURVIVES
[FROM THE GRAND HAVEN TRIBUNE, APRIL 2, 2012, REPORTER MELISSA TRACY]

A seventeen-year-old boy struck by lightning on Lake Michigan has died, authorities said late Tuesday night. A girl, who was also on the sailboat when the lightning struck, survived.

Ottawa County Coroner, Michael Wallen, told the Grand Haven Tribune that Conner Anderson died at the North Ottawa Community Hospital from heart failure, following injuries from the lightning strike.

Paramedic John Croley told GHT that the teens rented a sailboat around three o'clock yesterday afternoon, and Anderson was struck by lightning around eight. The strike caused him to fly off the boat and into the frigid waters of Lake Michigan. Since the teens weren't wearing life jackets, the seventeen-year-old girl, Olga Worontzoff, had to jump into the water to retrieve Anderson. After swimming back to the boat, with Anderson's body draped over a lifebuoy, she managed to dial 9-1-1 on Anderson's cell phone. That's when she apparently noticed Anderson wasn't breathing and administered CPR before being rendered unconscious when a gust of wind knocked the sailboat boom into the back of her head.

Anderson was in cardiac arrest when the Coast Guard arrived and was pronounced dead at the hospital an hour later. Worontzoff regained consciousness while being loaded into the ambulance on shore, Croley said, and was treated for a Grade 3 concussion and moderate hypothermia at the hospital before being released.

This article and others flashing on my laptop screen suggested the lightning strike wasn't the only factor contributing to Conner's death, that he didn't receive the proper care in time. Nicole and my parents had spared my feelings. I guess that's why the news crews were at school; they were trying to get my side of the story. Again, I'd agree with them. I was surprised there hadn't been a citizen's arrest for not doing more to save Conner's life.

I should be in jail right now.

No medicine existed that could help me get over losing my best friend, my soul mate. But a bottle of prescription pain meds the hospital gave me sat on my nightstand, next to a glass of water. It still had ice floating on top. Mom brought it in this morning with a cup of applesauce, a piece of peanut butter toast, and a sliced banana. I still wasn't hungry. I didn't think I would ever be hungry again.

I didn't want Mom to add anorexia to her list of worries for me, but how could I eat when I felt like puking all the time? My body shook with sobs.

Blood pounded faster than normal behind my ears, a panic attack on the horizon. My throat burned, so I sipped my water. The glass shook because my hand was unsteady, but I left the pills alone. I figured I deserved my pain and lay down.

Although I desperately felt the need to sleep more, I couldn't force my eyelids shut with the guilt of responsibility gnawing at my insides. Tears wouldn't stop, but after an hour of hearing myself weep, I couldn't stand the noise anymore. I reached for my iPod and scrolled until I found the playlist for Cantankerous Monkey Squad, then hit the arrow button seven times until the title *Haunted* displayed on the screen.

This was the most recent song he wrote before they laid down the tracks to produce their first album a few months ago. Conner's rich parents paid for the whole thing as part of his Christmas present. I cranked up the tiny speakers, drowning out my sobs, and heard Kyle tapping out the beat and Sean strumming his guitar at the beginning of the song before Conner's voice filled my ears.

"We ain't the same children who scared the other neighborhood kids/ When we made spooky sounds from the closet where he hid/ We ain't the same best friends who up on my backyard hill/ Engraved our initials on that old oak for summer thrills/ We ain't the same homies who to Detroit we'd go/ Just so my bro could hook up with some hoes/ Well, maybe I'll make my dreams come true someday/ Move to Florida and have a son that bears my name/ But in this haunted house there's danger in every direction/ I pray to God he would give me some protection/ And in this haunted house we're not the same people/ But you, my friends, are my sanctuary, my steeple/ I hope if I die young, I'll find my way back home/ So you'll feel me and know you're not alone/ In this haunted house."

Kyle went all out with his long drum solo at the end, and it felt like a metaphor for how I'd been battling my emotions. The words to Conner's song were truly haunting, like a premonition. He wrote the song in October, inspired by Halloween, even wanted me and the rest of our friends to spend the night in a real haunted house.

I'd joked with him, asking, "What—the one we created in sixth grade doesn't count?"

"Not a ghost of a chance," was his response, typical corniness.

The song told briefly about our haunted house. We didn't care if it was summer. We'd devised a plan, made invitations, and delivered them to the neighborhood kids' mailboxes. Nicole dressed up as a witch and stood in Conner's foyer, greeting children and stirring dried ice in her cauldron. She led them into the kitchen, where Conner's sister stuck the kids' hands in bowls covered with napkins. I thought she used JELL-O and put weird stuff in there, and the kids guessed what they touched. Then Kyle, dressed as a zombie, led them upstairs to where Conner and I told a scary story in the dark with the flashlights shining on our white-painted faces. Sean hid in the closet, making spooky sound effects. At the climax, I led them out of the room, screaming down the stairs. Except I tripped on the last step, and everyone tumbled on top of me. I split my lip open on the hardwood floor, and Loria took me for stitches. That was the only time I visited a hospital, until last week.

Last week... because of last week, Conner will never get to move to Florida, never have a son, and it's entirely my fault. Holding up the bottle of pain pills, I read the labels. I hadn't taken any yet. The directions said to take with a small meal because the medication may cause drowsiness or dizziness. The instructions stated I was only supposed to take one tablet a day.

Screw that, it wouldn't even make a dent in my pain.

Pushing down on the cap, I turned it counterclockwise, then dumped the tablets into my left hand. The pills were white, oval-shaped, and about two centimeters long. There were twenty or so pills in the bottle, and without thinking, I took them all.

The tablets didn't catch in my throat. In fact, they went down smoothly with my drink of water.

The word 'suicide' flashed in my mind.

No, I wasn't attempting to end my life. I just wanted to escape my pain. Although a small part of me knew I could be risking death. I should've Googled the name of the medicine first to see what the effects could be. Oh well, I'd let God decide what He wanted to do with me. If I awoke, I'd know there was a reason for me to go on.

A new kind of dizziness washed over me, much stronger than the concussion I sustained seven days ago, weighing down my muscles just as the cold waters of Lake Michigan had. But I didn't feel cool; I felt warm. Heat spread from the top of my head to the tips of my toes, sinking deep underneath my skin.

Soon the weight of my muscles disappeared, and I knew this was more than just a simple side effect. This tingling feeling took over, like being disconnected from my body, the air around me static with electricity. As I floated toward the ceiling, my bed seemed like a distant mile.

Closing my eyes, I let the sensation carry me away from the pain and guilt, heading toward numbness instead.

Now I lay me down to sleep, I pray the Lord my soul to keep. And if I die before I wake, I pray the Lord my soul to take.

"The boy they loved was gone, and the one they viewed as responsible still walked among them."

Chapter Two

"If you're going through hell, keep going."
—Winston Churchill

N ic leaned over the cash register, flipping through a 'Sexy Styles of Summer' article in *Cosmo Girl* magazine. The bookstore where we worked—that her parents owned—was super slow today. "I can't believe I got this huge frickin' pimple on my chest this morning when we're supposed to be beaching it in two days."

Yesterday was the last day of school, and Monday is the annual Memorial Day picnic at Grand Haven State Park. Not that it meant anything to me. When Mom and Dad found the empty pill bottle and hate letters, they agreed to let me homeschool the rest of the year. The only catch was I had to do my schoolwork at the marina clubhouse where they worked, so they could keep an eye on me, and I had to start grief counseling. I promised never to take another pill. I didn't know what I was thinking—well, clearly I wasn't.

I sighed loudly. *Lord, help me see past my feelings. I pray for your grace to mold me into the person you want me to be. Help me find the courage within to forgive myself, to face the ghost in the mirror. Please take away this relentless darkness, and help me find the light of your peace again. Amen.*

Nicole continued her diatribe about the upcoming summer, and I half-listened while washing the store windows with listless effort. They were spotless anyway. I kept my hands busy all the time now. Mom's mantra about idle hands being the devil's workshop made so much more sense to me as of late.

Fingers snapped loudly. "Hello? Are you listening?"

I walked to the counter, then set the Windex and roll of paper towels down. "Um. No. Sorry."

Nicole rolled her eyes and held out the magazine. "It's okay. I'm used to it. What do you think of this bathing suit? I'm thinking of ordering it off this website."

I reached for my glasses from atop my head but realized I didn't need them.

Weird. The print describing the suit was really tiny. *I'll have to Google if vision can improve on its own.* "I think it's cute. You should get it."

"I think I will. So it's almost time for lunch break. How about we go throw eggs at the guy in the chicken costume dancing like a freak outside Chicken King?"

Staring at her, I asked, "Am I missing something?"

"These days? Usually."

I threw my wet paper towel at her over the counter, and she laughed. I giggled with her for a few seconds before remembering I didn't joke anymore.

"Sean got hired there and starts today. He has to stand on the street corner, waving a sign about the daily specials."

I hadn't seen Sean or Kyle since the last day I attended school. Hanging out with them would make me think about Conner even more, and that just plain hurt too much. "Sounds finger lickin' good, but I actually need to head over to the hospital for my counseling session."

With a down-turned mouth, she asked, "On a Saturday?"

"Yeah. I missed Tuesday's appointment because I was studying for finals, so Dr. Judy rescheduled."

She stepped around the counter, purse in hand. "See you when you get back then."

By the time I reached Dr. Judy's office on the third floor, I was five minutes late. The secretary informed me Dr. Judy was on an emergency phone session with another patient, then asked if I'd mind waiting for ten minutes.

I agreed, then plopped down in the waiting room and noticed a guy staring at me. I stared back. He was cute if you liked Zac Efron look-alikes, and okay, I did. Clutching my purse tightly in my lap, I marveled at even noticing another guy. I'd been in a fog for the past eight weeks; I knew that at least. My grief-stricken, guilty self was my new normal. The ordinary world seemed foreign to me now. I didn't know how to live there without Conner. So, the fact that this attractive guy gazed at me really penetrated me to the core, as if someone unexpectedly threw a bucket of cold water on my face and woke me up.

He had perfect posture: shoulders back, straight neck, muscular arms rigid at his side. As if to challenge me to a staring contest, he leaned forward, but then he extended a hand and smiled. "I'm Nate Barca."

"Olga," I said, shaking his hand, which felt cold and clammy like a dead person, but my cheeks still burned with mortification. Since Conner was my soul mate, I never expected to find someone else so... hot. I wanted to undo my ponytail to hide my shame, but if I did, it'd look like I was flirting with him.

Tossing his hair back, which I affectionately noted was the color of coffee, he laughed. "Olga-who-doesn't-have-a-last-name?"

I cringed like always. My parents dubbed me Olga to honor my grandmother. I couldn't go by my middle name—it was more horrible— Gay, in honor of my other grandma, and, to top it all off, the Russian last name proved hard to pronounce or spell. "Worontzoff."

Air escaped his lips like a leaky tire. "Quite the name for a pretty seventeen-year-old to have."

I nodded. "It's after my grandmother. How'd you know I was seventeen?"

Wait—did he just call me pretty?

"I guessed. I'm seventeen, new in town." His voice was loud, conveying authority. "Just moved here last week, which sucks. And before you ask, because everyone always wants to ask these things but doesn't want to pry," he said the last word in air quotes and rolled his eyes. "I'm in therapy because I drag-raced my way home on the last day of school and ended up flipping my car and flying through the windshield. I wasn't wearing my seatbelt. My parents figured I had a death wish and needed some counseling. Actually, the court demanded the therapy."

I couldn't believe he told me all this so casually, and I wondered if he was this honest with everyone right off the bat.

"You're lucky to be alive." From what I could tell, there wasn't a scratch on him.

Adopting a pondering pose, elbow on knee, hand clasping his chin like *The Thinker* statue, he said, "Am I?"

I shrugged. "I guess. At least that's what they tell me."

He stretched his legs in front of him, then placed one ankle on top of the other. "Yeah, it's weird because there was this moment where I thought for sure I was dead. I was lying on the ground, covered in glass and blood, and then I felt like I was floating and staring down at myself. Before I could look around for the other kid, I blacked out. When I woke up, I was home. I don't even remember the hospital."

I shifted in my chair. The similarity of our situations made me uncomfortable. Two accidents, the feeling of responsibility I was positive we shared, the floating above our bodies, even though that didn't happen for me until the pills. I wasn't ready to tell him about the pills, though. "Did the other kid make it?"

He uncrossed his ankle and put the other foot on top. "My parents told me he was doing better but wouldn't even let me see him. I wrote a letter to apologize and mailed it the next day, then went to court. The judge revoked my license for a year, and I was sentenced to therapy." He smirked and twirled his finger in the air in mock fashion. "That's why I'm here so early for my appointment. I'm at the mercy of my parents' schedule to drop me off at places. So, what are you in for?"

Did I like this guy? He was confident and weird and cute and I dunno. But I realized I'd been at ease from the moment I saw him. "Conner, my best friend"—*and secret crush*—"since I was five, was killed by a lightning strike while we were sailing last month, and I feel responsible. I wasn't able to save him."

Nate's eyes were the color of the ocean, and he narrowed them at me as his eyebrows drew together. "You shouldn't blame yourself."

"That's what everyone tells me. But it's easy for you to say. Your guy lived. Mine died."

He stood, and I noted he was about average height, maybe five-foot-ten, then sat in the chair next to me. Nate shifted so we were face to face. "I'm really sorry to hear about your friend. And I'm sorry if I'm scaring you with all the heavy. I ramble a lot. My mom says I suffer from verbal diarrhea, among other things."

I looked at my hands in my lap, took a deep breath, and counted to ten, trying to decide if I wanted to laugh or cry. Instead, I just muttered, "Thanks, and it's okay."

"So, is this lady any good?" He nodded toward Dr. Judy's office.

I shrugged. "I dunno. I mean, I always thought talk was cheap. But maybe…"

He smiled, leaning a little closer. "Yeah, I've always been an action kind of guy. Some might call me an adrenaline junkie."

Dr. Judy swung open her door. "Olga, I'm ready for you now."

Looking over at Nate, I held out my hand this time. "It was nice to meet you."

"Same here."

Dr. Judy waved to Nate before inviting me in. Her wavy, butterscotch colored hair fell over her tiny shoulders, making her look angelic. "Did you bring your journal?"

I started my weekly grief counseling sessions with Dr. Judy the day after my pill episode. That's what I called it in my head, 'the pill episode,' not 'suicide attempt.' I still didn't think I was suicidal, no matter what everyone else said. Swallowing all those pills was a terrible mistake. The only thought I had at the time was *I'm tired*, tired of hurting, tired of guilt, tired of sadness, tired of pain, tired, tired, tired.

During our first session, Dr. Judy tried to get to know me by asking about my interests. Sailing definitely wasn't making My Favorite Hobbies list anymore, so I shrugged and mentioned writing. She suggested I keep a journal. Last week, she asked if I would bring in my journal and read a page aloud. Mostly the pages were filled with stories of Conner, so I wouldn't forget, but today, I read the one about my reoccurring dream where faceless Conner haunted me.

I'm alone, running home from the hospital in the dark. A black-hooded, faceless figure follows me. I sprint into Conner's massive Victorian house, locking the door quickly, then hurry down the stairs to his basement bedroom. There's a chair by the sliding glass door, with its back to me, rocking slowly. In the window, I notice a girl's reflection holding something, but I can't make out what.

I curiously approach the chair, then peer over the girl's shoulder. I spot the most beautiful baby I've ever seen, dressed in a white christening gown. I walk around the chair, to see who the mother is, and jerk back when I see myself. The only exception being I am faceless, just like the hooded figure chasing me moments before. Startled, I draw in a

29

breath. I turn to the sliding glass door, ready to run again, but it opens before I reach it. The hooded figure floats in, lifts his finger and points at me. "You were supposed to save me." It's Conner's voice.

Dr. Judy remained quiet for a moment. I was thankful for the secretary's reception area buffering Dr. Judy's office from the waiting room. Otherwise, I'd be a little paranoid Nate could overhear my whole psychosis.

Sweat beaded on my forehead, the papers shaking in my hands as I waited for her response.

"Well, the dream actually makes a lot of sense, doesn't it? I mean, Conner is wearing black, representing death. You're faceless, like his ghost, because you don't view yourself as having a future anymore. You feel dead spiritually and emotionally speaking. Not only did you suddenly lose your best friend, whom you love, but also the many dreams you had for your future, like maybe even having a child together some day. Am I right?"

I wondered how she became so wise. I was book smart but not wise. Of course she was right, but saying so would've hurt too much. My gaze flickered to the framed picture of Grand Haven Pier hanging behind her desk.

Dr. Judy turned, admired the photo for a moment. "Have you visited his gravesite yet?"

"He was cremated." My voice came out subdued, trancelike. I could force myself into a trance whenever I wanted, so I didn't have to feel things. The outside world disappeared around me, like staring into one of those 3D pictures for a really long time. "They scattered his ashes on Lake Michigan."

Why, why would they do that? No, don't think, don't feel.

Though thin and delicate, Dr. Judy stared hard at me now. "That's what I mean. I think it could be cathartic for you to take a boat ride again. Send up some balloons, or leave a message in a bottle. It's time to face your fears and release this guilt you're holding onto."

My heartbeat thundered in my ears. "I don't think I'll ever forgive myself, no matter how many balloons I release."

"A person with no forgiveness in their heart for the things they've done is doing nobody any favors. It's a punishment worse than death, worse than Hell. Is condemning yourself really what you want? What Conner would want?" She reached across her desk and grabbed a piece of pretty stationary and a fancy pen. "For you."

"For me? For what?" I asked, rearranging my position on the chair so I sat cross-legged.

Her mouth curved into a knowing smile. "Grief never ends."

Duh! Anyone who looked at my face could make that assessment. Some days my grief only hurt a little, like being electrocuted by a tiny spark when plugging in something. Other days, my sorrow used a jackhammer to excavate my heart.

"Are you listening to me, Olga?" She leaned across the desk toward me. "You won't ever forget Conner's death. But you can learn how to live with the loss, make the pain manageable enough to overcome it. Maybe you're not ready to let go of your guilt yet, but you could write it down as part of a bucket list."

I grimaced. "Bucket list, like the movie with Jack Nicholson?"

She nodded curtly.

"Sorry, but I don't think trekking around Nepal will help me any."

She waved away my words. "Life lists aren't just for older people. And it can be full of anything you want. Starting to make some new goals for yourself is a way you can honor Conner, living life to the fullest. It can be stuff you want to do, or things he wanted to do. Either way you'll be taking positive steps to move on."

I didn't know if I wanted to give in—*after all, she can't make me, can she?*—so I stood, wandered to her open window, arms hugging myself for what felt like a long time. "How long does this list need to be?"

"The length is up to you," she answered, her voice barely a whisper.

Dr. Judy lived for crisis management, but I admired how this strong woman kept her voice soft and controlled, especially when I felt like a ticking bomb all the time.

"I'd rather you decide. You're the expert."

While I waited for her answer, I kept my back to her. The air was thick with the smell of air freshener, lavender to calm the senses. If only serenity came so easily.

"How about eighteen?"

I leaned against the side of the windowsill. "Why eighteen?"

People walked the streets, enjoying the start of summer. People who were eating ice cream, walking their dogs, window shopping, bike riding, skate boarding. I didn't envy them, and none of them should've pitied me. I deserved this pain.

Metal grating against tile caused me to turn. "Well, you'll turn eighteen this year, correct?"

I nodded, even though I couldn't imagine celebrating.

"You could title your list, '18 Things'. Eighteen things to do the year you turn eighteen, a journey to remind yourself to stay positive as your soul is on its way to wholeness again. I want you to carefully think of each task, visualize yourself completing it, and then do it. By the time you finish, it'll be time for you to leave this place, hopefully with some closure, and ready to begin the next chapter in your… life."

Moving on should've sounded comforting, but her words didn't console. And why had she paused before that last word, like she wasn't confident I could do it? "You said hopefully. What if it doesn't work?"

Actually, that wasn't the scary part. Not the question, 'what if nothing ever works to fill this giant void left inside me?' The scary part was not having my pain, because then I'd have nothing.

Shaking my head, I reached in my pocket for my asthma inhaler but came up empty. I didn't have it. In fact, I hadn't needed it since the day after Conner's funeral, which was weird since I'd never been so panicked.

Judy's eyes widened. "Let's not focus on what ifs. One day at a time. See where that takes us, okay?" She stood and handed me my piece of paper and pen. "And one more thing: I think we're ready to cut down your weekly counseling sessions to twice a month. Does that sound all right to you?"

"Yes." I moved toward the door, but glanced backwards at the painting of Grand Haven Pier, unsure.

As I exited her office, she told Nate he could come in.

Now I was sad for another reason. I didn't want him to feel as alone as I had these past two months. Plus, if I was being honest, I was drawn to him in a way I couldn't understand, but I wanted to.

"Um, Nate, I'm going to the beach with some of my friends on Monday around noon for a picnic. You're welcome to meet us by the Grand Haven Pier and hang out."

He smiled and nodded, and I couldn't help but notice Dr. Judy did the same thing.

"I'll see you there," he said.

Focus Question:

Describe the way Olga feels like an outsider at school and at home.

Chapter Three

*"The only rules that matter are these:
what a man can do and what a man can't do."
—Captain Jack Sparrow*

Sucking in deep, calming breaths as I left Dr. Judy's office, I searched for a bathroom to have my nervous breakdown in private, and of course, I couldn't find one anywhere. I knew there was one in the ER lobby through the double doors up ahead, but there was not a chance in Hell I was going there. Too many haunting memories. Loria on her knees, Robert holding his arms around her shaking frame. Conner lying still on a table. I shook my head, trying to shake my thoughts away. Grief had become my smug companion. Maybe rushing into the ER and screaming at the walls would prove therapeutic. *Are you happy with yourself? Do you know what you've done? You took a seventeen-year-old kid away from his parents, from his friends, from a girl who loved him more than life itself!* Instead, I altered my course and backtracked. When I bore right, I spotted two nurses talking animatedly while Toe-touch Tammy stepped out of the elevator.

What is she doing here? Panicking again, I slinked into a supply room.

"What happened?" asked Tammy, her muffled voice filtering through the door.

With my ear pressed against the cold metal, I listened as a nurse explained. "Your father suddenly vomited up blood after drinking several beers at the bar up the street. The owner called for an ambulance right away, and the paramedics brought your dad to the ER. He had internal bleeding, part of liver failure. The blood vessels in his gut burst. Our liver specialist stopped the bleeding, using an endoscope—a flexible tube with a tv camera at the end. Then the doctor used a balloon to press on the vessels."

The elevator doors dinged, and I heard Tammy speak in an exasperated voice. "Thank you so much for coming."

The sound of heavy sobs followed, and my eyes glistened with sudden tears for my archenemy.

"I'm the Fitzgerald's neighbor," said a woman with a quavering voice, whom I assumed must have stepped out of the elevator since I heard the doors ding. "Tammy called me on her way over. What happened?"

"Alcoholic hepatitis," the nurse announced. "I've just finished telling her about it. We're treating him with a blood transfusion now, but he'll need to stay with us for the next three weeks to recover. Tammy, how much does your father drink in a typical day?"

"Six to eight beers." She sniffled.

"That'll do it," stated the nurse. "And how long has this gone on?"

"Since the day I was born," Tammy responded in a weepy voice. "I'm his only child. Mom died during childbirth, and he took up drinking afterward to deal with the grief."

Staggering backwards, I drew a hand to my heart and remembered the afternoon Conner died.

The school parking lot was nearly deserted while I waited for him by his Hybrid. My gaze flitted in search of Conner and then to the *Lord of the Flies* book I was reading for English class, never able to focus on either task for long. One of the vehicles, a Lexus, belonged to Toe-touch Tammy. As if summoned, she paraded like a peacock around the side of the building, with two other cheerleaders. I debated fleeing for a second, but then...

"Hey, Olga!" Tammy put out her cigarette on the asphalt and blew smoke in my face.

I coughed but managed to fight off potential asthma attack number two for the day. Waving a geekazoid prop like an inhaler in front of Tammy would be worse than pulling Star Wars figurines out of my pocket and playing with them.

"So, um, like, how was your day?" Tammy asked, as if she cared. Lately, she kept messing with me, as if making me miserable was high on her priority list.

I had no idea why, because honestly, I wasn't that important.

"You look so cute waiting here for Conner, like a lost puppy." One of her cronies scoffed. Oh yeah, there was her reason. She was in love with Conner, too. Half of the school loved him.

"I don't really speak cheerleader, but let me see if I can put this in terms you'll understand. O-M-G, my day was like *sooo* totally fabulous, girlfriend! Eww, I think I just broke a nail! Gotta go!"

As I bolted past her, figuring I'd head inside to search for Conner, she snagged my sweater and jerked me backwards. "Listen, go ahead and have your mercy sailing date with Conner—"

I shoved her hand away and wondered how she even knew he and I were sailing. "I don't need your permission."

My cheeks burned, but there was no way I was letting Tammy get to me.

She held up her palm in a talk-to-the-hand way. "I'm still the one he's taking to prom."

She flicked my hair, and I had a sudden urge to hurl my textbooks at her.

"In one week, I'll make *all* his dreams come true and beat you like the redheaded ugly stepchild you are."

A million insults flashed through my mind. Somehow, one of Mom's annoying life lessons popped into my head, telling me to be the better person, and I tried responding appropriately.

"Yeah, I get it. You're prettier than I am," I said. And she was, with her model tan legs, blonde hair with a cute inverted bob, blue eyes, and a chest too big to be natural. I was short, five-foot-two to be exact, with unruly long hair, fair skin with freckles dotting my nose and cheeks, glasses, and boobs that definitely couldn't match her Victoria Secret double D size. "Now that I've admitted it, why don't you get over yourself and get a life instead of messing with mine?"

She threw her head back in mock laughter. "Is that the best you got? Oh, I *really* don't have anything to worry about. You're ugly, poor, *and* pathetic."

My mind snapped back to the present, and I heard the nurse tell Tammy she could see her father now.

"Just beware. He won't look good. His skin and eyes are a bright yellow, and his stomach is very swollen from the fluid. We'll drain some of the fluid during the next three weeks, but the rest will need to drain on its own through alcohol abstinence. He'll need you to be strong for him. It's a lot to ask of someone your age."

"There's nobody else. So, if you'll excuse me." The roughness was back in her voice, and I heard her high heels click past me and down the hall.

"Sure is a beautiful girl." From the sound of the soothing tone, I think it was the nurse who commented.

"Yes," agreed the elderly neighbor. "She models to help pay the bills. She's quite successful though, even won a Lexus through some modeling contest."

My stomach slammed down to my feet, and I felt lightheaded as I tried to process all this new information about Toe-touch Tammy. *She models to pay the bills? She's not rich? Her dad is an alcoholic? She lost her mom and feels responsible for her death?*

Maybe it was possible—even probable—we had more in common than anyone else I knew.

I yelped as the doorknob turned and the nurse's face showed she was equally surprised to see me.

"Um… I'm looking for the bathroom?"

She squinted, seeming unconvinced, then pointed. "One door down."

Of course. Forcing a small smile, I muttered "thanks" and rushed into the stall.

I didn't walk back to The Bookman afterward. Instead, I took an extended lunch break. I didn't want to stay indoors. I didn't even want to stay in my skin, but I didn't have a choice about that. So I headed to the hospital cafeteria for some coffee and then sat outside in the courtyard. I sent a text to Nic so she wouldn't worry when I didn't return for a couple of hours, maybe even for the rest of my work shift. I just needed some time to think, about eighteen things apparently.

Thank you, Dr. Judy.

The air was the stuffy kind of humid, and I should've ordered something cold. Still, it seemed fitting for the temperature to match my personal Hell.

Was it too early to call it a day? Truthfully, I just wanted to go home and sleep. I wondered if the saying 'time heals all wounds' still worked its magic if I slept through all my days. I didn't feel like staying outdoors anymore, of hearing birds chirp and viewing the cloudless sky. But getting up seemed like too much work.

"Got a match?" Tammy's voice came from behind a pair of tall shrubs and startled me.

Breathing in slow and even, I barely shook my head.

She walked around to face me, pulled a matchbook from the pocket of her jeans, lit a cigarette then puffed smoke in my face.

"If you already had a match, why'd you ask me for one?"

She mimicked my smug tone. "I thought it'd be more ironic if I lit you on fire with your own match."

I did what I should've done the day Conner died: ignored her. I pushed past her to go inside, but she stepped ahead of me and blocked the door.

"What are you doing here? Punishing yourself for killing my prom date?"

Shaking violently, I took a series of quick, short breaths. She was only going to prom with Conner because she'd tricked him. I was about to tell her I knew about her scheming ways. Then I reminded myself of the conversation I overheard in the hallway earlier. "I'm sorry to hear about your dad. I hope he'll be okay."

Pursing her perfect lips, she asked, "How'd you hear about Daddy?"

I offered a sad smile. "News travels fast in a small town."

Flicking her cigarette in the air, the wind carried her ashes across the landscape. "Quit trying to change the subject. I don't hear any denials. I want to hear you say you're sorry for killing my prom date."

Usually I'd just agree and slink away, but a fire built inside me now. "I hope your plan for Kyle to take me to prom was worth it. I would've never asked Conner to go sailing that day if I hadn't been jealous."

Okay, I couldn't believe I just admitted that. Plus, my assessment was kind of unfair. Conner and I always took a first spring sail together, but asking him was a spur of the moment plan, one I thought up after he and Tammy agreed to attend prom together. Tammy's trick was this: she wanted Conner for herself. In the hallway before first period, she'd made sure I overheard her gossiping about him asking her to prom. That was a total lie, but I didn't know that at the time. Then, in the cafeteria when Conner was a captive audience, Tammy encouraged my friend Kyle to ask me to prom. I only said yes because I thought Conner was going with Tammy. She'd made her move then, practically throwing herself at Conner, and he asked her to be his date. The smirk on her face afterward still made me want to punch her.

I shook my head at the memory, angry I never got the chance to tell him the truth. "So, now you're actually responsible for your mom's death, possibly your dad's, and Conner's too." I regretted the words even as they flew out of my mouth, but like a lightning strike, I couldn't stop. "I'm sorry. I didn't mean…"

A ridiculous, loaded pause followed after my words failed me. I could tell she was trying to figure out how I knew about her mother and her Kyle scheme. She must have decided she didn't care how I knew, and she slapped me hard across the face.

I grimaced and stifled a sob. "I deserved—"

"Yes. You did." Tammy cut me off, cold as ice, then out of nowhere, she dropped to her knees and sobbed.

I didn't know what to do, so I joined her. We were both in hysterics, crying for what felt like hours, eventually handing each other fresh tissues from our purses and hugging.

The first rain of summer splashed across the grass. I hadn't been caught in the rain, let alone looked at it, since the night Conner died. But just to show me everything was gonna be all right, the drops mixed with the sunshine to create a rainbow.

"What does this mean?" Tammy asked, looking at the sky.

I held out my hands. Tammy had been so awful to me since the start of this year, but the truth 'nobody's perfect' hit me. I realized what she needed was a true friend. It was what everyone needed, and I sure could've used more of those myself.

"I think it means this is the beginning of a beautiful friendship."

Focus Question:

What significance does the flashback in this chapter have in the story?

Chapter Four

"It's not the years in your life that count.
It's the life in your years."
—Abe Lincoln

ammy and I brought up the rear, carrying a cooler full of waters, sodas, and a huge watermelon. We were almost to our picnic area at Grand Haven State Park for our annual Memorial Day outing. It's something Conner, Kyle, Sean, Nicole, and I started with our parents three years ago and continued by ourselves now. I invited Tammy before I left the hospital on Saturday, but my mouth went dry as we set the cooler down, gearing up for a nervous breakdown. Not only was I here without Conner, but I was at the beach near the very water where he died, where his ashes were now scattered

Tammy suspiciously eyeballed me. "Did you know they gave my dad a pair of Crocs at the hospital so he'd have something to easily shuffle in and out of?"

I turned slowly to study the expressions of my friends, wondering if I was missing something.

"Right," Nicole responded with slow delivery. She plopped down on the blanket and opened a soda. "I think all the toxic chemicals in your cigarettes are impairing your brain function."

Nobody was more surprised than Nicole when I'd informed her I invited Tammy.

Tammy laughed. "All I'm saying is if Crocs, the world's ugliest shoes, can be so popular, then anything is possible." She opened the cooler, took out two water bottles, then handed me one. "You can do this. STAR."

STAR was a copping mechanism Dr. Judy gave me. I told Tammy about it when we'd chatted on the phone yesterday. The acronym stood for: Stop. Take A Rest. When something seemed overwhelming for me, I was supposed to take deep breaths and go to my happy place. My happy place used to be here. Now, I took a deep cleansing breath and thought of riding up Five Mile Hill, my favorite bike trail in town.

"Thanks. I *can* do this." I said this more for myself than her.

"Of course you can. Never doubt my mad skills. I've been through enough therapy over the years for all of us. Now, if you'll excuse me, it's hotter than a mother out here."

Tammy stretched her arms overhead, pulling off her cover-up. She sported a leopard print halter-top bikini, which barely covered her massive boobs. She raced toward the lake, then splashed Kyle, who was already in the water. Tammy's boobs were like a train wreck; I couldn't take my eyes off them.

Kyle stared at her chest; even from where I sat, I noticed his eyes were wide, nearly the size of walnuts.

I wondered if at some point Tammy used a portion of her modeling money for breast implants. Either way, this beach moment kicked my self-esteem down a few notches—to below zero. I wished she left on her cover-up.

That's an odd thought.

Kyle splashed her back. With his blond hair and blue eyes, I noted he would actually make a very cute boyfriend for Tammy. They were even the same height.

Still studying her, I couldn't help but try to adjust the top part of my red lifeguard style one-piece suit.

Oh, but what do I care if Conner's not here anyway?

Then I spotted Nate walking toward us in baggy swim trunks, carrying a white boogie board. If his golden tan and defined biceps weren't enough to make me drool yesterday, this shirtless vision before us also sported six-pack abs that could've made any guy on the beach jealous. I waved to make sure he knew it was me, and because I was incapable of tearing my gaze away from him.

"Wow. Is he the guy you met at the hospital yesterday?"

I nodded. I hadn't exactly told Nic I met him at therapy. Even though he was so open and honest with me, I wasn't sure if he wanted everyone to know his business.

"Well, you better keep an eye on Mr. Hottie or you-know-who will snatch him for herself. Who does Dolly Parton think she is anyways?" Nicole chugged the last bit of soda, then threw the can on Tammy's towel.

Nic's sneer made me flinch. "She's not doing anything wrong. We can't hate her just because of her Victoria Secret measurements."

Nicole rolled her eyes, but I resisted the urge to tell her she needed a calming breath. "Whatever. Did you ask her if she wrote you those notes you found in your locker?"

A sudden burst of voices and cheering came from the pier. I looked over just in time to see a group of kids jumping, which wasn't really allowed. Rocks surrounded the area, and some people had gotten hurt in the past few years.

"Um, no."

She lifted an eyebrow. "Well, it's about time someone did."

Nicole stalked off across the sand toward the water.

I felt dizzy.

"Catfight?" Nate asked, plopping down beside me on my blue towel with the picture of Grand Haven Pier on it. His smile was contagious.

Sean was stretched out on Nic's beach towel on the other side of me, still fully dressed and listening to his iPod, but he sat up and introduced himself to Nate. "How'd you meet our girl Olga?"

I watched the sailboats way out on the lake, my eyes glazing over, waiting for Nate's response.

"It's kind of a funny story." He turned his incredulous gaze on me, and I nodded to show I didn't mind him mentioning Dr. Judy and tugged at my lip in anticipation. "We both have the same therapist to deal with our... issues."

I couldn't help but laugh.

Sean whipped off his sunglasses and stared at me. "It's not funny."

Knowing he was right, I tried to lighten the mood. "I've missed Jimi Hendrix."

I rubbed his afro for luck, a daily ritual for the five members of the Jedi Order, Conner's nickname for our group of friends. There were only four members now. *Maybe we should let Tammy in as a replacement.* Conner would've liked that. Maybe Nate could join us, too.

Sean nudged me. "We've missed you, too. Is today just a fluke, or are you rejoining our Jedi Order?"

I sipped my water and thought about his question. "Hand me a lightsaber and call me Ahsoka."

Tammy and Nicole stormed our way, Kyle lagging behind.

Tammy gave an exasperated sigh. "You really think I wrote you like, death threats?"

"Well, you and I didn't exactly have the best track record," I said lightly. My heart beat a little bit faster just thinking about it.

She contorted her face, agitation showing as she wiped a sheen of sweat from her forehead. "Right. And we all know I had no problem telling you exactly what I thought. I wouldn't anonymously send you death threats. I have way more dignity than that."

"Word," Kyle said.

I looked at him from the corner of my eye.

He shrugged. "What? She does keep it real."

I thought about her tricking me into believing Conner asked her to prom and then tricking Kyle into asking me to be his date even though he clearly dug Tammy. I laughed so hard I had to dig around in my beach bag for my standard pack of pocket tissues. Nate took my momentary lapse of reason to introduce himself to the rest of the gang.

After we finished our lunch of subs, chips, and watermelon, Sean and Nicole announced they were heading out to the water for a swim and invited me along. I declined with the excuse of not wanting to be a third wheel, which was really the least of my worries. There was some truth to it though. They'd dated ever since prom. I fumbled in my bag for some sunscreen and looked up to discover Sean sporting a Speedo.

"*What* are you wearing?" I screamed, pointing.

He turned around, modeling. The back of his swimwear read 'Real Men Wear Speedos.'

"Isn't it great?" he asked, not masking his pride. "Nicole bought it for me as a joke, but the joke's on her because I'm wearing this baby like a white man from Ohio wears tall white socks with shorts."

With my eyes closed, I tried to shake the image of Sean in a Speedo from my mind. "Which I'd like to point out, is *not* a good thing!"

I opened my eyes and caught him shrugging.

"Whatever. Every social gathering is a two hour countdown until we can chill in our underwear again. Wear a Speedo. Problem solved."

"Dude, you have the most convoluted thought process of anyone I know," Kyle told him.

Nicole flung her arms around Sean's back, and he carried her into the water.

I reapplied the sunscreen to my pale face and couldn't slip my sunglasses on fast enough. "I'm gonna need government spies to erase that image from my brain."

Nate laughed as I leaned back on my towel, watching Tammy and Kyle walk down the beach with some other GHHS students beaching it. Every guy she walked by checked her out, but I was glad she at least showed Kyle some love.

"Your friends are nice," Nate said.

I automatically turned to see if he checked out Tammy.

He didn't.

"Yeah. We call ourselves the Jedi Order. Conner thought of it. I just wish everyone would chill with the guilt trips. I mean, my best friend died." I kept my eyes steady on Sean and Nic playing in the water.

They make it look so easy.

I turned back to Nate.

He crossed his arms around his waist. "Yeah, but wasn't he their best friend, too? It's good you're coming around. The longest journey commences with a single step, and the first step is always the hardest."

I smiled. For better or worse, I liked his offbeat remarks. "Yeah, and one of those first steps includes writing a bucket list of eighteen things to do with my life over the next year." Pulling out the stationary and pen, I told him about Dr. Judy's order, then asked, "Any ideas?"

"Can my suggestions fall under things that may land you in jail?"

Raising my eyebrows, I said, "Jail? I can't wait to hear this list."

He cocked his head to the side. "Crash a wedding."

"Really? Isn't that kind of lame? I mean, why do people ruin somebody's perfect day just to hook up with some lonely bridesmaid?" My voice was kind of sharp, and I made a mental note to tone it down. I didn't want to scare off Mr. Hottie here, which was still the weirdest thing for me to be thinking.

"What? I wouldn't ruin their day; I'd add to it. And you're the one who is *lame*."

I didn't know what to make of him calling me lame. I couldn't tell if he was joking or serious, so I returned my focus to the piece of paper in front of me. "So, am I keeping wedding crashing?"

"Why not? A bucket list is all about trying new things, right? Which leads me to your number seventeen… firewalking." There was an unmistakable glint in his eyes.

I pursed my lips. "Something warns me you've already done crazy stuff like this before."

"Yep. Whenever I can use a little help focusing mind over matter, I go firewalk."

I wondered if the experience would've given me the faith I needed to tell Conner I loved him.

Too late for that now.

I didn't toy with the idea for long, or it may have brought on another nervous breakdown. "You know, sometimes getting cold feet isn't such a terrible thing."

Nate looked at me with vivid eyes, a mixture of blue and green, sporting a smile and wild look that said he plotted something. "Please, girl. Who in their right mind wouldn't want to leisurely stroll over coals hotter than an oven?"

I thrust my finger at him. "Fine, but the next one needs to be a little tamer."

His mouth curved into a slow smile. "You handle the lame—I mean—tame ones."

Laughing quietly to myself, I jotted down number sixteen.

He read over my shoulder. "Watch the one hundred greatest movies of all time. Wow, don't do anything I wouldn't do."

"Just trying to make it easy on myself. The Jedi Order has probably watched a good portion of those already. I think I'll write 'read *The Lord of the Ring* series' for the next one."

His eyes widened. "No offense, but you seem like a textbook only type girl, like you wouldn't even know how to read a book for fun."

I picked up a handful of sand, then threw it in his lap. "They were Conner's favorite books."

Tilting my head, I studied him, trying to find one flaw or fault. When I came up empty, I looked around and noticed a lady in a beach chair, typing on her laptop. "Nope. I'll jot that down. I'm also thinking of starting my own blog this summer. But I don't know. I'll already have a lot of stuff to do for the Bucs' Blade. Bucs' Blade is our Grand Haven High School publication. I've been on staff since freshman year, and Nicole joined me last year. We hold the coveted title of Business Managers next year."

He raised his eyebrows.

"Yeah, not. It just means we'll spend a good portion of summer trying to fill up ad space for the upcoming school year." I exhaled loudly. "What do you think about a blog?"

He flashed me a 'thumbs-up'. "Sounds good."

"You don't think I'm opening myself up to a whole new world of people who will ignore me?"

"I'm not sure the point is achieving one hundred followers to read your uncensored rants or anything. Just do it for yourself. I'll read it, so that's all that matters."

He squeezed my leg and I adjusted my oversized sunglasses, hoping they helped hide my flushed face.

I smiled at him, then gazed out at the horizon where the water met the sky. "I know this may seem silly because I've already done this so many times, but I think I need to add go sailing on my list."

My hands shook as I wrote it down and realized 'go sailing' was number thirteen on the list. Thirteen was also the number on the sailboat Conner and I rented the day he died. I don't know if I believed in bad omens, but this seemed like a big one.

Reaching over, he patted my back. "Great idea. I'm coming with you for sure."

"Where are we going?" Tammy pranced over and snatched a piece of watermelon from the cooler.

"Nate's just giving me suggestions for my list."

"You started without me? Uh, rude. That means I get to make suggestions and you have to take them."

"Come on, even your worst enemies don't deserve that."

"Well, I *am* your worst enemy. Remember, we have the whole love hate thing going on. So, you need to throw a big party and invite everyone you know."

It took me a minute to mentally calculate that everyone I really knew was at the picnic with me. After flashing my Cheshire grin, I said, "Fine, but you're underestimating how many people I actually know. Even my apartment is big enough for that, and you haven't seen where I live."

A breeze blew across us, ruffling our towels. "Okay, then we'll invite some of my peeps. Have you ever been to a party minus parents before?"

"My parents wouldn't allow that."

She threw her head back in bray laughter. "True dat. We better make the party at someone else's crib. It'll be epic. Oh, write down sneak out, too. You probably owe your parents a whole list of eighteen things for rebellion alone."

"Let's go, let's go, L-E-T-S-G-O!" I answered in faux cheer.

"Oh. My. Gawd!" Tammy squealed. "Put down 'try out for the cheerleading team'."

My mouth fell open, and I shook my head.

"Seriously. How many extracurricular activities do *you* have? You need those for your college applications."

She was right. Even as I jotted down her suggestion, it pained me to admit newspaper and math team probably wouldn't be enough.

"Hey, have you ever stayed up all night to watch a meteorite shower?" Nate asked.

"Nope. That makes eight things, ten more to go."

I wiped a hand across my sweaty forehead, toying with the idea of putting my feet in the water to cool down a bit. Especially since Sean was walking toward us with Nicole, flaunting his Speedo.

"Waz up, ya'll?" Sean shouted in a mocking feminine tone.

"Olga's metamorphosis," Nate said.

"Meta-what?"

"Our counselor asked her to write a life list of eighteen things to do. Metamorphosis means change. It's also a reference to the story by Franz Kafka, a highly symbolic tale dealing with the absurdity of human existence."

Tammy turned away and snorted at his explanation. "An-y-ways, suggestions? For the list, I mean."

Sean raked his fingers through his afro. "Enter a karaoke contest at Jumpin' Java."

I shook my head, my hair blowing in the wind. "I'll never recover my dignity after this list is done."

"What dignity?" Sean said, making a *tsking* sound under his breath. "Besides, karaoke contests are fun. I'll help you practice."

"Oh yeah. Didn't you win that contest three times already?" I asked, writing 'karaoke' down on the piece of paper.

"Yesss. I did!"

"Someone's a little too hyper today," Nicole said, handing Sean his shorts, which he thankfully slipped on. "Can I suggest a serious one, or is that not allowed?"

My skin felt like it was baking in an oven. I fanned myself with the paper. "Fire away."

"Start telling people what you really think."

A flag snapped in the wind, causing me to glance towards the lifeguard tower. A little boy cried for his mother as the tanned guy in red shorts spoke into his walkie-talkie. "Better yet—keep my parents happy, keep the little number of friends I actually have, keep my job, keep my mouth shut."

We stared at each other for a minute.

"I'm serious. You need to stop saying what you think everyone wants to hear and speak your mind."

"Sounds like a winner," Nate said, grabbing the pen and paper from my hands, then writing Nicole's advice down. "And I'm writing down another good one."

He scribbled a few words, then handed the paper back to me.

"Spend one day following what the Magic 8-ball says? Um, yeah, my sources say no."

"Too late. It is written."

I studied him from the corner of my eye. "This isn't the gospel."

"Practically. This is your freakin' personal Holy Grail encounter."

"Fine," I said through gritted teeth.

"Oh, I know one! I know one!" Tammy shouted. "Get a tattoo!" She pointed to the pirate skull and crossbones on her lower abdomen, right next to her belly button. As head cheerleader, I guess she really was zealous about supporting our GHHS Buccaneers. "I'm getting another one this week, a small one right here." She pointed to her chest, just above her left boob. "You should totally come with me."

"Yeah, when I have six-pack abs and boobs I can bounce a quarter off of, then I'll do that."

She laughed. "Okay, then. How many more things do you need for your quest?"

I looked down at my list. "Five."

"Yesss! Final five—time to get serious."

Nicole's eyes went wide. "I know number five. Ride the biggest roller coaster in the U.S."

Tammy cleared her throat. "I don't know. Sounds a bit clichéd for a top five pick."

"Maybe. But Olga's never even been on a roller coaster."

She stretched out a hand to me, gesturing. "Oh, then write it down. We won't even have to travel far because I've already done that one before. It's Millennium Force at Cedar Point in Ohio."

My stomach did a nervous drop just thinking about the amusement park. "I know a good one for number four," I said, looking from Kyle to Sean. "Help Cantankerous Monkey Squad sign a record deal. If I'm supposed to move on, then maybe it's time you guys start auditioning for a new singer."

Their mouths fell open, but then Sean nodded. "Alrighty. I'll put a shout out on Twitter tonight."

Nate caught a stray frisbee and then threw the disc back to the owner. "This is weird, but I was actually the lead singer and guitarist in a band back home. I was gonna ask around about other musicians when school started, but it'd be cool if I could jam with you guys."

Kyle drummed his palms against his knees. "What kind of band was it?"

"Alternative rock with an indie style."

Sean and Kyle squinted at each other.

"That's exactly what we are," Sean told Nate.

"Well, why don't we all jam at my house tonight?" Kyle asked.

Nate and Sean nodded in agreement. The situation was eerie, a little too convenient—like Nate was planted here in our lives by God or something.

A few moments of silence passed, aside from the sound of Nate chomping on a bag of chips, while we all thought.

"Maybe it should be renamed fifteen things," I suggested, reaching over and then shoving a few chips in my own mouth.

Nate snorted. "Just Zen. We'll think of something."

Tammy rubbed some tanning oil on her legs. "So, are we all *doing* this list, too?"

"I like the sound of that." I winked. "I mean, you don't have to do everything with me, but it'd be nice to have company for most of these if I'm gonna get through it."

"Wimp." Sean coughed the word loudly.

I jerked my head up, surveying him from the corner of my eye.

He looked at me, holding up his soda can before taking a sloppy sip. "You checking me out?"

"Yes, but only with this eye." I pointed to my right pupil.

"Which eye?"

"My good eye, so don't try any malarkey," I said, looking over my list.

"Oh, crap."

Nate smacked my shoulder. "Number three—break a world record."

"You already sound like a broken record, and I just met you, Plato," I said, writing his suggestion down. Sweat dripped off my arm, and I pulled my hair into a sloppy ponytail with the standard hair tie I wore on my wrist.

"Oh, we got ourselves a wise guy here," Nate cracked, stretching his arm around my waist and tickling my sides.

I laughed in a please stop, that's not fair kind of way, until Nicole stuck her head between us and shot me a look, making me quiet down.

She picked up my pen and paper, wrote something down, then handed it back to me. "Go on a date/get a boyfriend/fall in love?"

"Don't look at me like I got my forehead pierced or something. I'm sure I'm not the only one here who thinks you should *at least* go on your first proper date."

Gosh, she made me sound so pathetic sometimes! Her condescending remarks drove me crazy, but I knew she didn't mean anything by the comment.

"You've never been on a date?" Tammy practically screamed. "Well, call me the Jehovah girl of matchmaking."

I shook my head. "Thanks, but no thanks."

"Aw, come on. I'm practically the role model for getting guys to ask me out. What kind of frenemy would I be if I didn't hook a sister up?"

Looking at Kyle, I suddenly felt angry about the last time she tried hooking me up with a date, when she robbed me of the experience of Conner finally asking me out.

"Did you get your brain amputated or something? I said no."

Tammy stood, hands on her hips, accentuating the curves I'd never have. "I was just trying to help."

She turned on her heels, then marched down the beach to her other friends.

"It's not like I've *never* been on a date," I grumbled under my breath.

Nicole rolled her eyes, sighing dramatically. "The bowling alley doesn't count as a *proper* date."

"Bowling alley?" Nate asked.

I shrugged like it didn't matter, but the truth was never going on an official date really bothered me. "When we all went to Rock'n'Bowl at Starlite Lanes last summer, we ran into some guys from school. One of them offered to drive me home because he lives in the same apartment complex as me. Then he tried to kiss me when he dropped me off."

"Yesss! Olga got game!" Sean held out his hand for a fist bump.

"What a butt munch," Nate said.

"Yeah, and my mom was watching the whole thing through our living room window and started flipping the porch light on and off rapidly, signaling for me to come in. You should've seen her total menopausal breakdown when I walked through the front door. Lecturing me about getting a reputation and how I should wait until I'm ready to get married before I date and even then the guy should be courting me."

The boys stared at me with their mouths open.

"Yep, that's what happens when you have parents from the fifties."

"I do have that," Nate said. "But they're called *grand*parents."

We all laughed, and I buried my face in my hair.

It was so hot, from heat and embarrassment, I imagined my cheeks matched the fire engine red color of my curls. "The sun is the most annoying thing ever today. I can't stand how hot it is."

Nate nodded toward the water. "I don't know if you've noticed, but the lake is right there."

He stood, brushed the sand off his shorts, held out his hand, then pulled me up.

When we got to the water's edge, I stopped short.

"Seventy percent of the world is covered by water; you can't ignore it forever."

I smiled. "Conner used to say my blood was seventy percent coffee."

Stabbing hurt rose up in my chest, and I sucked in a deep breath.

"When you look that sad, it breaks my heart." His voice was as smooth as silk, like an angel's.

Gesturing with my hand toward the lake, I said, "He was killed out there."

In my head, I thought back to my last sailing date with Conner. I remembered it perfectly, as if it happened just yesterday, no matter how hard I tried to forget.

So many days since then I wished it was me who died instead of him.

My breathing came fast now. "He had a pulse. I should've noticed sooner he wasn't breathing. I should've pulled him up and administered the rescue breaths as soon as I got to the boat. We should've been wearing life jackets, too. I wouldn't have had to dive after him if we were, wouldn't have wasted all that time." My voice was unbalanced, trembling like strings on a guitar. "Everyone thinks the lightning killed him instantly, but it didn't. That's what keeps me awake at night. This guilt, knowing his death could've been prevented. It wasn't some freak accident. It was plain stupidity. Just like my hate letters said. I may be a genius, but I'm a complete idiot."

I sobbed and he tried to hug me, but I untangled my body from his arms and then shoved him away.

"Stop it!" My voice rose. "I don't deserve to be comforted. I stood there and let my best friend die. Don't you see that? Don't you get what I'm telling you?"

Nicole was at my side now, putting an arm around my shoulder and smoothing my hair.

"He had a pulse," I confessed to her, too.

She shook her head. "Olga, I wasn't there, but I didn't have to be there to know you would've done everything humanly possible to save Conner's life. You can't beat yourself up over it. Let it go. Remember how he lived more than how he died."

Nic took my hand and gently led me into the water, my legs wobbling.

I looked over at Nate, and he gave me a sad half-smile. Realizing I still held my pen in my hand, I stuck it behind my ear. The water rhythmically lapped against my knees, and I closed my eyes.

S.T.A.R.

I knew my last item for my life list now. What Dr. Judy suggested to me in her office: Let go of my guilt about Conner's death.

Sliding my sunglasses to the top of my head, I squinted at the sun and a cloud moved in front of it, finally. I blocked out all the sounds around me, and all I heard was the water and the wind. A warm, soft breeze blew across me, like Conner whispering from the grave, *It's okay. Go on, go on.* Those words are something I'd heard many times before but never listened to.

Life does go on, and it shouldn't.

*"A warm, soft breeze blew across me, like
Conner whispering from the grave, It's okay.
Go on, go on."*

Chapter Five

"Courage does not always roar.
Sometimes courage is the quiet voice at the end of the day saying,
I will try again tomorrow."
—Mary Anne Radmacher

Today would've been Conner's eighteenth birthday: June thirtieth. Ugh, that hurt so bad, but there it was. The Jedi Order hadn't heard from Conner's family since the funeral, but two weeks ago, we received an invitation for a celebration.

I was surprised I got an invite. I figured they held me responsible for the accident.

Standing next to my parents on the front porch, I rang the doorbell, my hand shaking. His mom, Loria, let us in and even gave me a hug.

His dad, Robert, pulled me aside.

"We heard from your parents that you've been going to counseling. How have you been?" He smiled, but it wavered at the edge.

"Um, okay. Better this past month, I guess. The Bookman keeps me busy with the tourist season and all." I thought of the last time I saw him, at the funeral, and looked down at my hands.

"We've started seeing Dr. Judy, too. Megan made us before she left to go back to college. She's taking summer classes."

There was an awkward pause. I bit my lip, unsure of how to talk to him anymore. I thought about telling him how the party was a nice idea, but the more I thought about it, the more I felt wrong for coming to the whole shindig in the first place. Taking a step backward, I surveyed the house of my childhood where most of my best memories were built, and counted to ten. I thought I'd need to count all the way to fifty before I could really calm down. Then Robert placed his hands on my shoulders, and my body eased.

"He loved you, you know? More than anything. You were his best friend."

The words were meant to comfort, but his sentiments felt more like an accusation, slapping me hard in the face.

Yes, I was his best friend, and I let him die.

I knew I was supposed to be over this now, moving on with my life. Breathing in and out, letting my guilt go, visualizing my future. Everyone kept helping me with the list, trying to make me forget. Moving forward was all part of the war I engaged myself in daily. I knew I owed it to everyone else around me to remove myself from my emotional prison, but I didn't want to forget. Dr. Judy kept telling me moving on didn't erase what happened or my friendship with Conner, but enabled me to integrate the disappointment, sorrow, and injustices of life into learning opportunities as the foundation of my growth. *Blah, blah, blah.*

"Anyway, Dr. Judy is the one who suggested this party," Robert explained. "Since we really didn't have a celebration of Conner's life after the funeral. It was just too much to handle then. And she's been making us go into his room once a week to get rid of or donate one of his things."

I flinched a little, the realization he's dead hitting me again and again like bullets to my heart.

"We had left his room alone, until a few weeks ago. I wanted to let you know you're welcome, along with Sean and Kyle, to go down to his room tonight and keep anything you find sentimental or of use."

I cleared my throat, hoping my voice didn't squeak when I said thanks, but it betrayed me. I turned slowly, unwillingly, and headed for the stairs leading to Conner's basement bedroom. If I put off the visit, I knew I'd chicken out.

The room was cold and dusty, and I could barely see as I descended the steps, my only light from the glow of the kitchen upstairs. I strained my eyes and reached for the switch at the bottom but wished I hadn't. Every inch of me felt suffocated, seeing his room almost exactly the way it looked when he still walked among us. It definitely showed they hadn't gotten far into cleaning out his stuff, adding to the haunted feeling. His video games littered the center of his floor where an old brown couch sagged in front of a widescreen tv, the cords to his PlayStation 3 stretching across the coffee table.

But would coming in here have been easier if they'd cleared out his room? Probably not.

Sucking in a deep breath, I pushed forward, my stomach in knots and tears in my eyes. The plaid patched quilt Loria sewed years ago for Conner twisted into lumps on top of his bed. Resting my head on his soft, plump pillow, I inhaled his amazing scent still lingering on the sham, a kind of earthy outdoors smell. I stared at the black and white Green Day poster on his ceiling, thinking about how things used to be simple, everything laid out in black and white.

Now, everything in my life hung in this gray area called the unknown. I wanted to convey a brave face tonight but didn't want to be a poser. Because truthfully, I was terrified, and no amount of therapy or life list would fix that.

Huddling my legs close to my chest, I rocked back and forth in the fetal position until I glimpsed two things—an unframed photo of Conner and me at the beach, sitting on his nightstand, and a hair scrunchie I lost featured prominently on his bedpost. No matter how many months these items rested here, they now served as signs to pull myself together and honor Conner's memory.

I grabbed my old hair scrunchie and the picture of Conner and me, then slid them into the pocket of my hoodie.

"Find something worth keeping?"

I jumped at the sound of Kyle's voice. "You scared the bejeezus out of me."

"Sorry." He narrowed his eyes, eyebrows pulling down in concentration. S.T.A.R. "It's okay. I guess Robert gave you the message, too?"

"Yeah. There's only two things I can think of wanting though." He rubbed a hand over his face, and I could tell being here killed a little part of him too. "His song book, because I know there were songs in the works in there, and I think he'd want us to use them, and his guitar. His dad said he'd want us to have it."

I pointed to the dresser beside Conner's bed, the mirror mounted on the wall above the chest of drawers reflecting all our sadness. "I know the song book is in the top drawer."

When Conner was alive, his room was a mess. I came over every Thursday night to help him study for Friday tests, and I often tidied up for him.

After retrieving the items, Kyle turned and faced me. "You ready to head outside to the bonfire?"

My eyes watered at the mirrored reflection of just us two standing alone in Conner's room, knowing he'd never come back. "Yes, it's a little weird being in here now."

"Lewis Carroll for sure."

I shook my head, thinking Nate's offbeat remarks were already influencing Kyle's vernacular.

"I mean, yeah, weird."

Someone stomped down the steps. Conner's room took up the Anderson's spacious basement, a perfect practice venue for the Cantankerous Monkey Squad. We looked over and found Sean staring back at us.

"This is weird," Sean said.

Kyle nodded. "We were just discussing that." He held up Conner's things. "Got the song book and guitar."

"Great minds think alike." Sean tapped his finger against his temple and walked to the closet. "That's what I was coming down here for. And one more thing."

"You want one of his shirts?" Kyle asked.

Even though Conner's family was loaded, the majority of his wardrobe consisted of Goodwill finds.

Sean held out two white tees. One featured a hot dog and said, 'The dog kids love to bite.' The T-shirt was an advertisement for some food company and so was the other, which said, 'My fanny has no fat.'

Kyle meandered over, then took the fanny one. "I guess it would be cool to wear his shirts to gigs sometimes, honor his place in the band."

Sean grabbed one more T-shirt from the closet, a black one that said, 'Trust Me. I'm a Jedi Master.' "Nothing honors Conner more than a Star Wars shirt, and we need one for each member of the band."

Suddenly, a moment of silence struck us. A crushing disappointment weighed on me, and maybe them too. We'd never see Conner again. As we all stood there, I felt so small, so insignificant, contemplating how quickly life could end.

I picked at a loose thread on my sweater and thought about Nate instead, wondering if the band picked him as an official replacement yet.

"Now, can we get outta here? Not to sound insensitive, but I don't need Conner's stuff to remember him. And being in here creeps me out," Kyle said, clearing his throat while sliding Conner's guitar strap over his shoulder.

"True dat," Sean said, leading the way out the sliding glass door to the backyard, slinging the shirts over his shoulder.

I followed but took one last look around Conner's room; the memories of our childhood together made my chest ache.

Lawn chairs and blankets littered the backyard, adding to the outdoor glider and two sitting hammocks, always a standard around the Anderson's fire pit, which burned bright. Most people crowded around the fire, telling their favorite stories about Conner. Loria dashed up the stairs of the deck leading to their dining room and kitchen to fetch more food, her dozen beaded necklaces swinging as she went. Mom trailed behind her.

Nicole sat at our favorite spot on the glider, so I joined her. I eyed a basket, packed with s'mores ingredients, on the grass by my feet and then noticed Tammy and Nate relaxing in the two hammock chairs adjacent to the glider. The guys must've invited him to the 'party.' I didn't even know he was here, and the sight of him next to Tammy made me cringe.

Odd.

As soon as he saw me, he got up and then squeezed himself into the glider with Nicole and me.

"Where have you been?" Even in faded jeans and an olive green hoodie, he looked handsome. "I've been looking all over for you."

I swung the glider back and forth and admired the way he swept his hair back from his face. "Stalker."

He grinned, the smile quickly becoming my favorite. "Totally."

"What are those boxes of sparklers for?" Sean asked, nodding to a stockpile on the ground.

Nicole handed me and Nate sodas from the cooler next to her. "Loria and Robert already handed them out to everyone. Kinda like party favors, I guess, since Conner liked them so much."

Kyle's lips turned up into a huge smile, and he sat in the hammock next to Tammy. "He really did. This is actually kind of perfect."

Nate turned to me and whispered in my ear. "By the way, you look really cute tonight."

In Conner's honor, I'd dressed up a bit. I borrowed Nicole's brown sequined V-neck tunic, pairing it with my old jeans featuring a few torn holes in them and Tammy's fur trim boots.

I couldn't fathom looking cute to a guy. Taking in Nate's smile again, I met his eyes for a second, but I was sure I blushed because heat rose in my cheeks, so I looked away.

"Did you get it?" I asked Tammy, because I let her and Nicole in on my plan earlier today about accomplishing number four on my list. I figured getting the *Cantankerous Monkey Squad* on the radio was a definite step in the right direction for landing a record deal.

Tammy nodded just as I spotted Loria and Mom coming down the stairs with cheese and veggie trays.

Perfect timing. I glanced at my watch. 8:00 p.m. I nodded to Tammy, signaling for her to make the announcement.

"Holla, holla, holla!" she shouted, holding up the radio. "Shh! Olga has a surprise."

A few seconds later, the DJ delivered the introduction. "It's time! Every Saturday at eight o'clock I play ya something new. So, here's one from a local teen band called Cantankerous Monkey Squad. Today, I met their biggest fan, Olga Worontzoff, and asked her how the band got their name. She said their lead singer, Conner Anderson, thought of it. Their self-titled debut explains it all. Here's to you, Conner; may you rest in peace as your music plays on."

Everyone listened quietly, seeming to savor the moment just as much as I did. Kyle tapped out the drumbeat over the speakers, Sean strummed his guitar, and Conner belted out the lyrics. "Down on Washington Street/ I saw a deal I couldn't beat/ Fifteen dollars for a cymbal-banging cantankerous monkey/ I thought to myself, ain't that funky/ You had a red and white striped shirt and yellow pants/ But there was something disturbing I didn't see at first glance/ Red rings painted around wide open eyes/ Could take home Most Scary prize/ I reached into my wallet, but it was empty/ But that's okay, 'cause Mom and Dad have plenty/ So I'll just wait till I come around/ Back to this side of town/ That night, I'm sitting at my coffee table/ Wondering if I'm able/ Coming up with the band name is the hardest part/ I wish I could shop for one at Discount Mart/ Then, I remembered those cymbals in your hands/ And I knew what to call the band/ Cantankerous Monkey Squad/ Our problem finally solved/ I screamed Oh My Gawd, Oh My Gawd/ Next day, I walked back to Washington Street/ Not caring at all about Grand Haven's heat/ But the cashier said we're all sold out/ And I became the same boy who used to pout/ But I'll always remember the way you bobbed your head/ Cantankerous Monkey Squad is what you said."

After the three-minute stint ended, the song was rewarded with applause, and goose bumps spread over my arms and legs. Then, Robert's firm hand was on my shoulder, Loria next to him. We just stood there for what seemed like a long time. I think each of us tried hard not to cry, to say something meaningful. But words failed to express what we felt, so silence hung in the air. Sometimes, I realized, you just had to show up, to be there for someone. No matter what my future held, Robert and Loria had been a huge part of my past, and a piece of them would always go with me. I was glad I came tonight, after all.

"That was really special," Robert finally said.

Loria leaned closer. "Thank you. And I want you to know, we don't blame you for what happened. I'm sorry if it seemed like we did, at the hospital. We were hurting, but we should've handled it better. You were always like a second daughter to us, and we loved you like Conner did. If you ever need anything—she tilted her head toward Robert, seeming to draw strength from him to get the words out—"you have our number."

Then, she ducked her head, avoiding eye contact as tears fell, and walked away.

I broke into a cold sweat as Robert followed her across the yard. Leaning to the left, I stole a marshmallow off the paper plate in Nicole's lap, then shoved the sugary substance in my mouth, fighting the urge to cry.

"You're supposed to toast that first, silly girl," Nate said, handing me a skewer. He stood, his back to me for a moment, then handed another metal stick to Sean.

"Here you go, buddy."

"Wow. What a gentleman this guy is, fixing my marshmallow stick for me and everything"—Sean held it in the air in a toast—"To Olga, for getting our song on the air." He placed the wooden skewer over the fire.

I studied Nate's face like it was the most important thing in the world, searching for his motive for doing something so oddly kind. As he plopped down on the glider again, I scooted closer to him and whispered, "What was that about?" I hoped this form of homosocial intimacy toward Sean was as far as their bromance went.

He slid his arm around me. "The least I can do for letting me in the band."

"Wait, so it's official?" I asked, because they'd only been practicing together for the past month, or messing around as they put it, making sure he'd be a good fit. I think they just hadn't been ready to replace Conner yet, and of course, I could relate.

A huge burst of pops sounded like Independence Day came four days too early as Sean's marshmallow stick exploded. Gooey fluff flew everywhere, like the scene in *Ghostbusters* when the Stay Puff Marshmallow Man blew to pieces.

"*What was that?*" Sean said, jumping back a step or two.

Nate's face prominently featured a mischievous grin.

"Dude, did you just put my marshmallow on the end of a firecracker?"

Nate nodded, laughing.

"That's freakin' *awesome!*"

They high-fived each other, and everyone burst into laughter.

"I knew that wasn't just some random act of kindness," I told Nate.

Sean took long, gasping breaths. "How'd you think of that, man?"

"These things just come to me. It's not so hard to pull pranks when you're surrounded by gullible people."

"You kids be careful." Mom propped her hands on her hips. "Someone could've really gotten hurt. What if Sean had gone to check on it and it exploded in his face? You could've shot his eye out!"

I rolled my eyes. "Relax, Mom. This is no *Christmas Story*." I turned to Nate and took a bite of my s'more. Then, forgetting my manners, spoke with my mouth full. "You should put 'pulling the perfect prank on your life list'," I mumbled, the best my lips allowed, before shoving the rest of the s'more into my mouth.

His gaze darted around the fire, then to each of our friends. "But I don't have a list. You do."

I sighed. "Precisely, and I think we should change that. You should all write your own."

"Mission number one accomplished," Sean said. "Find a new singer."

"I think I want to join or start a book club," Tammy said, folding her long legs.

"Like school doesn't provide you with enough reading homework for a lifetime," Sean said.

Tammy waved her hand in the hand, as if dismissing his remark. "Please, I hardly ever do my homework. Popularity takes up a lot of time. But maybe I can put it to good use. Get kids to read and bring in some commission for Olga at The Bookman."

I tried picturing Tammy reading an old classic like *Little Women*, but I couldn't. Though the music blasting from the radio didn't help my concentration any. "I don't make commission."

Tammy raised her eyebrows. "Really? Oh well. Truth is I only read magazines. I'm starting to feel a little ignorant since I started hanging out with you."

Kyle held up his hands. "Wait, time-out. Starting to?"

Tammy gave him a purple-nurple that, no doubt, would've made school bullies everywhere proud.

"Mercy! Geez. It was a joke, girl. Way to defend your band mate," he said to Nate and Sean.

They laughed.

"Sorry, dawg," Sean said. "You got an idea for your list?"

Kyle turned to Tammy. "Just one. Would you like to go out with me?"

A light flickered across Tammy's face as a car pulled out of the Anderson's driveway. The headlights highlighted her blush. "Aww. Sure I would."

"Okay, get ready to laugh," Nicole said matter-of-factly. "I'm thinking maybe I can postpone college and live on a cruise ship for like five years. You know, save money for college. I could be their resident photographer and teach scrapbooking classes and stuff, since I absolutely love doing that and am actually good at it. Like Tammy here, I'm no bookworm."

"Hey!" Tammy swatted at Nicole's arm.

Nic tipped her head back toward the sky. "No offence. I don't even have popularity as an excuse. And my parent's own a bookstore."

"Don't sweat it, babe. You always have your looks to fall back on," Sean said. Then, in a somewhat more serious tone, he turned to Nate. "You've been quiet over there."

"I don't know. Maybe just returning to the simpler things in life." His voice was soft, and he stretched his hands behind his head. "Take up skateboarding again. Learn to play the piano. Adopt a dog from a shelter. Become a regular at a restaurant every Saturday morning. Pulling the perfect prank." He looked right at me as he said all this, and I wondered what he saw when he looked at me.

"You said simple stuff sounded lame when I wrote mine." I thought back to Memorial Day. Even though our beach picnic took place only a month ago, it was already so easy to imagine completing all the things on our lists together. Moving on still scared me, but it suddenly felt like it was happening with Nate.

"Only because that's not what you needed, so I encouraged other things."

I shook my finger at him. "Don't get all Freud on me again."

"Well, I'm down for Saturday morning breakfast," Sean said.

"How about Morning Star Café?" Nicole rested her head on my shoulder. "Olga and I can meet ya'll there before our shift every Saturday."

Everyone nodded.

Reaching down, I fixed another s'more, then shoved it in my mouth. All this talk about food made me hungry.

"Enjoying yourself?" Tammy asked, grabbing her pack of cigarettes from her purse.

"Hmm, I can never get enough of this chocolaty goodness."

Sean laughed hard, tossing his dread-locked hair. "Well, you might want to take it easy. A moment on the lips is a lifetime on the hips."

Nate joined me in my gluttony, smashing an entire s'more into his mouth, making a huge mess on his face while everyone chuckled.

"Sweet tasting all the way through, just like you," he said, looking straight at me.

I glanced over his head toward Tammy who mouthed the words 'I told you so,' referring to our conversation earlier today when she claimed Nate was interested in being more than 'friends.'

Standing, I collected everyone's paper plates to distract myself. I needed a moment to absorb all this.

"Okay, I think you've fulfilled your corny comments quota for the day. Congratulations." I winked at him and then headed to the trashcan at the side of the yard.

Ugh, did I just wink at him?

That moment of flirtation caught Mom's attention. I swear she always watched me with eagle eyes. "You ready to go home?"

I tucked my hair behind my ears. "Um… I dunno. Do you and Dad want to leave?" I was surprised I didn't want to head home, considering how badly I wanted to avoid coming here tonight. But I followed Mom's line of sight to Tammy smoking her cigarette, and I knew Mom wasn't really asking but *telling* me it was time to leave. She wasn't a Tammy fan, and she always said hanging out with someone like her made me look ignorant.

Well, ignorance is bliss, right?

Focus Question:

Nate loves to play pranks. What is the perfect practical joke that you would love to pull off one day?

Chapter Six

"Never, never, never give up."
—Winston Churchill

Tonight, I attempted something else for the first time. I threw on a pair of jeans and a Grand Haven High Bucs sweatshirt at 2:00 a.m. to sneak out of my apartment. As I tiptoed out of my bedroom, worry jolted through me like I'd drank a dozen cups of coffee. My parents' room was further down the hall, and they slept with their door shut. It only took me a few seconds to realize how easily I could sneak out of my house. We didn't even lock our windows and doors. Ever. Dad said as soon as we needed deadbolts, we'd move. He was very big on safe, small-town living.

Tammy had sent me a text message thirty minutes ago with the plan, telling me to meet at Nate's house. He lived two miles away, and keeping a steady jog, I arrived in twenty minutes, albeit a little out of breath and sweaty and probably with messy hair, but that last one was nothing new. He waited in his driveway, a bulky backpack slung over his shoulder and his guitar case in his left hand.

Just seeing him gave me goose bumps. I didn't know what that meant, and I tried not to think about it.

"I grabbed you one of mine in case you need an extra at the lake," he said a little too boisterously with his deep voice, holding out a blue Michigan hooded sweatshirt.

"Shh!" I warned as we set off down the sidewalk, the leaves of the overhead trees rustling as a breeze blew over us. "Did you leave your parents a note in case they wake up to find you gone?"

"Yeah. Right on my bed. Even signed it Cantankerous Little Monkey. But they'd be fine with it. They've woken up to find me gone before."

"Wow, I wish my parents were so forgiving."

"Did you leave one, too?"

"Yup, on my desk. But I'm dead if they find out." I gave him a flat look, letting him know I meant business.

"No worries. We'll be back before they wake up." He lifted his hand, then raked his fingers through his shaggy hair.

"I can't believe I'm fully awake and haven't even had my cup of coffee. Must be the adrenaline of sneaking out."

In the dead of the night, his big shoes sounded too loud against the concrete. "Good, because we got places to go and people to see."

He kicked a rock, sending it skittering across the sidewalk, then into someone's driveway.

I watched him walk, temporarily distracted by the handsomeness of his tan face... the coffee colored hair sweeping across his forehead, the golden brown eyebrows always drawn together in thought, those laughing ocean blue eyes and long lashes, the square jaw and wide, slightly smiling mouth. I tripped over a rock and lost my footing, falling down entirely.

"Whoa! Are you okay?" Nate reached down and held out his hand. I just sat there, feeling my heart beat rapidly, and then he grabbed my hand when I didn't respond. He tugged me up and inspected me. "You look like you'll live. Can you handle walking, or do I need to carry you?"

I smiled at him, in spite of basically making a total fool of myself, and moved my feet forward. "I can walk. So, what exactly is the plan?"

Letting loose of my hand, he said, "All I know is Tammy orchestrated the whole thing. She's picking up Kyle, Nicole is picking up Sean, and you met me at my house since we're closest to the beach."

Footsteps were the only sound for moments. It was weird how quiet the dark could be. I thought about all the people resting inside each house we passed, oblivious to us walking by in the middle of the night. So much happens in the world. I wasn't used to this type of calm, and I should've sensed peace. Instead, the silent night disturbed me. Then, we crested a hill, and the sidewalk turned to sand, and I felt at home again.

"Where do you want to set up camp on the beach tonight?" he asked.

I took a few steps forward, scanning the beach. "I get to pick?"

Nate jabbed my arm. "It's your list."

Pressing a hand on my stomach where I felt butterflies, I said, "Oh, right. Number eleven: sneak out. Are you sure we should do this?"

He pointed skywards. "How about hiking to the top of the sand dunes?"

I gawked at the hill, but he shoved my arm lightly.

"Race you to the top!" His hair whipped in the wind as he sprinted a few steps, then looked back at me.

I ran, feeling my feet under me. I was sure Nate purposefully slowed his pace or I never would've caught up with him. Up ahead, all I could see was sand and sky until finally, we were at the top.

We almost collapsed with laughter as we reached the peak of the mini mountain. Nate retrieved two blankets from his backpack, then we stretched across the warm polyester, listening to the song of waves rolling in and watching the stars twinkle.

My own mind remained tranquil for once, and I hummed the old Christmas carol, *Silent Night,* while mapping out the constellations... then sighed. "Shouldn't we text the others to let them know where we set up?"

"Yeah."

He pressed his lips together and slowly pulled a cell phone out of his pocket, and I thought maybe he was just as content as I was with only the two of us being here.

He typed a message to Sean and Kyle.

"I know this probably sounds strange since I just snuck out for the first time, but I've never felt more at peace than this moment," I said.

Fireflies flitted past us. I wished I had a jar to capture them, like Conner and I did not too many years ago.

"I know what you mean," Nate murmured.

The moon rested full and bright, the same way it looked the night lightning struck Conner. And with Nate and me sitting on the blanket alone, it seemed the lunar effect caused strange things to happen again. Not that I was complaining, this time.

We traced our names in the sand, then he snapped a picture of us next to our designs. We lay on our backs, staring at the cumulus clouds in the light of the moon, and looked for pictures in the piles of puffy cotton. He saw a hand pointing at him, an eagle, and a hamburger. I spied a dragon breathing fire, a crab, and a woman's face.

"Nate and Olga sitting in a tree, K-I-S-S-I-N-G," Tammy said, hiking up the hill with the rest of the Jedi Order.

I pointed at her. "Don't even open that Pandora's box."

Nate bowed his head.

Did I offend him? That was so not what I was going for.

What would've Conner thought about all this? Whenever I pictured him, he was buttoning his Kurt Cobain grunge style flannel, holding up three fingers in the Scout Sign, reminding me to always be prepared. But you can't prepare for falling in love, which is why I didn't want to. Give me my place on the school math team over having a boyfriend any day. Algebra, Geometry, Calculus, that's something I could fall in love with. Something precise, a formula I could figure out that always worked and never disappointed, never hurt.

"What took you guys so long?" I asked, trying to avoid staring at Nate's frown.

He fidgeted with his phone, flipping it over as though he'd never before looked at it.

"Well, I can't speak for Nicole and Sean." Tammy eyeballed them with a quirked brow. "But Kyle and I stopped for supplies at Meijer Grocery. Thank God they're open twenty-four hours."

She overturned a plastic bag, dumping a package of peanut butter cookies from the bakery, a Family Size bag of SunChips, and an assortment of king-sized candy bars.

"How do you keep your model figure?" Nicole asked.

"Cheerleading." Tammy bounced on her toes and winked at me. "Pretty soon, Olga will have a rocking body too." Turning to Kyle, she asked, "Did you bring the energy drinks?"

"Got 'em in here." He retrieved a six-pack from his bag, then gestured for Sean to take one and pass it around.

The sounds of cans popping open echoed around our circle of friends.

"Alrighty then. Who wants to bury my butt in the sand?" Sean rubbed his hands together.

"Just your butt?" Kyle slapped Sean's behind like a good-natured football player, and Sean jumped. "Or your whole body?"

Sean massaged his tooshie. "The whole enchilada. I'm making it number two on my life list, baby." He lay down in the powder soft sand. "But be careful of Jimi Hendrix."

Nicole patted his afro, which was especially poofy with his braids gone.

"Just bury your head in the sand and wait for your friggin' prom," Nate blurted out as we all grabbed a fistful of dirt and dumped it on top of Sean.

Tammy pursed her lips. "Okay, that was random."

But I wasn't confused. "Nice, Bender," I told him before turning to Tammy. "It's only right he quote The Breakfast Club since we're starting one of our own. You're all still coming next Saturday to The Morning Star Café, right?"

Nate nodded and Tammy's eyes darted between the two of us.

"Oh, so that was like, a movie reference?" she asked.

"Yes, an eighties classic," I answered in a slow, exaggerated voice as everyone laughed.

"Very funny," Tammy said as we finished covering Sean's legs and worked on his arms. "Speaking of prom, remember when Kyle asked you to be his date because I told him to? Let's see if that can work again. Nate, I think you should ask Olga out on a date. Oh yeah, let's get this bucket list started tonight!"

She punched Nate in the arm.

I seized her hand in a Vulcan death grip. "Yes, let's get it started by telling people *exactly* what I think about them."

Nicole launched her hand in the air. "I second that one!"

"You know who was good at telling people what they think?" Calm emanated from Kyle's voice, the way he always spoke. "Conner. That's why he was such an epic songwriter. And we found one for Olga in his song book this past week. I think he wrote it as a birthday present for you."

My heart raced, and a warm feeling hit my core. Not just because of Conner, but because Kyle's a good buddy, changing the subject like that. Really, all my friends were awesome, the way they protected me and stood up for me, even when Tammy stuck her nose where it didn't belong.

"Really? Why do you think that?" Tears formed in my eyes.

"Because it says 'Olga's Birthday Song' next to the title."
I leaned toward him. "Which was?"

"You'll see. Okay, where'd you put Breedlove?"

Nate pulled his guitar out of its case, as way of answering, while Sean punched and kicked his way out of the sand.

"That was short lived," Nate said, waving toward Sean.

"Word. It's not as fun as it sounds. Can I play? Huh, Nate? Can I?"

Nate smiled and nodded his head, then handed Breedlove to Sean. "Stop wiggin', man. Play *Time of Your Life* by Green Day."

Sean stroked the guitar like a pro, but then again, we didn't nickname his afro Jimi Hendrix just because of his hair.

"Conner titled this one *Ode to a Septic Tank,* and from what I gather, it's written from Olga's perspective," Nate said.

A sidesplitting laugh escaped my lips. On Halloween of our kindergarten year, we decided to dress as army men, girl in my case. At the time, my parents rented a small house, and after trick-or-treating, his family along with his sister's best friend all came over for a bonfire and some cake… since it was also my birthday. That night was really the beginning of our parents' friendship, and the four of us kids raced around the acre of land we had out back, playing a combination of tag and hide-and-seek. Conner and I clearly losing, he sought out a form of camouflage, but there hadn't been any rain for days. Poop replaced mud when he came upon our ruptured septic tank and dared me to jump in, saying, "This is war! Don't be a girl." I didn't want to be labeled a sissy, least of all by my comrade, so I answered, "Yes, Commander!" He claimed he never meant to almost drown me, didn't expect me to actually plunge into the foul mess, or for the poop pile to go so deep. But the truth was I could never say no to him, something he used to his advantage frequently.

"Wait, don't sing yet! Let me get out my iPhone to record." Nicole dug in her purse. "Okay, hit it."

Sean strummed the acoustic bass guitar, Nate sung, and Kyle drummed a beat on his lap.

"Experience comes in many forms/And one I remember, breaks all the norms/Playing outside with Conner, his face wears a grin/When all of the sudden, a septic tank I fell in/Swamped in poop/I couldn't breathe/I flapped my arms and tried to scream/A septic tank is what I fell in/A few minutes felt like hours, nobody prevailed/Then my mom came around/Her face went so pale/She rushed over with great alien speed/Like mothers do when their child is in need/She lifted me out of the fume/A bath could not have come too soon/A septic tank is what I fell in/I got washed up and was put in a dress/Never again did I want to see that awful mess/All of you can have your laughs/Like I do when Sean raps/Mom often does when she says I'm full of crap/I answer her defensively/Conner tried to drown me/A septic tank is what I fell in."

Nicole, Tammy, and I rolled on the ground as Sean set Breedlove down and shouted, "Boo-yah! Stop, drop, and roll! You just got burned from the grave, Olga! How does it feel?"

A patch of sea grass bowed in the wind, directing my attention to the sparkling water like an omen, a good one this time. The perfect, round moon shone brightly on the horizon, illuminating everyone's smiles.

"Pretty good actually."

"Sure did," Nate said, jumping to his feet. "Body Slam!"

Nate lifted Sean, then slammed him down in Hulk Hogan fashion.

"Boys, please." I clasped my hands in faux prayer. "Last time you started your WWE tricks, Conner broke a toe!"

Anytime one of the guys impressed the other, their reward was a Body Slam, and apparently they'd already acquainted Nate with this tradition. Again, another example of why I'd never understand boys.

"You're right, 'Mom'. We should really be more responsible." Sean sat next to Nicole and ripped open the bag of SunChips.

"I'm loading this onto YouTube as we speak." Nicole had already reviewed *Ode to a Septic Tank* on her phone. *Nice.*

I smiled. "I don't know whether I'd kiss or slap Conner for the song if he was here right now."

"Definitely kiss," Nate said, staring at me, like he was ready to fill in.

Well, he did sing the song.

"You two are weird." Tammy chucked a Twix bar at my head.

"Right you are," Nate said. "Which is why it's time we all form a love circle and hold hands and sit crisscross applesauce." He picked up Breedlove. "No beach night is complete without a rendition of Kumbaya."

Nicole joined in last. "Nate Barca, you're gonna make me barfa. This is the first and last time I sneak out with you."

I saw the song as another tribute to Conner, who no doubt sung this tune many times on Boy Scout trips. I looked out at the waves as we belted out the lyrics, the violent surf pounding in and clinging to the shore with frothy fingers.

Does Conner see me crying, praying, laughing, and now, singing?

Water inches over my bare feet. I wake up and check Conner's Storm Trooper watch. He looks at me, like he's preparing for something. I smile, and he rips me off the beach

towel and plunges me into Lake Michigan, holding me under. I convulse in horror, unable to plea for my life. Finally, my body stops flopping, lifeless now. Conner gathers me in his arms, looking down at my dead eyes. He brushes water from my face and lays me on the towel again.

He scans the horizon and laughs as Sean and Kyle walk toward him on the beach, carrying a poker table. They set it up right at the edge of the water, next to my towel.

Kyle nods at my stiff body. "Will Olga be joining our game?"

Conner deals the cards. "Nope. I'm disappointed in her. She wasn't able to save herself. I loved her, you know? I just hope she'll do the right thing now."

"Enough with the heavy. It's Guys Night Out!" Sean reaches behind him and places a bag of potato chips and a container of Heluva Good Dip on the table.

Seagulls circled over us, squawking like maniacs. I blinked a few times and absorbed my surroundings, but all I could think about was the dream. They were really something lately, weird enough to send me into cardiac arrest just thinking about them.

Crap. We weren't supposed to fall asleep.

Lifting Nate's arm, which was strangely draped over me, I noticed the time on his Storm Trooper watch, last night's initiation gift from the Jedi Order. We gave one to Tammy, too. The tiny display read six-thirty. The sun graced the horizon.

I was supposed to be sleeping in my bed! Frantically, I shook Nate. But then something white and nasty hit my forehead. I looked up and saw three seagulls circling above us before heading for the lake.

Double crap.

"Eww, ewwey, eww, eww!" I touched my finger to my hairline.

"Well, it is all fun and games until some bird poops on your head, and then it's freakin' hilarious!" Nate pointed at me and laughed so hard he woke the others.

"Stop it," I managed through giggles, jumping up and down. "You're gonna make me pee my pants!"

"Usually number one comes before two, not the other way around," Sean said, holding out his hand to Nate for a fist bump.

I crossed my arms and grimaced even though I was tempted to smile. "The lame jokes keep on coming today, guys, don't they?"

"I'm sorry. But really, it's tomorrow, so I haven't nearly filled my lame joke quota for the day." Nate winked at me.

"Seriously, can you go dunk your head in the water?" Kyle asked. "You're starting to smell stank."

"Wouldn't be the first time," Tammy said.

I kicked off my sneakers and socks, then rolled up my pant legs.

"I swear it's like I have a bounty on my head from the poop gods." I raced down the hill toward the water, feeling like Conner had something to do with this. Or maybe getting pooped on was just bad karma for sneaking out. Trudging ankle deep in the cold water, I scrubbed poop off my hair and skin.

"If it's any consolation, I think a bird pooping on your head symbolizes good luck." Nate handed me a towel.

I ran a hand through my tangled hair. "I'm pretty sure people just tell you it's lucky so you'll feel better."

Nate shrugged. "Hey, I'm not the one full of crap."

I splashed water on his face. "Whatever. I'll take seagull poop over the human variety any day."

"You need a ride home?" Nicole asked, arriving at the shore with everyone, and every*thing* in tow.

"Yeah, we're starting to cut things close, so I don't think walking is an option. I'll have to crawl through my window as it is."

When we were a few streets down from mine, we caught sight of Dad too late. He drove his Ford, on the way to get his Sunday morning paper before church, and spotted me passing by in Nicole's car.

Busted.

"I watched him walk, temporarily distracted by the handsomeness of his tan face, the coffee colored hair sweeping across his forehead."

Chapter Seven

"Never take cues from the crowd."
—Unknown

So, I guess I'll be ungrounded soon," I told Dr. Judy. Repeat anxiety attacks over going back to school on Tuesday landed me in her office for an emergency visit… the Saturday before Labor Day!

Dr. Judy's eyes grew bright as she leaned forward. "How do you feel about that?"

I shrugged. Since Dad busted me for sneaking out, I spent the rest of my summer, a whole two months, grounded from everything except work.

"Being grounded wasn't so bad. I still got to work at The Bookman and on newspaper stuff with Nicole, and come here. And the list wasn't on total hiatus since I was able to watch a lot, *a lot*, of the hundred greatest movies of all time, read *The Lord of the Ring* series, and start my own blog. The only people who read it are Nicole and Nate, but that's still two more followers than I thought I'd have. Truth is being around Nate is like an escape from my unhappiness, so not being able to see him much was like the only thing that majorly sucked about being grounded. But maybe I don't deserve him anyways."

Leaning across her desk, Dr. Judy asked, "Do you really believe that?"

I shrugged again and changed the subject, something she allowed me to do most of the time when I didn't want to answer a question. "Do you want to hear something weird?" I pulled out my journal. "I never remembered my dreams until now. I mean until after I took that bottle of pills. It's like the whole experience of almost dying altered my state of mind or something."

Dr. Judy crossed her arms and gave me a knowing smirk. "In my experience, many patients return to their near-death experiences through their dreams. Maybe it's your brain's way of trying to make sense of your memories, or maybe like you said, almost dying altered your state of mind. It could've awakened some muscle memory you never used before."

"But these dreams don't contain my memories. Well, they kind of do, but they're altered." My breath tucked itself away in my chest, refusing to come out until Dr. Judy told me I wasn't crazy.

She nodded to my journal, then closed her eyes and sat back in her seat. "I assume you wrote it down. Will you read it to me?"

I gripped the black leather-bound book tight enough to cause bruising, but I loosened my fingers and then turned to the last page I'd written on.

Mom tiptoed into my bedroom. The only light came from the setting sun, through a slit in my curtains. She crept closer, nose turning up at the funky smell. She untwisted the zebra blanket clinging to my body and reached out to touch my face. Her hand froze as she muttered, "Oh, God."

She put her ear to my mouth to listen for breathing. She checked the pulse on my wrist and gasped. I could tell she wanted to scream, but the sound curdled into nothing as she realized I was dead. Finally, she looked around the room, sucked in a deep breath, then let the sound loose.

Dad came running in, then pushed past her. He was the one to dial 9-1-1, tears in his eyes as he reported the empty pill bottle on my nightstand.

In the ambulance, I heard another distress call over the radio, and it was for Nate Barca.

When I arrived at the hospital, every room I passed had the number eighteen on it. I was there, following the dead me on the gurney all the way to the autopsy room in the basement. They stuck me in a refrigerated area, and when the medical examiner left, I unzipped the plastic bag. As I examined my corpse, it rose to life again and fought me. The whole time, I kicked and punched myself, and I heard whispered prayers for my soul. The dead me knocked the other me unconscious and then Conner came in and told me to wake up, and I did.

Cringing, I closed my journal and then hugged it to my chest, praying Dr. Judy could help me decipher what this dream meant.

She gave the office a crisp sweep before returning her gaze to me. "Dreams are about taking the focus off ourselves and taking a break from our every day lives. Sometimes when we have those really weird dreams, it's simply us taking all the events from our day, or past, throwing them together and then trying to make sense of everything."

Pulling in a deep, cleansing breath, I said, "Okay, I get that but Conner…"

My voice drifted off as I spotted the Grand Haven Pier photograph behind Dr. Judy's desk. A small whimper escaped my lips, remembering everything I'd been through. I craved a better explanation than the one she gave me. It almost felt like Conner tried to communicate from the grave through my dreams or something. I also knew how crazy that sounded.

Dr. Judy rolled up her sleeves, then fidgeted, tapping one long fingernail on her chin. "I think Conner keeps popping up in some parts of your dream because of the bond you shared. You were very close over the past twelve years, so you shared many of the same experiences, including the most tragic event of your life. Logic tells me that he would be the one to help you make sense of everything even now, if only through your dream state." She picked up a pen and twirled it between her fingers. "I don't know how comfortable you are with spiritual stuff, but maybe you should meditate on these dreams and seek God's opinion on them. The book of Romans in the Bible speaks of the spirit interceding for us because we don't know to pray as we should. You said you heard whispered prayers for your soul in your dream. Maybe the Spirit is trying to relay some information to you through your sleep."

I stared at the polished metal crucifix hanging on her wall. "Wouldn't it be easier if you just put me under hypnosis or something? Maybe I could try to meet Conner in my dream and try to figure all of this out."

Dr. Judy wiggled in her chair. "Hypnotherapy won't help with understanding your dreams. I could use it on you to help deal with your guilt and grief, but I've always felt that was a bit like cheating."

I reached into my tote bag and put away my journal, the subject of dreams clearly closed.

"What's that other book you have in there?" Dr. Judy asked, peering over her desk.

"A memory scrapbook Nicole brought me from the bookstore a few days after Conner died. She helped me fill it up. Do you want to see a picture of him?"

She nodded. "Very much so."

I took a deep breath and opened up the scrapbook, tears falling from my eyes.

Dr. Judy handed me a tissue. "He was really handsome, wasn't he? Do you mind if I look at some more of the pictures, or is it too painful?"

I stood and laid the scrapbook on the desk, then leaned over her shoulder. Flipping through the snapshots, I gave her detailed explanations for each. Birthday celebrations, holidays, sailing competitions, the annual Coast Guard festival. The memories all there, in case I ever forgot. The last one I came across was from two Octobers ago, the surprise sweet sixteen birthday party Conner and Nicole threw for me. It was a small gathering. Both of our parents were there, Megan because she hadn't left for college yet, and Sean and Kyle. I had thought Conner was just taking me out to dinner to a fancy French restaurant along the Grand River channel, but when we arrived, everybody was waiting for me in the back room. The picture showed me seated in my chair, sixteen balloons behind me, Conner down on one knee. His present, besides the party, was re-gifting the Morticia Addams gumball machine ring I'd given him when we were eleven. *The Addams Family* was one of our all-time favorite movies.

"I didn't think he possessed a single sentimental bone in his body until that night," I said.

Dr. Judy closed the scrapbook, then rested her hand gently on mine. "Where's the ring now?"

I walked around her desk, then shoved the book back into my tote. "In my night stand at home. It's too painful to wear."

I sat in my bedroom after counseling and a long day at work, staring at the sweet sixteen picture. Deciding not to leave this one in the scrapbook, I walked over to my backpack hanging on my swivel chair, all ready to go for Tuesday. I taped the picture to the inside of my planner, where I'd see Conner's face the most. Then I opened the drawer on my nightstand, debated for a minute if wearing the ring would be too painful like I thought, then slid it on my finger.

Hurt like hell.

But I'd keep wearing the ring as a reminder of my pain. Conner would be the only guy I ever loved, because if I never loved again, I'd never have to be this sad again.

In a rare act of kindness, Mom agreed to end my sentence one day early so I could attend the last day of the annual two-week long Coast Guard Festival downtown. The leniency was probably only because we'd signed up the Cantankerous Monkey Squad to compete in the Battle of the Bands. It was part of the festival's concluding events. Bands came from all over the midwest to compete because the festival attracted such big crowds every year. So Mom knew I'd be forced to sneak out again if she tried to keep me from attending.

Sitting at our cozy glass-top kitchen table, I sipped my vanilla flavored coffee and hoped this little bit of comfort would last me through the day. Looking up, I counted the coffee mugs I'd purchased for Dad over the years. Ever since they started letting me drink coffee, mugs were the only thing I gave him for birthdays and Christmas. Eighteen cheap porcelain cups with cutesy pictures of snowmen, stockings, lakes, and golfing greens lined the top of our kitchen cabinets.

Mom wasn't so sentimental. She'd never hung my school work on the fridge, never told me good job for all my straight A's, only, 'Why did you get a B on this test?' Perfection was the standard in my house, not the exception. Picturing those formative years when my parents were my best friends proved difficult now. They didn't conceive until their late thirties, so all their friends' kids were much older. Having no playmates my age until I started elementary school meant I'd developed an old soul from the start, participating in their grownup conversations and drinking coffee—starting in third grade—albeit, only miniature cups back then.

Sighing, I flipped open my laptop and typed another blog, keeping time.

I feel small and tired today. Forget today, how about every day. Things have been so tough in my life lately, and I can't remember when life was good. Minute by minute, I struggle not to think of the accident. I wish I had courage to face tomorrow. I wish I had peace over what happened. I wish I felt like there was a purpose to my life.

Right after Conner died, I thought I'd never go on, like the only thing ahead of me was suffering, loss, grief. Then I started my life list. The 18 Things helped push me toward a goal, but now I feel like all my dreams have fallen flat. I've worked hard all my life, but what's the use? Things didn't work out for me. I don't know how to handle all this grief. Before Conner's accident, if someone would've asked me what the most powerful weapon in the world was, I wouldn't have known the answer. I might've guessed a nuclear bomb. A knife in the hands of your enemy. A United States Marine and his gun. A missile. But now, I know the answer with absolute certainty: the most destructive force isn't anything you can hold physically with your hands, it's something you hold in your heart. It's a tiny five-letter word, not even hard to pronounce: g-u-i-l-t. It kills you slowly from the inside out, and there are no drugs to numb the pain.

I almost typed, 'I would know,' but I also felt too guilty about that incident to even admit to the deed. The only people who knew about it were my parents and Nicole. I sighed, pounding the keyboard while I summed up my thoughts.

Sometimes I'm tempted to daydream about my future, then I stop myself, wondering if the future is really in my hands. Life is so not fair.

"Life is so not fair," Mom repeated over my shoulder, making me jump.

I hit the post button and then shut my laptop with a little more force than necessary. "You wanna argue with me about that, too?"

She sat next to me and took hold of my hand. "I have your father as a husband and you as a daughter, so anyone would be hard pressed convincing me life is *all* unfair. You just need time to heal. And that's okay. But I think everything happens for a reason, even if we don't see the why just now."

I cleared my throat, so over the 'everything happens for a reason' right now. "Yeah, well, if you'll excuse me, I gotta go."

Sean pulled his truck into the last parking spot in front of Buffalo Bob's skate shop downtown, and Nicole was forced to Parallel Park her Civic on a side street nearby. All sorts of folks were packed in the blocked off areas. Nate and Kyle helped Sean gather the band gear out of the trunk, while the girls helped me retrieve my supplies. During my time spent in Mom's Boot Camp, I bought a box of thirty plain red T-shirts and another box of thirty plain blue T-shirts. I experimented in Photoshop and created different iron-ons featuring angry chimps and the name of the band. I wanted to see how they sold tonight at twelve bucks a piece. Increasing their fan base was my first step in helping Cantankerous Monkey Squad land a record deal.

I arranged the shirts on the table the event coordinators set up for me, and Tammy came over to help.

"So what's with the hippy skirt you're wearing tonight? New look?" she asked.

I harrumphed. "Kind of. Mom let me borrow it. Her old hippie look matches the band better than any clothes I own, and I wanted to dress the part since I'm selling these shirts."

I tugged my own Cantankerous Monkey Squad shirt over my stomach, admiring the logo I designed.

Tammy blew a bubble, and the gum popped in her face. She wiped off the sticky substance with her hand.

"Nice," I said.

She laughed. "Just like that skirt."

I fluffed my hair with my newly polished fingernails. "Well, at least my hair and nails look great for once. Nicole helped me get ready when she came to pick me up."

Tapping manicured nails on the table, Tammy said, "Totally hot. And you can still wear cool jewelry even if your clothes suck. Come and look at this stuff."

She dragged me to a tent where necklaces dangled from an Eiffel Tower Jewelry Stand. "Check this one out."

Tammy held out a blue glass pendant on a sterling silver necklace with a diamond in the middle.

"It's beautiful." I searched for the tag, then whistled at the five-hundred dollar price. "Wish I could afford it. It'd probably be the only diamond I ever get."

She unclasped the necklace, then held it around my neck so I could see what it looked like in the tiny mirror mounted on the canvas. "Nonsense. And you should splurge. I never see you spending any money you earn from the bookstore."

A flush crept across my cheeks as I caught a wistful look from Nate in the mirror. I hadn't seen him standing there.

I cleared my throat. "Nah. I'm saving money for college. But what do you say you, me, and Nicole grab a bite to eat before Battle of the Bands starts?"

"Sounds perfect," Nicole said from behind.

I glanced at the table where she taped her poster advertising our T-shirt sales.

"Your bubble letters haven't changed a bit since third grade," I said as she steered our little group toward the sub shop. "And do we really need to eat at the Pavilion Wharf Pizza and Sub Shop again? We go there on our lunch break almost every day."

"Hello? A submarine sandwich is a very fitting meal for the Coast Guard Festival."

The automatic door slid open, and we all sailed in, the sky behind us as blue as the sea.

We got so wrapped up in our convo at dinner that we almost missed the start of the boys set. I took my seat in Waterfront Stadium as Kyle picked up his sticks, ready for their first song. The guys looked adorable in their matching ensembles: frayed jeans, a mixture of red and blue Cantankerous Monkey Squad shirts, tweed jackets they found at a thrift store, and a pair of two dollar reading glasses they bought at The Bookman. After their self-titled song, I shifted the water bottle I held to underneath my arm, then clapped with the rest of the captive audience. They adjusted some of the settings before the next and final song while I snarfed down the bag of SunChips left over from my value meal.

They announced they were ready and the small crowd cheered, clearly the hometown favorite.

"Thanks for your patience. I'm Nate. On electric guitar, we have Sean, and on drums, we have Kyle. To our right, you can buy the CD. It's underneath the green tent with white stripes. Also, starting today, we have available the newly handmade Cantankerous Monkey Squad shirts. Olga, stand up, please, so we can thank you properly for all your hard work."

I wanted to crawl underneath a slide, as I did when I was in kindergarten, and make myself small, then wait for Conner to rescue me. All eyes trained on me, and suddenly, I found the ground very interesting. At least I had my merchandise table to hide behind.

"This next song is titled *Return*." Nate's ocean blue eyes rolled in the back of his head, reminding me of Conner's death.

Shivers tingled down my spine.

Several girls to my left held up their hands, swaying to the music and batting their eyelashes at the guys, like real groupies. The entire crowd forgot about their lawn chairs and danced around, a blur of red, white, and blue, complete with a standing ovation as the cymbals hummed the last note.

The crowd cheered and clapped.

Nate found me and stared, but a guy to my left distracted me, repeatedly yelling, "Yeah, baby!"

Clapping my hands, I joined his praise, and for some reason, I felt compelled to speak with him. "Seems you liked what you heard."

He nodded and took a sip from his red solo cup. "They are really entertaining. There aren't a whole lot of young bands that can play well and still be interesting to watch live."

I rocked back and forth on my heels and checked him out. He wore a red spandex muscle shirt, but I tried not to hold that against him because I got a hunch this guy was someone important. "My name's Olga. I'm kinda like their groupie. Uh, not in every sense of the word. I make their T-shirts."

I wiped the chip grease onto Mom's skirt, then held out my hand.

His handshake was firm. "I'm Alan. I scout out talent at different events like Music Walk and Battle of the Bands."

A girl walked by, distributing a business ad in the form of a hand-fan made from heavy cardstock and a light wood handle like a Popsicle stick, which reminded me how Conner and I could go through a whole box of Creamsicles on a summer day like this. I wondered if he had anything to do with this serendipitous meeting with Alan. "So, do you like, work for a record label?"

He nodded. "Yes, for a small, independent label Mixed Tape."

Taking another sip of water and fanning myself, I tried to keep my cool as I felt the perfect timing of divine intervention clicking together. "So, are you gonna offer them a record deal?"

Wind blew a thick cloud of his bad cologne my way and I coughed as he cocked his head to the side and smiled. "I wish. I don't have that kind of clout. I can only meet with the band and report what I like to my boss. If he thinks they're sellable, then he'll tell me to set up a gig for them so he can see them play. If he likes them, that's when the ball starts rolling."

The guys cleared their equipment from the stage, and Nate stepped up to the microphone. "We're Cantankerous Monkey Squad. Don't forget to like us on Facebook and check out a bonus track on YouTube. And go buy a T-shirt! Peace out."

"Well, duty calls," I said, holding out my hand to Alan.

His cell phone rang, and he mumbled a 'Nice meeting you,' then took off.

A warm glow spread throughout my body as I headed toward the tent. Nicole and Tammy helped me for the next two hours, but I was too excited for the band to think straight. Making correct change proved too difficult for my brain.

"Who's talking to the band?" Nicole asked, accepting a twenty from someone, then she handed them back a five and three ones, completing the sale of the last T-shirt.

I couldn't believe we sold out.

I spied the guys talking to Alan by the stage and smiled. "Number three on my list."

We gathered the tin full of money and the now empty boxes and then headed back to the stadium seating. Twelve bands performed two songs each, and now they were ready to crown the new winner.

"Thank you," the lead singer from last year's winning band announced as the huge crowd screamed. "First, on behalf of the promoter for this event, Big Jimbo, I'd like to thank our five local celeb judges. They stepped up to volunteer for the impossible task of choosing the top three performances. Today's extremely talented bands came from all over the country.

"All three will take home a cash prize, but top dog will also leave with some free studio recording time. Third prize, all the way from Cleveland, is Jasperwal. Second place, from just across the lake in Milwaukee, Under the Joshua Tree."

Weird both band names are references from the Bible.

"And first place, from right here in Grand Haven, our very own Cantankerous Monkey Squad."

I closed my eyes, appreciating the applause and all the support the band earned from the community, and I wished Conner experienced this achievement with me. After a minute, I looked around Waterfront Stadium, the setting sun shining the last of its rays on the stage.

I sighed at the official end of summer, and prayed I didn't get any death threats tomorrow.

Focus Question:

What type of symbolism does Olga's dream sequence suggest?

Chapter Eight

*"If you're going to do something tonight
that you'll be sorry for tomorrow morning,
sleep late."*
—Henny Youngman

I n déjà vu fashion, school was the last place I wanted to be. I dressed for the first day of my senior year in a mesh Michigan football jersey and a pair of skinny jeans. Nicole had taken pity on me and brought me a new outfit yesterday when she picked me up for the festival.

Looking out across our back porch, I noticed the ducks waiting by the pond for their bread or cheerios. Since I hadn't much company this summer, I'd taken it upon myself to feed them as part of my morning routine. Leaving them high and dry just because I was returning to school seemed cruel. I grabbed a bagel, ripped it into pieces, then threw them into our backyard while repeating a pep talk Dr. Judy gave me at our emergency session on Saturday. First, she told me to list all my blessings to help stay focused on the positive. *Okay, good things. The Jedi Order, newspaper, The Bookman, books, coffee, a second chance, the beach, Jesus, school. School?* Somehow school worked itself into my subconscious. Well, Dr. Judy said challenges are our real opportunities to know who we are and what we have the potential to be. If I could get through this year, the next one would be easier—it had to be. I had to press on and finish the race of high school, so I could apply for tons of scholarships this year. College was my only ticket out of here.

Nicole's clicking high heels snapped me out of my reverie. "Oh, you look truly amazing in the jersey!"

I gave her a hug. "Thanks. Whoever bought it for me must have really good taste."

"I totally do. It's all sexy with attitude on you."

Mom approached from behind and cleared her throat, as if she couldn't stand to hear the word sexy describing her daughter. "Hello, Nicole. Olga, you girls should hurry so you're not late."

She poured herself a cup of coffee and clinked her spoon against the mug. I grabbed my backpack off the floor and clutched some books in front of me like a security blanket. Not one goodbye between us, like these past five months taught us nothing at all.

We headed toward Nicole's shiny, silver Honda Civic in the parking lot, and Nic studied me the whole way. "What's with the tone and glare? Your mom still mad about us sneaking out?"

I nodded. "Did you forget who my mom is? If there was a world record for grudge holding, she'd be listed in Guinness."

"Man, parents really suck."

"That may be the truest statement you've ever made. Ready to roll?"

She smiled and swaggered to the driver's side, keys in hand. "Let's go meet my peoplez!"

I laughed at our contradictive emotions. I couldn't feel any less enthusiastic.

When I walked through the front doors with Nicole, everyone stared at me.

"I have a really big nose," I told her, joining everyone else's whispers.

Slamming lockers echoed through the hallway, making me jittery.

"What? No, you don't. You have a strong nose."

I blinked and swallowed the lump rising in my throat. "I was just trying to delude myself into thinking they're gossiping about some other aspect of my life. But you really think my nose is strong? What does that mean?"

She laughed, but I held out my hand and she grasped my fingers, keeping me near, keeping me safe. A memorial plaque with Conner's school photo on it hung on the wall to my right, a poem about Heaven beside the picture. Suddenly this place didn't feel like a high school anymore. It felt like a funeral home.

My body shook, and I squeezed my eyes shut. "I think I'm gonna puke."

"S.T.A.R.," came Tammy's perky voice behind me. "Turn around and open your eyes. You're about to become yesterday's news, baby."

Two girls who'd always hung out with Tammy last year walked in together, each sporting a preggo bump.

A small gasp escaped my lips. "Baby is right."

"God bless them both," Nicole blurted.

I turned to Tammy. "Did you know already?"

She shook her head and put her hand on mine, then pulled me down the hall. "Nope. They've been M.I.A. this summer; guess now we know why. It appears everyone is just finding out. I bet they got themselves knocked up at prom. They hooked up with some guys from Lakeview that night. Anyway, they should provide a nice distraction from the Conner and Olga gossip for the rest of the year. Plus, that means two less people to compete for a cheerleading spot."

We spotted Nate, Sean, and Kyle up ahead, standing under a handmade poster for this Friday's pep rally. A yawning student approached them, then handed Kyle a couple of bucks in exchange for an energy drink. Kyle, always the entrepreneur, started selling them on the down low last year after the school banned energy drinks and sodas from the vending machines.

Nate turned and saw me, his goofy grin warming me from the top of my head to the bottoms of my feet.

"Good to see you," he said.

He was no stranger to The Bookman this summer. Nicole said there was no way he really needed all those books and stuff. She thought he used 'reading' as an excuse to see me since I'd been grounded. As I restocked books and dusted shelves, we shared lots of animated conversations about life and dreams. Even when I handled the register for hours, he still stayed near, sharing secret smiles with me over grumpy costumers while he sat in the armchair by the window. The Jedi Order also started our Saturday morning breakfasts at Morning Star Café before my shift. My parents thought I went in early to unload shipments.

The lies came easily now.

My hands felt sweaty, so I stuck them in my pockets. "You, too. Guess Kyle is open for business already?"

Nate nodded, his hair falling over his forehead lower than usual, and I wondered if he planned on ever cutting his locks again. Nate looked like a younger, hotter version of Bono with his dark curls and sideburns. Nicole and Sean locked lips to my left, and Tammy and Kyle did the same thing to my right.

Annoyed with the awkward silence, I shuffled my feet, and my yellow sneakers squeaked against the hardwood floor.

Tammy came up for air, her face flushed, reaching underneath her shirt to push up her bra.

"Classy," I said.

She fluffed her teased, blonde hair. "Thanks. So, you're like totally ungrounded as of yesterday, right?"

I reached up, then tucked a stray curl behind my ear. "I think so. I mean, they said I was grounded until school started, and it's the first day, so—"

"Great! It's settled, then. Your first big party is this Saturday at Kyle's house. His parents are going out of town."

Looking around, I noticed the crowd in the hallway thinned and figured I should head to class.

"Yippee," I said dryly, twirling a finger in the air. "I'll catch up with you guys at lunch."

Nate walked beside me, apparently headed in the same direction. "Where you going?"

"Multivariable Calculus," I answered, looking down at my schedule to triple check.

"I don't even know what that means."

"It means I took regular Calculus last year, so this is a step up. I'm not taking it easy my senior year."

He laughed, patting me on the head. We arrived outside my classroom. "Good for you. That stuff's all Greek to me."

"Yeah, well nothing is more like a punishment out of Greek mythology than high school."

The bell tolled five times, the sound of a ship, reminding us Grand Haven was the Coast Guard capital of the good ole U.S.A.

Nate followed me into my class, then stepped in front of me. "Hey, have a good day, okay?"

A fluttery feeling settled in my belly.

He stretched out his hand, swept the long strands of hair out of my face, then turned on his heel and loped out the door, travelling in the same direction from where we just came.

I took my standard spot in the front row. Everyone stared, making me feel like a mannequin on display. Whatever, I was used to that. What I was not used to? My skin tingling strangely, making my head spin.

Mr. Propert skipped the introductions and jumped right into the lesson. The students in this class were serious about learning. Math wasn't even required for seniors, unless a student took remedial course as a freshman.

The teacher pointed to the first problem on the Smart Board, and I smiled. A calculus theorem I could figure out and prove. But trying to decipher my new feelings... butterflies in my stomach, dry mouth, heat rushing through my body in waves? I didn't have a clue.

I sat cross-legged on the floor of the gym, wrapping my hands around my neck, giving myself a massage.

"It's on your life list. You can't back out now," Tammy propped her pom poms on her hips.

In front of us, dozens of girls who actually wanted to be here learned tryout cheers. I took a swig from my water bottle, inhaled a deep breath, then tried to roll the stress from my shoulders, which were killing me after some not-so-skinny junior girl stood on them for my first pyramid formation.

"I just didn't think cheerleading would be so hard."

She brushed the blonde hair from her face with perfectly manicured nails and held out a hand to help me up.

"I love it when geniuses find the simple things difficult." She smiled widely. "But you're not terrible. If you work hard enough over the next few hours, I think you have a shot at making the squad."

I knew she was just being nice; let's not sugar-coat this... I stunk. Outside of sailing, I'd never been good at sports. That whole coordination thing was something I'd never mastered. In fact, I was prone to falling, and every time I did, the Jedi Order all shouted, 'Gravity Check!'

But for some reason, I did work hard during the next three hours, knowing it'd still take a miracle for me to make the team. There were plenty of other girls better than me. Maybe I channeled Conner's spirit. He always excelled at everything. Or maybe knowing I should have some sort of athletics for my senior year on my college application motivated me. Sailing team was no longer an option. Best of all reasons was perhaps it'd tick

Mom off if I made the team. I didn't even tell her I planned on trying out. Whatever my logic, when the coaches and Tammy, still head cheerleader, finally announced the roster for this year's squad at seven-thirty, my name was on the list.

Tammy ran over, then wrapped me in a hug. "Congratulations! I knew you could do it!"

Nodding, I didn't fully comprehend why I made the squad. Then it hit me. "You pulled your head cheerleader rank for me, didn't you?" Pressing my lips in a fine line, I broke away from her grasp. "Tammy, I don't want a pity spot."

Her hand flew to her halter-top. "I didn't. I mean yeah, I recommended you, but Coach agreed. You may not have been the best one out there, but you had the most heart, and you worked the hardest. I mean, you'll be like the cheerleader for our cheerleading squad."

I never thought of earning a spot that way, but her words were actually kind of touching. I headed straight home and told my parents the news. I figured a congratulatory dinner or speech or anything displaying a sense of pride in their daughter would be out of the question, and they didn't disappoint.

"We need to talk," I said after walking through the front door. "Here. Incase you ever want to come watch one of my games." I handed Mom the cheerleading schedule.

She sighed so hard I think actual smoke fumed from her ears. "You've got to be kidding me. You are way too intelligent to become a dumb cheerleader."

I sat on our seen-better-days lumpy couch, a permanent staple of our living room since my childhood.

Dad relaxed in his Lazy Boy across from the television. "I didn't realize you wanted to…" He stopped and cleared his throat. Then he looked at Mom and I saw her calculating stare, warning him not to get involved.

Mom stood over me, her usual power position. "Is there a permission slip I need to sign?"

I retrieved the form from my bag on the floor, then handed the paper to her.

She didn't even read the paper before tearing it up.

Propping my socked feet on our wooden coffee table shaped like the state of Michigan, I pulled a power play of my own.

"Whatever, Mom. Tear it up. I'm eighteen next month, and I won't need your permission then to join the squad. And by the way, cheerleaders *aren't* dumb." I wanted to add, only your rules are, but thought better of it since she could still ground me.

With each exhale, her face burned redder, and she flashed me a look with fire in her eyes, like I wasn't her daughter any more but rather the spawn of Satan. But I just gritted my teeth and stood my ground. I needed a change. No more depression. No more life on autopilot. No more unconscious thought behind my actions. No more heading toward some pre-determined destination chosen for me by my parents. For the first time in my life, probable valedictorian or not, I finally thought on my own.

For the first time in my life, probable valedictorian or not, I finally thought on my own.

Chapter Nine

"Memory is the diary that chronicles history that couldn't possibly have happened."
—*Oscar Wilde*

When I arrived at Kyle's, the only light in the living room emanated from a few lava lamps and black light sets around the room. The band already played loudly. I headed to the back corner where a folding table served as a makeshift all-you-can-eat junk food buffet. All ten of the extra large pizza boxes were empty.

"The early bird gets the worm," Tammy said, appearing beside me with a plate of brownies. "Want one? They're fresh outta the oven."

I eyed the brownies suspiciously. I couldn't picture Tammy in the kitchen wearing an apron Betty Crocker style. Up until a few months ago, I thought she was rich enough to have maids waiting on her hand and foot. "Um, yeah, if they're regular brownies."

She loaded one onto a monkey-themed paper plate, then handed it to me. "Like, if you're insinuating what I think you are, then don't even. I only smoke cigarettes. I wouldn't do anything to get fired from my spot as head cheerleader."

Nodding, I grabbed a handful of salty chips and a chocolate chip cookie, then searched the cooler on the floor next to the table until I discovered the last root beer.

The door slammed behind us, another carful of guys arriving, and Tammy said, "The dinner of champions."

This group already seemed drunk. I recognized one boy, Dave, from my Driver's Ed class. I chomped on my cookie for a few seconds, watching the boys head straight to the back porch where several people played Quarters. Like Zeus sitting on his throne surrounded by worshipers, the beer keg sat prominently on the patio table.

"Did you make these cookies, too?" I asked, my mouth full.

She struck a match, and smoke formed a cloud around me. "Yep. Good, right?"

"Sweet. Maybe you can teach me how to bake sometime." I grabbed another cookie, then excused myself to the leather couch sitting against the wall. I wanted to listen to the band.

For the past five years, I heard Conner play guitar and sing every week. He had such raw talent, and I knew it'd be tough to replace him. But as I listened to them playing *Haunted*, I didn't think I'd ever heard them play so well in the two years' time they'd been a band.

Mostly the stoner non-conformists clique from school littered the green carpet, moshing as Nate hit all the right notes, Sean nailed the rhythms on his bass, and Kyle whaled on his drums.

The song ended, and Nate cleared his throat by the microphone, ready to address the crowd of twenty-something people. "We'd like to thank everyone for coming out tonight and supporting the newly regrouped Cantankerous Monkey Squad."

Whoops and hollers rang out.

"I'm sure all of you know they lost their previous singer to a tragic accident five months ago. This last song we're playing for you tonight is one we found in Conner's song book after he passed away. *Return* is its title."

Nate belted out the lyrics Conner wrote. "I am the branches, and you are my vine/ Most of the time, we sit and wait for a sign/ But I don't know if I can wait much longer/ I intend to face all those things I've pondered/ All those broken bridges I've burned, I'll mend/ And become someone on who you can depend/ So don't be afraid, I will return/ After my life lessons, I have learned/ I will return/ I'll try not to get lost in all the chatter/ And find a way to make my life matter/ And you do the same to find your own place/ And don't wish our mistakes, we could erase/ We'll grow into the people we're meant to be/ Lovers who eat afternoon picnics under Sycamore trees/ So don't be afraid; I will return/ After my life lessons, I have learned/ I will return/ So no need to cry/ This isn't goodbye/ For you, I will always sing/ Like eagles, we will soar with our new wings/ When the curtain tears in two at the end of the day/ My love for you will never fade away/ So don't be afraid, I will return/ After my life lessons, I have learned/ I will return/ I will return."

The band never missed a beat, but my heart did. I pretended Conner wrote the words of the song just for me. All the 'What if' questions plagued my mind, and pain throbbed in my chest. I hung my head low, my hair falling over the sides of my face, and I stared at my sneakers very carefully, trying not to cry. Paralyzed on the couch, my mind flashed to the weekend before he died, the last time I unofficially heard him sing.

The Jedi Order had taken me out to a fifties diner called Dee-Lite Bar and Grill. Getting my first 'C' on a test at school depressed me, and they thought breakfast for dinner would cheer me up. Still, Conner didn't like the way I wasn't laughing at his usual jokes, so he convinced Sean to stand with him when open mic started, and he sang *Don't Stop Believin'* by Journey. I'd give anything now to have something, *anything*, to believe in.

Nate spoke loudly into the mic, pulling me out of my flashback. I frowned, feeling all the blood drain out of my feet. The memory felt so fresh, like that night happened just yesterday.

"We'll have T-shirts made up with our name and logo next show, so be prepared to fork out some money! No freebies here, suckers! Anyway, hopefully you liked us and will spread the word."

More loud cries of agreement.

Those cheerleaders screaming from the kitchen are really getting on my nerves. I giggled. *Oh yeah, I'm one of them now.*

Nate continued, "Yeah, you like that, ladies? *Anyway*, there are movies in the den off to the left and video games in Kyle's bedroom to the right. You can stay right here and chill if you want. Just please, no slobbering on the furniture, homies. Peace out, everybody!"

I had to tell the band what a great job they did. Leaning forward, I attempted to stand, but Dave blocked me, shoving a beer in my face. "Hey, Olga. You want one?"

Ugh. He reeked of beer.

"Um, no thanks. I'm D.A.R.E. president," I joked, but sarcasm was lost on him.

"Nice outfit." He grinned from ear to ear, holding up his can as if giving cheers to my ensemble, a knee-length gray sweater dress.

"Thanks."

99

Spilled beer streaked his shirt was streaked with spilled beer and an open fly graced his jeans.

I scanned the room for Nate only to discover Brittany, another big haired, big boobed, blonde cheerleader, wrapping her arms around his waist from behind.

I looked again at Dave, his eyes wide and unguarded. "So, how about me, you, and my Porsche get out of here?"

In Driver's Ed, Dave constantly talked about his car, so I heard this annoying pickup line of sorts from him a lot. "Sorry, but I don't date underclassmen."

Nate shuffled over. "Oh, epic fail, dude."

Dave, a sophomore, pressed the can to his lips and chugged. "Why don't you date underclassmen?"

"Because," I said, my gaze bouncing from Nate to Dave. "Boys my own age are already immature. Now, if you'll excuse me, I'm gonna go watch Star Wars."

"And I'm immature," he slurred.

Nate lifted an eyebrow. "Dude, shut up, and XYZ."

I stood and crushed the empty soda can with trembling hands. I couldn't pinpoint the exact cause of my anger, but it drummed inside me as I entered the movie room, *A New Hope* already playing. As young Luke Skywalker began discovering his destiny, and while I contemplated mine, someone rubbed my shoulders. I had an inkling as to whose those hands were, based on the boozy smell emanating from them, but I didn't know how to turn around and tell Dave to knock it off.

He scratched my back and got dangerously close to brushing the sides of my ta-tas in doing so.

I jumped up so fast I knocked over a bowl of popcorn sitting on the floor, a sick thudding in my abdomen.

Some angry nerds shouted, "Hey! Watch it!" as I scurried out of the room, but not before confirming my suspicion it'd been Dave who tried to molest me.

Heading for the slider, I caught a glimpse of Nate and Brittany sitting together on a Detroit Lions inflatable chair. He looked at me, and caught off guard, I ran head long into the sliding glass door.

That'll leave a mark. Surprisingly, my head didn't even hurt. I trudged through Kyle's spacious backyard to the sound of party-goers laughing, hoping the snickers weren't directed at me. Ninety-nine percent of the time I felt certain people laughed at me, not with me.

"Hey, Olga. Wait up! Where's the fire, huh?"

I turned around and glared at Dave.

Can't this guy take a hint?

A sure sign a girl's not into you: she bolted from the room after you nearly touched her ta-tas. I continued hiking through the overgrown yard as fast as I could to get away, but then I stepped in some dog crap. The blood drained out of my face, and I sighed.

Why is it always the crap?

I scraped my shoe against a tree.

Dave came up from behind and placed two enormous hands on each side of me, resting them on the bark, his thumbs caressing my upper arms.

I turned sharply. "Look, Dave, I don't mean to be rude but…"

"Then don't, baby." He caressed my face with his hand. "I know I'm not your first choice, but I'm alive."

Panicked now, my head spun, but I tried to harness all the misery of this night and direct it toward him without my voice shaking. "Really? That's your best pickup line? You're *alive*?"

"I'm just saying," he slurred. "You have choices, ya know?"

He leaned in, mouth open.

On impulse, I slapped him hard. *Wow, that felt incredible!* I'd never actually witnessed a girl slapping a guy in real life, only in the movies and books, and suddenly, I felt as erratic as Scarlett O'Hara in *Gone with the Wind*.

"Oh, you like to play it rough, my little dominatrix." Cupping one hand behind my head and the other around my waist, he tried to force me into a kiss.

I shifted my head side to side, trying unsuccessfully to push away.

My mind raced; I couldn't overpower him or scream. He settled for kissing my neck instead, and his lips sucked my flesh like a vampire.

I spotted Nate at the edge of porch, peering through the black night. My eyes widened, convinced he wasn't there just a second ago, and my whole body shook, praying he'd spot us and come to the rescue. I heard him calling my name. Somehow, my prayers were answered.

"Olga?" He rushed through the darkness. "Are you okay?"

Dave's hands flew off me, and I let out a huge breath.

"This girl's into some freaky crap, dude," Dave said.

Nate stood face-to-face with Dave in less than a second, then hit him square in the jaw. Dave fell to the ground, blood dripping from his bottom lip.

"I'm well aware of Olga's bad luck with pieces of crap; just look at you. Now, do I need to count to three, or are you gonna leave on your own?"

A passive expression spread across Dave's face as he stood, wobbled, then reached for the keys in his pocket.

"Don't be stupid." Nate yanked them from his hand. "Walk or get another ride home. You can pick up your precious car tomorrow. One—"

Dave raced up to the porch, covering his mouth with one hand.

Nate shrugged. "Personally, I didn't care if he did run himself into a tree, but I was worried about the Porsche."

I shook my head. "I can't believe you saw us in the dark all the way out here."

He chewed on his lip for a few seconds. "Olga, I always see you."

I leaned on the tree trunk again, feeling like the drunken one now.

Nate extended his hand, and I took it, letting him lead me back toward the light.

Focus Question:

How would you describe the music of the Cantankerous Monkey Squad? Think of an event in your life and write a song about it.

Chapter Ten

"It is difficulties that show what men are."
—*Epictetus*

Maybe trials are part of helping us discover our purpose in life. Because even though I've been living for almost eighteen years, I feel like this is the first time I've had a life. I'm not running in circles any longer, doing the same things over and over. On this new path, I hope I don't make the same mistakes. Maybe we're meant to experience life like this, one day at a time, without complete answers to all life's questions. I don't want to leave my 18 Things list with items unchecked. I want new adventures, because one thing Conner's death taught me is this: Live every day as if it were your last. YOLO!

Chairs scraped against the hard floor of the Journalism room, and I hit the post button on my blog.

Mrs. Cleveland entered carrying her clipboard. "All right, people, we have exactly eight hours 'til deadline. So don't just sit there, hustle, hustle, hustle!"

Nicole and I headed to the back room office and laid out our business ads, making sure they were camera ready. She popped a Cantankerous Monkey Squad CD into the computer, then cranked it up.

"Can you pass me the X-Acto knife?"

She swung her arm back, knife in hand.

"Don't throw it!"

"You're too easy." She reached across the table and placed the tool in my hand gently.

"That's what she said," I retorted.

Nic giggled, swaying to the music.

"What ad's supposed to go here?" I pointed to the left-hand corner at the top of the page.

"Mario's Pizza."

I licked my lips. "Oh, El Pizza-O! I'm gonna ask Mrs. Cleveland if we can order from there for dinner tonight. You think we'll stay until ten again?"

"Don't we always?"

Half-smiling, I drifted out the office door and found Mrs. Cleveland reading my blog.

"Um, sorry. I guess I forgot to close out the window on the computer," I said.

I reached over, about to click the red 'x' with the mouse, but she placed her hand over mine to stop me.

"Why didn't you tell me you started your own blog?"

I shrugged and stuffed my hands in my pockets. "Oh, I don't know. I don't really advertise it. I mean, I only have ten followers. It's just part of a bucket list I'm doing."

Her eyes sparkled. "Yes, I read about your eighteen things under your list of previous blogs. We have a limited space available, only one-fourth of a page that the editor and I were trying to fill for a regular feature this year. What do you think?"

I blinked hard. "About what?"

She gestured excitedly to my blog. "About starting a monthly *What's On Your Bucket List?* feature. We could highlight a different student or teacher each month."

Rain plinked against the window, and I gave a mild smile. I didn't know when the shower started, but I thought of how motivating others to start a list could bring new life into this place. "I think that's a great idea. Except eighteen things like mine would be too long for a one-fourth page. So, maybe we could ask them their top three? Oh, and we could like, have a graphic of a beach bucket for the feature. Get it, because it's a bucket list."

She squeezed my arm, laughing. "I get it."

"Mrs. Cleveland, the printer's not working again," Steve yelled across the room.

Wiping her eyes, I noticed the lines under her lids and felt so much appreciation for the countless hours she spent in this room with us during and after school. "Duty calls. So, you'll take care of getting that graphic for the story and creating a cool headline, too?"

The thought of what this list turned into made me warm all the way down to my toes. "Sure thing. But who should I feature first?"

She rubbed her hand over her chin and then pointed to me. "You."

"Me?"

But she walked away. Either she ignored my objection or just didn't hear me.

I returned to the business manager's office.

Nic stood and stretched her arms over her head. "What'd she say about the pizza?"

I ran a hand through the frazzled curls of my hair. *Should've known it would rain today.* "I have to pick three things from my life list and publish them in the *Bucs' Blade* this issue."

"Huh?" Nic said, rubbing spit over a fresh ink mark on her shirt, smearing the blue color in a wider stain.

I piled my long curls on top of my head and crisscrossed two pens there to hold my hair, gearing up for our monthly race against the clock to meet our deadline. Newspaper was all about multitasking, so I searched for my bucket graphic on the computer and explained everything to Nic. She multitasked too, half listening as she searched the phonebook in an attempt to sell one last ad space.

"Well, that's cool, right?" she asked.

Leaning across the desk, I peered at her more closely. "Are you serious? I mean, yeah, it's cool to feature *other* people, but not me. I didn't write the list with the intention of sharing it with everyone in the world."

Rain pelted the window, hard. So hard, in fact, I thought maybe the water turned to hail.

"Whoa, take a Prozac already. It's not the whole world, just the student body, and most of whom don't even read the paper anyway. Plus, you already posted your eighteen things on your blog over the summer."

"Yeah, for my own documentation, Dr. Judy, and the Jedi Order."

She opened my blog on her computer, then turned the screen toward me. "So, what three will it be?"

"Well." I scanned the list, thiking. "Firewalking and spending one day following what the Magic 8-ball says are kinda cool."

106

Nicole hunched over the computer screen. "And I think you should include a more personal one, too. Like sailing, because everyone will get that's about Conner."

A half-hearted shrug is all the agreement I mustered, the thudding inside my brain getting worse. After I helped Nic organize the business ad layouts, I put all my energy into creating the ideal bucket graphic and typed my top three bucket list tasks in the center of the pail. Only the clicking of a camera snapped me out of focus. "What's that for?"

Nicole smiled, her face always picture perfect. "We need a photo of you for your feature."

"We do?"

"Yep! I'll load it into the computer now. See the space next to your headline? Put it there."

I wasn't smiling in my picture, but I didn't think I should be anyway. Underneath the heading, I typed up a short synopsis: A bucket list is something pushing you toward a goal to live every day as if it were your last. Because if Conner's death taught me anything, it's life is too short to do something you don't love, or waste time posing as someone you aren't. So what's on your bucket list? Drop me an e-mail at peaceloveandponcho.wordpress.com with your ideas, and you might just be next month's featured student.

Nic's eyes were big as she paused for a second. "So, you went from not wanting anybody to know about your blog to advertising it in the school newspaper?"

Closing my eyes to give them a rest from the computer screen, I nodded. "I figure go big or go home."

She patted my shoulder. "That's my girl. You know, you never did tell me why you named your blog that. I mean, I get the peace and love thing, but why poncho?"

Opening my eyes, I rubbed a hand over my face. "To honor Conner. That was my nickname for him, our inside joke. One day when we were on this bike ride to Five Mile Hill, it started raining, and he pulled out two pocket ponchos from his jeans. I thought it was so random he had stuffed those in his pockets. We put them on and cut through the woods back to his house, the tires splashing mud on our ponchos as we laughed so hard I thought I'd crash my bike."

That day was all fun, one of the best I spent with him. My chest ached. Ironic how I nicknamed him Poncho and then he died when in the rain. He was prepared for everything, but not dying. I wondered what was better: dying slowly from an illness so you'd have time to say goodbye and check things you wanted to do off your list, or dying quickly without suffering.

Through the window, I saw lightning fork the sky. I felt a wave of nausea when the power flickered on and off.

"Ah, Mrs. Cleveland, our work!" shrieked Veronica from the middle of the room.

Everyone scrambled to turn their computers back on to see if their final layouts were saved.

But I stayed rooted to my chair, watching rain streaking down the window like tears. I wondered if this empty void left by Poncho would be filled by the time I crossed all eighteen things off my list.

The *Bucs' Blade* was distributed yesterday, Friday, and today I woke up checked my blog, and discovered 401 e-mails, all about bucket lists. I almost choked on my waffle.

I pulled my legs up Indian style, tucking my feet into the warmth of my own skin. My laptop sat open on the patio table. The September mornings were cold, but still warmer than the inside of my apartment.

Mom's almost total silent treatment approached the three-month mark. Just when I thought she'd talk to me again, I joined the cheerleading squad, effectively throwing the baby out with the bath water.

At least the fall weather provided a beautiful distraction. The sky streaked with the light orange and reds of sunrise, matching the color of the surrounding evergreen trees. Studying the screen again, I shut the computer abruptly. I expected to answer ten e-mails tops. No way could I think of how to respond in the little time I had now. My shift at The Bookman started at nine, but first I needed to meet the Jedi Order for breakfast in a half-hour.

I pulled open the patio door, then stepped inside to tell my parents goodbye and gather my things, laptop bag already slung over my shoulder. We kept my bike in the foyer of our apartment building, since the ten speed was better protected from the elements there. I yanked the handlebars off the wall, then pushed my Ladies' Beach Cruiser outside.

A black cat appeared from the row of bushes just below our front window, flicking his long tail just once. I stooped to stroke his fur when the squeaking wheels of Nate's skateboard startled me.

"What is that?"

He soared down the slope of the sidewalk, arms out like a surfer. "Saw your feature in the *Bucs' Blade*." Reaching an arm behind him, he pulled the paper from the back of his corduroys. "It inspired me to start crossing things off my list, like riding my old skateboard, remember?"

I hopped on my bike, put one foot on the pedal and kept one on the ground. "Yeah, well it looks like the feature inspired the masses. I have 401 e-mails to sort through today."

Nate circled around me twice before he stopped, pulled a wildflower from beside the sidewalk, then handed it to me, clearly not surprised. "You belong among the wildflowers."

I blushed but tried to iron out my face into a cooler expression, sniffing the white petals. "Tom Petty?"

Nate's mouth dropped open. "You caught that reference? Nice."

Pedaling, I pulled into the parking lot so there was enough room for him to skate beside me. "Why am I a wildflower, exactly?"

"Because a wildflower grows wild."

I waved a palm in the air as though swatting away a fly. "Thanks for the articulate explanation."

He threw his head back in laughter.

His amusement kinda hurt to hear when I felt so tense. My tired mind clicked off the things on my to-do list: respond to hundreds of e-mails, take inventory after The Bookman closed tonight, write a ten page research paper tomorrow for my English class, wash and fold all my laundry since I wore my last clean outfit, complete my extra homework for Math Team, practice two new cheers for this week's game, and somehow let go of my guilt over killing my best friend.

Nate slowed down his skateboard to turn onto the main road. "I mean, it wasn't intentionally planted. Just like you and your revolution."

"I don't know if I can do this. Spotlights, revolutions, cheerleading… they're not my area of expertise." Just thinking about all the tasks gave me a fresh wave of nausea.

He blinked at me several times, looking flabbergasted. "Didn't anyone tell you? You can be anything you want to be, do anything you set your mind to!"

I looked at him and swallowed the urge to reach out and touch his face. Sometimes he didn't feel real, like this was all a dream. People like him were too good to be true. "Um, no."

Releasing the grip on my handlebars, I balanced and tried to imagine the feel of Dad's hand on the back of my bike seat, Mom's footsteps slapping the pavement behind me, shouting encouragement. But things didn't happen that way. If it weren't for Conner, I would've been on my own while learning how to ride a bike, or for any childhood milestone. I was on my own now.

Nate smiled at me. "Well, now someone has."

His statement was so simple, but also freeing.

A tear trickled down my cheek, and I dried it with the back of my cold hand.

"Are you crying?"

Meeting his gaze for a second, I sneered. "Just shut up. I knew there was a good reason I didn't want a philosopher for a best friend."

His expression fell. I hated that look. Maybe Tammy and Nicole were right; maybe Nate did want to be more than 'friends'.

"Oh, come on. If you're going to start a revolution, I think a philosopher is exactly the kind of best friend you want."

"Right on," I said, pedaling faster, thinking of how tired I'd be after typing answers to 401 e-mails… and counting. "Does that mean you'll help me respond to all my e-mails?"

Nate waved the *Bucs' Blade* in the air as he bumped over the curb. "You're going to answer all the bucket list suggestions?"

"It seems like the right thing to do."

"It seems insane, but I like it. Sure. I'll help. Excellent clichéd advice at your service, ma'am." He took a bow.

"While you're at it, got any advice on how to deal with my mother, who's barely spoken to me in three months?"

He rubbed a hand over his goatee. "Honesty is the best policy. You don't want to get caught up in saying things just because you think that's what she wants to hear, so until you're ready to practice the item on your list about telling people what you really think, mum's the word."

I smiled. The whisper of the autumn leaves drifting to the ground had always been my favorite sound, but Nate's voice was coming in at a close second.

I wondered what was better: dying slowly from an illness so you'd have time to say goodbye, or dying quickly without suffering.

Chapter Eleven

"Forget safety.
Live where you fear to live.
Destroy your reputation.
Be notorious."
—Rumi

My pathetic score flashed on the screen, and I set the microphone on the couch. "This is gonna be so embarrassing."

Tammy tugged at my white sweater. "Oh, sweetie. You're wearing white after Labor Day. What could be more embarrassing than that?"

We were all at Sean's place, practicing for the big karaoke contest tonight by playing Rock Band 3 on his Wii.

"The key to winning a karaoke contest," Sean said, "is to choose a song everybody knows."

I opened my laptop, then Googled nineties rock—tonight's theme. "How about *Blister in the Sun*?"

Nate struck the four colored drumheads, hitting all the right notes. "Violent Femmes did that one in the eighties, but it can still work since Indigo Girls did a remake in the nineties."

"Perfect." I smiled at him over my shoulder.

"Pull up the song online." Tammy bounced from foot to foot. "You need to practice dancing, too."

"Dancing?" Nicole asked. "It's a singing competition."

"Duh! But Olga can't just stand there singing a song like that, especially if there are any interludes or whatever."

I sighed. "She has a point."

The music blared from the laptop speakers and Tammy grabbed my hands, swinging me through the air as I squealed. Dancing in public didn't seem so scary since I joined the cheerleading team. I was worried only about the singing. After Tammy and I shook what our mama's gave us for a few minutes, we collapsed in a fit of laughter.

Nicole rolled her eyes. "Well, I guess it's good you discovered your hidden dance talent, because as your best friend, I must inform you of something before tonight's contest. You sound like the teacher from the Charlie Brown cartoon when you sing."

This only made me roll around on the floor more, laughing. "How long before we need to be at Jumpin' Java?"

Nate checked his watch. "Two hours."

Tammy stood, stretching slowly before reaching out her hand and pulling me up, too. "Let's get a move on. A nineties costume, we shall find."

This was the first time I'd been inside Tammy's house. The two story home consisted of three bedrooms and two bathrooms; definitely nicer than my apartment but nothing to brag about.

Her dad snored on the recliner, television on, and he looked like he hadn't showered in days.

"Just ignore him; I always do."

She headed up the stairs and I followed on her heels, tiptoeing around the junk piled on every step.

"What is all this?" I asked.

"Stuff my dad won't get rid of, my mom's things. It's ridiculously unhealthy." She pushed open her bedroom door, flipped a switch, then the ceiling fan turned lazily overhead. "Take a seat on my bed, and I'll pull some clothes out of the closet."

Tammy stalked off across the hall to another bedroom, and I took a moment to rest my head against her plump white pillows. They smelled like roses. At the window next to the bed, I gazed through the sagging lace curtains. In the backyard trees swayed in the wind. I expected pages from teen magazines to litter her wall. Instead, one large framed photo hung on her wall of a woman standing in a garden with hands on her hips and a pair of come-hither eyes.

Tammy returned holding at least five outfits.

I figured it best not to point out if she didn't take up two bedrooms, then the piles of junk could probably be stored in a better fashion.

"Who's hanging on your wall? A beauty queen?" I sat ramrod straight, my fingers moving across a tie-dyed top with a plunging neckline. With Tammy, there was always a plunging neckline.

She held a pink neon shirt against my chest. "Yes, but she's also my mom. She won Miss Michigan back in the day."

After laying the discarded shirt on her bed, she quickly picked up another tee.

The picture couldn't have been more beautiful if Michelangelo painted it.

We'd never discussed her mom before, and I felt like I should say something. But I just sat there, wondering why I didn't try to at least hug her. Five months after Conner's death, and I still sucked at letting people get close to me, or vice versa. I wished for more in the future, but right now the broken me offered little. "I'm really sorry you lost your mom."

My sentiment sounded lame, but genuine, hopefully.

Tammy shrugged. "Thanks. Life sure does suck sometimes, don't it?"

I turned around, then fluffed her pillows. "Do you want to talk about it?"

She studied me, a third shirt in her hand now. "Not really. We have more pressing matters, like what you should wear tonight."

I reached out to touch her hand, but then let mine drop to my side. When she wanted to talk to me, she would.

A half-hour later, I was dressed in black boots stretching up to my knees, just where the red plaid dress ended. We decided to aim for nineties grunge. As I sat at her vanity, Tammy tried to perfect my look.

"Are you almost done? Drag queens don't wear this much makeup."

"Rome wasn't built in a day, my dear," Tammy said in her cheerleading voice, high and clear and steady.

I scowled at her reflection. "What's that supposed to mean?"

"It means shut up."

We met the Jedi Order inside the coffee shop at eight-thirty sharp.

"Any last minute tips for me?" I forced a laugh.

Sean pointed to the long line for drinks. "Hydrate."

"Right," I said shakily, my stomach twisting in on itself. Coffee pots gurgled behind us, and I was thankful for this sound to calm my nerves.

Nate gently placed his hand on the small of my back. "I'll get you something. You and Sean should sign up for the contest."

I bit my lip, trying to stop the panic as others in line chatted happily.

Kaylee, a girl from my computer class, turned and saw me. "Oh, hey, Olga. Loved your bucket list ideas in the *Bucs' Blade*. Is this an 8-ball challenge?"

"Um, excuse me?"

"Ya know, signing up for this contest? Did all signs point to yes?"

"Oh, yeah. I mean, no. This was all Sean's doing."

I rubbed his afro, and Kaylee and her friend smiled. Others eavesdropped on our convo with raised eyebrows and under-the-breath remarks, then talked to me about their bucket lists as we waited in line. When it was finally my turn, I bent over the small square table and wrote my name down for the contest. The lady at the table knew my name before I even wrote it. I took a step back and gave a slow, disbelieving shake of my head as Sean and I made our way through the crowd.

"What is it?" he asked.

Leaning in, I told him, "It's like people see me now. I didn't think I cared before if they did or not, and maybe I didn't, but I do now."

His eyes widened, and a smile illuminated his face.

We rejoined our group at the table closest to the karaoke stage, and Nate handed me a cup.

I took a huge gulp and groaned after swallowing. "Who the *beep* are you?"

"Beep?" Nate questioned.

"I don't swear, and that was code for this isn't the coffee I requested."

He nodded. "You didn't actually request coffee. You just wanted to hydrate. And I thought this herbal tea would help calm your nerves."

I tugged at the collar of the plaid dress. "Listen, Bucko."

"Bucko?" Nate grinned. "That's the best you could come up with?"

"It's the first thing that popped into my mind. I'll think of something more insulting to call you later, okay? But that's not the point. The point is coffee is always implied. If you knew me at all, you'd know that."

He shifted in his chair, leaning toward me, and butterflies swirled in my stomach.

"I do know you." He revealed another coffee cup in his other hand. "Chocolate-drizzled Snickers flavored mocha with whipped topping. And you should know, I get face palmed every time I order that for you."

I sipped tentatively, never a fool twice. "You are a gift from the gods, Nate Barca. Truly."

Taking another gulp, I realized I wasn't really addicted to coffee like I used to be. Usually I drank the stuff like water, especially during the school year while I stayed up late at night to study. But for a long time now, I hadn't even felt tired. I slept because I knew I had to. Still, I woke up every hour, on the hour. I forced myself to bed at midnight, then one, two, three, four, five in the morning, up like clockwork. Needless to say, my days started early, more productive than ever. Still, I couldn't shake the feeling I didn't belong here and that I was missing something.

I didn't feel that weird twinge right now though, so I shook off my thoughts and settled back into my chair, taking in everything around me.

The next couple hours were filled with nodding along to the beat of nineties pop rock songs. The little ball bouncing over the words on the screen mesmerized me. Judging rested with the audience, so we chose our cheers wisely. Sean sang his rendition of *Crash Into Me* by the Dave Matthews Band extremely well. He must've been in the top three so far.

Only one person left to perform before my turn. My hands jittered on the table so badly that Nate placed his hand on top of mine, holding my fingers still. This did nothing to calm my nerves. To make matters worse, the guy performing on stage started singing my song.

I clutched Sean's shoulder. "What? Why are they playing that? Don't they rule out repeats and stuff?"

Sean shook his head. "Nope. Usually they're not back-to-back like this though. You can change it. Just tell them when you go up there."

"Yeah. Wow. So easy." Silence hung in the air for a moment. I swallowed, hard, then took a deep breath and counted to ten. "Any ideas? Help me, people!"

"*I Don't Want To Miss a Thing,*" Kyle yelled.

The uneasiness in my stomach grew deeper. "Love the song, but there's no way I can pull off Steven Tyler."

"*Pictures of You,*" said Nicole.

"Technically, The Cure did that one in 1989." Nate knew music trivia like most guys knew sport stats.

Nicole rolled her eyes.

"*I Will Remember You,*" Tammy said.

Now I rolled *my* eyes. "Ugh, I get enough depressing at home without throwing Sarah McLachlan into the mix."

Nate cleared his throat. "How about *Closing Time* by Semisonic?"

I looked at Nate, eyes glazed as the crowd went wild at the end of what was supposed to be my song. "That could work."

But as I made my way to the DJ, I knew what I should sing. I leaned over the sticky counter where coffee had probably been spilled a gazillion times. "Do you have *Good Riddance* by Green Day?"

He handed me a microphone. "Sure do. Good luck."

My breathing was loud in my ears as I introduced myself. "Um, okay. Hi, my name is Olga. It occurs to me now that I should've bought you all ear plugs, because I totally suck at singing. But this is for my life list, and for Conner. So, here goes nothing."

The music started playing and I looked out at the crowd. I understood why many karaoke contestants made a habit of becoming inebriated before taking the stage. Since April, so much had happened, all started by an act of God that took the life of my best friend. It took another act of God to get through the words of the song, singing about the end of a relationship, a turning point, something unpredictable but in the end right, reminding me whatever happened in life was meant to be.

"*Ol-ga! Ol-ga! Ol-ga!*" The whole coffee house cheered, giving me a standing ovation. It felt like an out-of-body experience. Everyone surrounded the stage and high fived or slapped me on the back as I floated back to my chair. The high was better than when I swallowed those twenty pills. Then I shuddered, ashamed for my thoughts.

"You sucked, but you totally rocked it, girl," Sean said as I sat back down.

"Yeah. That was kinda perfect." Nicole had tears in her eyes.

Nate gave me a playful nudge. "What happened to my suggestion?"

His eyes were unreadable, and I hoped he wasn't upset I didn't take his advice. "Well, it just popped into my head while walking up there. I mean, that song could be the anthem of my life over the past six months."

"I could tell," Kyle said. "I mean, no offense, but I think you know you don't sing well. But you felt the song, so we felt it. It totally gave me an eargasm."

I laughed. "I hope you brought protection, then."

He pulled out a pair of earplugs from his jeans pocket. "Of course I did. I'm a drummer."

Nate motioned hitting a drum set as I said, "Badabum tsch."

We hadn't even planned it, so our timing was a bit weird.

"You two are so cute," Tammy said, smiling mischievously.

I wished I had two drumsticks to beat her over the head with.

Another hour later, with my fourth espresso in hand, a barista named Leah announced the winners. Sean won the third place prize of twenty-five dollars. Then Leah declared I won an equal amount of money for the Best Worst Performance of the night. I just sat there, stunned. Winning felt like waking up in a foreign place—only I knew I hadn't gone to sleep. Things like this only happened in my dreams, but this, *this* felt like living.

Focus Question:

Name the six friends that make up the Jedi Order and name a character trait that best describes their personality. Which one of these characters do you most identify with and why? Which one is your favorite? Compare and contrast the Jedi Order to your own group of friends.

Chapter Twelve

"A long thing expected
takes the form of the unexpected
when at last it comes."
—*Mark Twain*

Homecoming activities kicked off with the Powder Puff games on Monday night. The junior girls beat us at flag football, but the senior boys won the cheerleading competition. To celebrate, we took Nate, Sean, and Kyle to Dairy Treat. We were in the middle of coordinating our outfits for Wednesday's Theme Day, where each class dressed according to a certain movie. Fittingly for the Jedi Order, the senior's class movie was *Star Wars*.

"So," Nate gestured for me to come closer with his hand as Tammy tried convincing Nicole to dress up as Princess Leia, assuring her she'd look hot. "There's a meteor shower this Saturday. I thought maybe you could come chill at my house for it, since I have a telescope."

We sat outside at a picnic table under a buzzing street lamp, shoveling ice cream into our mouths. I felt the same curious fluttering in my stomach I always felt when I got this close to Nate.

"Um, aren't you going to the dance?" Even though I was cheering at the Homecoming game on Friday against Muskegon, I opted out of going to the dance. The memories associated with almost attending my first high school dance six months ago were still too fresh.

Nate ran a hand through his tousled hair and looked away momentarily. "The girl I was going to ask is unavailable."

Still in his Powder Puff outfit, which consisted of my borrowed navy blue cheerleading skirt, a white school spirit shirt stuffed with inflated balloons, and knee-high socks; he looked ridiculous saying this, and I suppressed a laugh.

"I thought you could come over for dinner, watch a movie, and then head outside for the meteor shower."

My ice cream dripped on my knee, and I licked the sides of the cone. "What time will the shower start?"

He squinted at the sky, and spoke to the air. "It'll start in the evening, but it's best to view after midnight."

Cars whizzed by as the light on Harbor Drive turned green and someone beeped their horn, yelling something inappropriate to Tammy out their window.

"Oh, that's my curfew," I said.

Tammy poked me in the ribs, apparently half-listening to our conversation. "So just say you're spending the night at my or Nicole's house and that we're picking you up after the dance."

Nicole harrumphed, grabbing her ice cream cup, then stomped off to the trashcan. She told me earlier today that she thought Tammy was a bad influence on me, but whatever; I didn't know when Nic turned to such an old stick-in-the-mud.

Usually I starred in that role.

Tammy lit a cigarette, then blew out a huge cloud of smoke, staying calm as ever.

"Yeah, but when the meteor showers end, I won't be able to go home, and you and Nicole will still be out. Aren't the four of you renting a room together on the beach?"

Cool air whipped around us, carrying the scent of fresh waffle cones.

"Well," Nate said, his voice shaky, "the meteors will go all night, so I figured we'd just stay up the whole time. My parents won't mind."

Tammy flicked her cigarette and winked before breaking into a chorus of *Lets Get It On* by Marvin Gaye.

I brought a finger to my lips, signaling for her to knock it off. "Okay. I told Nic's parents I'd work at The Bookman until eight since I'm not going to the dance, so is it cool if I just walk over after my shift?"

He stood and shot his empty chocolate shake cup into the trashcan. "Perfect."

Nate turned, then conversed with Sean and Kyle as Tammy openly gawked at me.

"What?"

She smiled and leaned next to my ear. "It's kind of a big thing, crossing your first date off your list. Have fun, but don't do anything I wouldn't do."

I cringed, because her last piece of advice covered nothing and because this wasn't a real date. I wanted to tell her so, but she'd already turned back around, doing what she did best. Flirting.

Walking up to Nate's house, a beach cottage not quite on the beach, I remembered I'd never actually been inside. I'd never even been up to the front door. I always sat in the driveway, inside Sean's truck or Tammy's Lexus or Nicole's Civic, when we picked Nate up to go out on the weekends.

The two-story cottage, surrounded with unkempt bushes and climbing vines, made me think of the Boo Radley house from *To Kill A Mockingbird*. Autumn's here, the yard more brown than green, but I almost tripped on a hose snaked across the grass.

Apparently someone was trying to keep it nice.

One tall tree stood in the center of the yard, skeletal with a mass of weeds at the base of its trunk, and all its dead leaves covered ground cover.

Crisp air blew across me and stirred them up as I approached the half-open gate and walked up the creaky steps to their front porch. The outside light was on, and I used it to check my reflection in the window of their red wooden door.

I didn't care that I still wore my work clothes. Since we didn't wear uniforms, my outfit consisted of a pair of khaki pants, a plain white tee, and a ruffled blue cardigan. I straightened my hair in the morning, but small waves returned. I dug out some lip-gloss from my purse and applied the cherry vanilla flavor with a vengeance before sighing, wondering why I suddenly cared so much about my looks. I fingered the cross on my necklace and rang the bell.

Nate's mom opened the door. She had golden eyes, dark brown hair like Nate, and looked a few years too young to be his mother. "Hi, Olga. Come on in. Nate's in the kitchen."

She pointed down the hallway, which was lit with four giant, glowing fish aquariums with all kinds of creatures swimming around inside. To the right was a family room, where his dad watched the evening news from the couch.

Following the sound of sizzling food, I found Nate lingering over a skillet on the stove.

I inhaled deeply. "Whatcha cooking?"

He turned, welcoming me with a gentle pat on the back and a kiss on the cheek. "You're supposed to say 'Hey, good looking' first."

My stomach fluttered with panic. *Is this a date?* Tammy kept teasing me tonight was, but I thought she was reading way too much into the whole thing.

"I'm making comfort food—southern fried chicken, green bean casserole, and apple cobbler for dessert." Turning his attention back to the stove, he flipped the chicken with his fork.

"It smells delicious, but why do we need comforting?"

The way he bit his lip and avoided eye contact told me my question made him *un*comfortable, but I had no idea why. "I didn't know if you'd be sad about not going to the Homecoming Dance tonight."

I leaned my hip on the counter, watching the grease pop in the pan. "Oh, well that's very thoughtful of you. But I'm not sad, not about missing the dance anyway."

He pressed his knee against mine. "Hence the comfort food."

"How do you know how to cook all this?"

Nate darted to the fridge, and I took the opportunity to check him out. He wore a pair of faded jeans with holes at the knees and a white graphic tee with a picture of a skull guitar strapped across the front as if it were a real one.

He held up an energy drink, then threw it. I jumped and somehow managed to catch the can, then set it on the counter gingerly.

"Um, can I just have some water?" I asked.

After pouring me a glass, he grabbed a plate. "Cooking's easy. You just keep turning the chicken until it's browned, then drain the grease on paper towels."

Gesturing for me to follow his instructions, I stabbed a piece of meat with the fork, but while I transferred the chicken strip to the plate, the poultry broke off and dropped to the floor.

I cocked my head to the side. "Yeah. Easy for anyone but me."

Nate picked up the fallen poultry, then tossed it in the sink. "Come on now. What's that supposed to mean?"

"It means I'm really good at figuring out complicated equations, but I can't do a simple task, like cooking or driving, to save my life."

He narrowed his eyes. "So, you have tried driving?"

I squared my shoulders. "Tried being the operative word, in Driver's Ed. It's why my mom and dad won't let me get my license. I'm horrible."

"I'd teach you, but I'm horrific, too. Obviously."

Before I could stop myself, I hugged him. Every muscle in Nate's body tightened against me, then he relaxed into my embrace, gathering my hair in one hand, his other planted firmly on my hip. I cleared my throat and backed away slowly, and Nate seemed to sense my awkwardness as he rocked back and forth on his heels.

"Well, your parents won't be able to prevent you for long." He hooked a finger under my chin and tilted it toward him, and I prayed he didn't feel the sheen of sweat forming there from his touch. "You've got a birthday making you legal soon."

"True." I couldn't muster a better response, and even with that one little word, my voice cracked.

Nate opened the oven door, slipped on a blue and white-stripped mitt, then took out a shallow glass dish.

"So, I suppose this casserole isn't complicated either?" I asked.

"Nope. You mix some Cream of Mushroom Soup, milk, pepper, green beans, and French Fried Onions together, then bake it for thirty minutes. We'll let this cool while I show you how to bake the cobbler."

Nate removed a kitchen gadget thingy from a drawer, and my eyes widened.

"What is that?"

Wrapping his arms around his stomach, he hooted with laughter. "You've seriously never seen an apple slicer?"

I leaned against the counter, taking a long, therapeutic breath. "My mom is very controlling about everything in our house. Nobody steps in the kitchen when she's cooking. So, that's an apple slicer?"

He nodded, grabbing some apples out of a basket on the counter.

"Well, it looks like a torture device from the middle ages."

He waved the slicer around. "It's not exactly horror flick material."

I pat his broad shoulder. "Famous last words."

Putting a hand on my arm, he asked, "When is the last time you saw some vixen sliding up against a wall, cowering in fear from an apple slicer?"

Straightening, I thrust my hands in my pockets. "Actually, just before I came over, I saw a preview for a Halloween movie showing that exact thing. Yeah, they were in the kitchen. The villain brought the apple slicer over the woman's hand, then cut off three of her fingers. In fact, if you read the warning on the side, it probably cautions against that little scenario."

Squinting, he said, "Now I know you're lying. You came from work, so you couldn't have been watching tv."

"Yes, I could." I shook my head, hair falling into my eyes. "I'm a total slacker. And there's a television in the break room."

As if I exasperated him, he sucked in a deep breath. "Stop it, silly. You're going to do this. I've used the slicer a million times, and I'm fine."

I raised my eyebrows. "Maybe, but you put one of those in my hands, and suddenly it becomes a killing machine."

He placed the slicer in my hands anyway, stretching his hands around my wrists. "I'll help you. The initial push is always the hardest."

We pressed down, and I couldn't stop myself from saying, "That's what she said."

His head snapped back in laughter, losing what little control he had over the situation. Nothing protected my index finger when the sharp edge sliced through my skin. Blood flowed everywhere.

Nate yelped. "Ah, I'm so sorry!" He grabbed a wad of paper towels, then pressed them over my finger while leading me to the kitchen table to sit.

"I'll be right back." He headed out of the kitchen to the right, I assumed toward the bathroom. A minute later, he returned with a Band-Aid and Neosporin and set them on the counter, flipping on the faucet. "Come rinse your wound with soap and water first."

Fittingly, the soap dispenser was shaped like an apple, its little leaf squirting liquid into my hands. I faux whimpered.

"Again, I'm so sorry."

I let out a shaky little laugh. "Well, I hate to tell you I told you so, but you should learn now I'm always right."

He handed me a fresh paper towel. "Should we go to the hospital? This looks like you may need stitches."

My nerve endings crackled at the word hospital. "No, I'm fine."

A weak smile let me know he understood. He applied the cream to my cut, wrapped the Band-Aid around my finger, then kissed it.

I blushed and wished he were the one blushing sometimes, too.

Rubbing his fingers over mine, he smiled. "That's what my mom always did when I got injured. Figured it couldn't hurt, right?"

This was one of those moments where I should've nodded in agreement, remembering all the times my mother did the same thing. But my mind was a total blank. "My mom was never that nurturing, but whatever you say."

"Okay, that's just sad." He still held my hand and led me back to the chair. "You relax. Want some ice?"

I half-closed my eyes, searching for pain, but none existed. "Nah. I know it looks bad, but it actually doesn't even hurt."

"If you say so."

Nate sliced four apples with no problem and arranging them in a baking dish, pouring a can of cinnamon spice apple pie filling and a package of yellow cake mix over the apples. Then from the fridge he retrieved a stick of butter and cut it up before placing the margarine all around the pan. He sprinkled chopped walnuts on top of the cobbler. For some reason, I found all of this fascinating.

My stomach grumbled, and I licked my glossy lips. "When Cantankerous Monkey Squad is famous, I'll be able to say I knew Nate Barca when he still cooked his own food."

After arranging two plates of fried chicken and green bean casserole, he walked them to the table. "Whatever. I don't want our fans to buy into the whole rock star image. I didn't join this band with the mindset of becoming big. I'd be just fine with doing acoustic versions in small clubs my whole life."

While I shoved a mouthful of green beans into my mouth, I idly traced the patterns on the plastic tablecloth with my free hand. "No sold out pretty boy rocker for you, then."

"Nuh-uh," he answered around tiny bites of chicken.

A long, low sigh escaped from my lips. "So, should I keep helping the band get a record deal on my list?"

In the center of the table a stack of napkins piled high, and he reached for some. Nate's fingers brushed my fingers as he handed me one, and I pulled back. This time, I didn't mean to shut him out, not like I did with my parents and so many others around me. Even more sad, Nate didn't seem surprised by my actions, like he expected the cold shoulder routine. I could tell by the way he grabbed the salt and responded to my question rhythmically, never missing a beat.

"It's up to you. I mean a record deal wouldn't suck, so if you think you can help us get one, then by all means do."

"Yeah. Well, don't hold your breath. I don't have any ideas for that one yet."

He frowned. "If it's meant to be, it'll be."

We ate in silence for several minutes, the voice of the local news anchor still blaring from the living room.

"This meal is fantastic." I lifted my water glass. "Cheers to the chef."

Clinking his drink against mine, he said, "The company is what made it so great. Thanks for coming."

When the oven timer buzzed, letting us know the cobbler was done, our dinner dishes looked like we had licked them clean.

"Have you ever seen *Citizen Kane*? I thought we could watch it in my room until the meteorite shower starts."

I cleared my throat. "No, but that's one on my list of movies to watch."

Nate flipped his hair out of his face. "I figured, especially with the newspaper ties to it."

We loaded the plates in the dishwasher, scooped out a helping of the cobbler, then brought our bowls with us to his room, where it smelled like incense. "What have you been doing in here?"

"Yoga."

"Really?"

He furrowed his brow. "Yeah. Denise Austin is da bomb. You ever try it?"

"Um, no." I flipped my index finger at him. "And you can't make me. I already have eighteen new things to try this year."

He laughed. "Fair enough."

To the left of the doorway a flat screen tv, a Blu-ray player, a PlayStation 3, and a massive pile of CD's cluttered his sticker-encrusted desk. After hitting a button on the remote, he popped in the movie. On the opposite wall clothes covered a black futon. He cleared away enough of them for a load of laundry.

"Shall we?"

I nodded and sat down, then balanced the bowl of apple cobbler on my knees and took a bite. Of course, this, too, tasted delicious.

A breeze drifted in through the open window behind us, and I sucked in a deep breath of fresh air. I distracted my nerves by looking around his room while the previews played. The shelves to my right were stacked with books on world history, religion, philosophy, and most of all, Greek mythology. Miscellaneous items like a wallet, keys, a half-burned candle, alarm clock, and Conner's old song notebook peppered the dresser.

For some reason, only one wallet-sized photo graced the mirror above the dresser. My fall school picture.

Curious. He must've hung it up right before I arrived—as a joke. Sticky notes featuring song lyrics covered the rest of his mirror, making a clear reflection almost impossible. *I like a man who's not into appearances.* I did not know where that thought came from, but I felt dizzy, strange too, entirely too strange. Desserts make everything better, so I scooped another bite of cobbler and ice cream into my mouth.

The movie began to play, and Nate stood on his futon and pulled the string to turn off the light but left on the fan. After a while, the wind from the fan and open window made me shiver.

Nate put his arm around my shoulders.

I shivered again, but not from the cold. I didn't dare look at him though, and it was difficult to concentrate on the movie.

Two hours later, I swept crumbs from my second helping of apple cobbler off the futon. As we watched the final scene in the movie, with the workers throwing Kane's sled, Rosebud, into the furnace, I rolled my eyes at Nate. "So, his last dying word, R-O-S-E-B-U-D, was about a childhood sled?"

Nate shut off the movie, plunging the room into darkness. He stood on his futon again and pulled the light cord. "You don't really think it was about a sled, do you? The sled was meant to represent the innocence of childhood. It was something he lost too early through a bad experience, like most of us. And most of us spend our entire lives looking to regain hope we had as a child but can never really seek it out because life always gets in the way."

Tumbling my hands through the air in a faux bow, I said, "Thank you, Mr. Philosophy."

"It's what I want to get my degree in. Can you tell?" He nodded to all the books on his shelf.

I ruffled his shaggy hair. "Might as well. You've been majoring in BS ever since I've known you."

"Hardy har-har." He meandered to his closet, then retrieved two sleeping bags and a pair of massive flashlights. "You ready?"

Following him through the back door, I carefully kept to the stepping stones past the fish pond to the edge of his yard where a telescope was already set up. The brilliance of the stars outshone the moon, like a million flashlights of the gods on this cloudless night. Each twinkling star made me wonder about the universe and my place in it. I studied Nate's relaxed disposition. Somehow I knew this was the only place I wanted to be in this moment.

He coated his arms with bug spray, then handed the can to me and asked, "So, what do you know about constellations?"

I smiled. "I can point out a few. There's the Big Dipper, four stars making up the bowl and three for the handle. The Little Dipper's there, a smaller version of the same thing. The really bright star in the Little Dipper is Polaris, also known as the North Star, which is at the end of the handle. Polaris isn't the brightest in the sky but shines directly above the North Pole, and as Earth rotates, all the stars appear to us like they whirl around it. There's Orion, also known as The Hunter. He has a human figure, and you can best spot him by his belt. Over there is Leo, the bright stars forming the outline of a lion. Then there's Scorpio, named for the insect. The constellation that looks like a cross is called the Crux—"

"Okay. I get it. There's no use trying to show off for you."

When he fell silent for a few minutes, I felt bad. I wasn't trying to steal his thunder, just teasing him.

"Wow! What's that?" I shouted after a piece of yellow brightness decorated the sky.

"The meteor shower." He lit up his watch and laughed a little. "Yep, it's after midnight. Right on schedule."

I turned a full-watt smile on him. "But it was so big, so bright! Will all of them be like that?"

Shrugging, he said, "The news said we should see ten, fifteen, maybe even twenty meteors every hour. But that one was the brightest one I've ever seen, which is weird since it's a full moon. That usually makes them seem dimmer."

My shoulders fell as I looked up at the sky. "So we just wait?"

"We wait."

Both of us spread out our sleeping bags, then took a seat.

I pointed to a short lattice fence covered by netting to the right. "Who does that belong to?"

The garden was the only neatly kept area of their front or back yard.

"Mine. I planted raspberries, blueberries, and blackberries this summer. I'm gonna dig up my potatoes tomorrow. It's the envy of all the kids on the block."

For some reason, I melted at the thought of Farmer Nate digging around in his garden. "You, Nate Barca, are a complete mystery to me." My body felt like Jell-O, probably just a strange side effect of the meteorites.

Nate chuckled, and it sounded too loud in the quiet darkness. "I like to keep the ladies guessing."

Through his telescope, we took turns watching another meteorite shoot across the black sky, and it seemed so close, as if I could reach up and touch it. "Ya know, I had a new dream last night that meteors were falling from the sky, like crashing into Earth."

"What happened?" he asked.

"Well, one hit me, and I woke up."

"Where'd it hit you?"

"Right here." I pointed to my big forehead.

He leaned in and kissed my fake owey. When he pulled back, I knew my eyes were wide. "Kissing makes everything better, remember?"

My breathing was suddenly rushed. *Oh my gosh! This is a date, isn't it?*

"It's kind of funny because you know how we always talk about how dreams have meanings? I read when they involve meteors, it symbolizes a truth which wasn't realized at first, something you just couldn't imagine before but then suddenly hits you."

I felt the sudden urge to take ten.

"Um, I gotta pee." I jumped up, then followed the little stones back to his house and headed for his room as my heart throbbed. "Okay, Olga, get it together," I whispered aloud to myself. "There's nothing to freak out about."

Except there was. I knew a part of me craved Nate as more than just a buddy, but I wasn't ready for this. He was supposed to be my safety zone, and suddenly he felt like the most dangerous person I knew.

I scanned his bookshelf, hoping to find one book on philosophy that could give me a gleam of truth to calm myself down. One titled *Wisdom for Dummies* caught my eye, and as I pulled it out, something fell to the floor. Sucking in air through my teeth, I opened the book and read the first thing I saw.

"Our physical bodies are often a sign of what's going on with our emotions."

No dip, Sherlock!

After replacing the book on the shelf, I bent down and retrieved what fell a moment ago. It was a journal, Nate's personal journal, filled with written accounts of his dreams. I knew I shouldn't be looking at it. I didn't know if I consciously searched for my name or not, but I found something more curious in the form of a poem.

Today I had this vision of what's to come.
It's of you standing in the morning sun.
It came afar by a gentle wind,
The speaker invisible, had a message to send.
Although this speaker possessed no form,
He saw you and no longer mourned.
He knew you still had many tasks to do,
And the courageous path would be the one you choose.
He said to tell you death you need not fear,
For he is here, drawing you near.
This vision, I hope is a wonderful sign,
For I see it clearly through my pondering eyes.
It's complete with a union, full of purpose and plan,
And it's of the day when I'll ask for your hand.
This dream comes from impractical thoughts, but I wish it were true,
Because since the day we met, I can't imagine life without you.

Tearing the poem out carefully, I felt faint. I positioned the pages so they were hidden in my purse, then replaced the journal on the shelf. I knew I couldn't stay.

I scrawled a note, then left it on his dresser.

"Is everything okay?"

I looked him straight in the eye and immediately regretted it. "Um, no. I'm not feeling well. I'm just gonna head home."

Brows drawing together to form a perfect unibrow, he asked, "But what about the meteor shower? And your mom?"

A long pause followed as I considered his point, but one look at Nate stopped my blood circulation, and I knew I had to jet. "Uh, rain check, and I'll figure it out. Thanks for dinner."

With my chin dipping to my chest, I rushed past him.

"Wait. Let me walk you."

A thin sheen of sweat formed on my forehead, but I fought the impulse to wipe it. "No. I told my parents I was with Tammy, remember?"

He followed me to the front door. "Well, then, I'll walk with you until we see the entrance to your apartment building."

I'd learned control from almost eighteen years of living with my mother, so I forced my voice to remain dry and calm now. "I'll be fine. My house isn't far. I can send you a text when I get there if that makes you feel better."

Nate curled his fingers into his hair and said, "Olga, I'm so sorry if this date was too much for you, if you weren't ready. I didn't mean to…"

A silence more awkward than anything I'd ever felt hung between us as he finally called this night what it really was. A date. Immediately my mind flashed back to the day Conner died. I knew however much I cared for Nate, I had to give him the cold shoulder now. "No, it's fine. It's not that I can't handle being here. I just don't feel good. I'll see ya later."

I quickly descended his porch steps, not giving him another chance to debate. The stinging tears I'd fought back finally flowed freely. I knew I was a coward for running away like that, but fleeing the scene was what I did best.

Focus Question:

What events in your life changed you? What future choices await you, and how do you think they will change you?

Chapter Thirteen

"Yesterday is a memory, tomorrow is a mystery
and today is a gift—which is why it is called the present."
—Unknown

Happy Halloween," Nicole said when I opened the front door. She handed me two presents. "And happy birthday."

I'd always thought it ironic Mom birthed me on the only day of the year she viewed as pure pagan evil.

"Thanks." I automatically knew the one wrapped in the fancy orange paper and lavish bow was from her, and I didn't need to read the card on the other one either, wrapped in green, to know who it was from.

"That one is from Nate."

"Yeah, I figured," I said, my voice irritated.

Nic cleared her throat. "So, let me get this straight; you bail on your first date, even steal his poetry, avoid him for two weeks, but he still buys you a present, and you're the one annoyed?"

I shuffled to the couch, in my comfy slipper socks; Mom's only present to me. "I just wish he'd get a clue."

She plopped down next to me and grinned. "I don't think someone who dreamed asking for your hand is giving up easily."

I'd shown his poem to Nicole. She took that line to mean marriage and figured it had to be about me because who else could he like? Her assessment totally freaked me out. I reminded myself daily about the vow I made to myself after Conner's death: never fall in love again.

My life list definitely didn't include that one, no matter what Nic and Tammy thought was best for me. Better safe than sorry. That didn't mean I stopped thinking about Nate though. I wished there was a switch to turn off those butterfly-inducing feelings. Oh wait, there was, it's called guilt. So any time he tried to call my house and I saw his number pop up on the I.D. display, I let the phone ring and told my parents not to answer, that the caller was unknown or just spam. When I spotted him in the halls at school, I walked the other way and on occasion, engaged a random stranger in a convo so he wouldn't be tempted to invade my space and start talking to me.

"Does he ever say anything about me?" I asked Nic, peeling away her bow, carefully unwrapping the paper so I could reuse it.

"Not to me," she said, gathering her long black hair in her hands and laying it across one shoulder. "And if he does to Sean, he's not spilling the beans."

I nodded and studied the contents in my lap. Inside Nicole's box were chic black leather shorts, a shimmering gold sweater, and a large pair of feathery earrings.

"Those earrings look like the ones girls wear at strip clubs," Mom said, on the way to the kitchen for a coffee refill.

I rolled my eyes. "How would you know, Mom?"

Nicole tried not to laugh as Mom shot us a don't-mess-with-me look.

"Oh, come on. It's my birthday. You have to be nice to me."

Ha! That shut her up. She pursed her lips, then turned her back on me and left the room.

I hugged Nicole. "Thanks for the outfit. It's perfect, just like my best friend."

She shoved Nate's present in my lap. "Don't forget this one."

Inside Nate's box awaited a Magic 8-Ball wrapped in tissue paper and a voucher for a free firewalk in Cedar Springs, a town about an hour from Grand Haven, and a note. "Happy birthday to a real groovy chick. I'm glad I got to know you this year. Good luck with crossing all the stuff off your list before your next birthday. Thought I'd help you out with these two things. Ask the 8-Ball if you should come firewalking with me tonight to commemorate becoming an official adult. Call me if the outlook is good."

Nicole let loose a snort of laughter, and I chuckled to myself.

"He sure does have a way with words. Go ahead and ask the Ball," she said.

After shaking the plastic ball up for a good ten seconds, I peeked at the transparent window on the bottom of the Ball for my answer. "As I see it, yes."

"Yesss!" She pumped her hand in the air. "Call Nate and tell him."

"No way. I'm not going on another date with him."

"We'll all go. It'll be fun."

"From your mouth to God's ears."

"You know, you're starting to sound like your mother now that you're an adult."

I wanted to punch her in the face. Instead, I hugged her goodbye, then completed my chores so Mom would let me go out later. *Do I really want to go?* The wondering made me restless enough to take a walk, but I got distracted by Dad walking across the parking lot, tinkering in our one-car garage.

"Whatcha doing, old man?"

Dad looked at me, his face rosy and shiny. "Just cleaning out some old junk."

I smiled. "Don't you know how to kick back on the weekends?"

He threw his head back in laughter. "Now you know your mother would never let me get away with that. Heard you got some big birthday plans with your friends tonight, eh?"

Shrugging, I perused the shelves hanging on the wall of the garage. I hardly ever came in here. Even when I went somewhere with my parents, Dad pulled the car out first so Mom and I could get in without banging the doors against the sides. But it was no surprise the garage appeared very neat and organized, just as my parents liked every aspect of their lives.

"So, you traded all the cardboard boxes for rubber bin storage? Nice…"

I spied the retro mahogany trunk that used to be in my room. Back when I was a child, the trunk was filled with stuffed animals, but we donated those long ago. I pulled it off the shelf and gawked. The trunk must've weighed at least thirty pounds. After popping open the lock, I discovered a much different kind of child's treasure inside, although there was a Winnie-the-Pooh bear that Aunt Tara brought to the hospital the day I was born. I quickly picked through the award certificates, spelling bee medals, school folders with pictures of Tiny Toon characters containing samples of my work, and classic fairy tale books.

I didn't know what I searched for until I found it, which happened often in my life. But what I really wanted was nothing new. It came in the form of an envelope stuffed with my letters to the Tooth Fairy, Easter Bunny, and Santa Claus. The one dated from the year 2001 mentioned him.

Dear Santa Claus,

I have not been good or bad but okay. I've had a few fights with Conner. This year I want world peace, a new name, a basset hound, a DVD of the Lizzie McGuire show, and the joy of Christmas. Oh, and for Conner to get everything on his list too.

Love,

Olga

A stabbing hurt rose from my heart, came out as a strangled cry, and tears streamed down my cheeks.

"Hey, hun, you okay?" Dad leaned over my shoulder. "Oh, maybe we should put this away."

Dad's voice sounded worried, and I couldn't blame him after I swallowed that whole bottle of pills after Conner's death. Still, I was irritated and just wanted to be left alone. And since it was my birthday, I should've been able to demand that one thing.

"I'm fine, Dad. Can you give me a minute out here by myself?"

"Well, I was finished in here anyway, so I guess it's okay, if you're sure you're alright."

I nodded and glanced toward the parking lot, watching him go while some kids zoomed by on their bikes. I couldn't help but think that just like them, life goes by so fast. It's like I blinked, and everything I thought was there disappeared. I'd give anything to be a kid again without a care in the world.

In another envelope, I found some goofy pictures my friends and I took in middle school. One of me and Nic showed her talking on a cell phone and me holding my Pooh bear. Obviously the photo shoot was one of those deals where we could bring our own props from home. To make it even cheesier, we wore matching outfits: denim miniskirts with red turtlenecks and black penny loafer shoes without socks—so we could show off our friendship ankle bracelets. My hair was in the standard pigtail braids, a frizzy mess, and her black hair was neatly woven into a half-ponytail.

In Conner's picture, Sean leaned down on a huge white Bengal tiger that stood to his waist, and Conner wrote a caption from the tiger's mouth: "This kid on me is weird."

A snort of laughter escaped me as I studied Conner's trademark cocky grin, Sean's closemouthed smile—an effort to hide the braces he wore back then—and Kyle smiling wide, his blue eyes twinkling of mischief. I turned the photo over, and sure enough, there was Conner's handwriting. "Eighth grade has been fun. Now you have this awesome picture to remember us! Have a great summer. I'll probably see ya around, like tomorrow! Hahaha. Yeah, baby, we're gonna be high schoolers next year!"

A silent sob rose in my throat. My elementary and middle school yearbooks lined the bottom of the trunk, but I ignored them, piling everything back in and shutting it fiercely before placing it back on the shelf. I felt terrified all of a sudden, like nothing was familiar, not even my past. I pushed the button to close the garage and climbed into Dad's Ford. He always left the keys in the truck, trusting in the safety of our small town. But this place hadn't felt safe for me since Conner died. Sure, Nate's presence had been helping, but I'd screwed that up. Maybe I should've just reopened the garage and drove right out of town, not stopping until I reached the California coast. Better yet, leave the garage closed, turned on the car, and let carbon monoxide poisoning take me away to that place somewhere over the rainbow like Dorothy sang about in *The Wizard of Oz,* some place where Conner still lived.

A lump formed in my throat as I turned the key in the ignition. The automatic light from the garage door opener shut off just as Dad's headlights flashed on.

Perfect timing, something that never happened in my life.

I sighed and turned the dial on the radio, searching and praying for a song that would speak to me.

Norah Jones' version of *Somewhere Over the Rainbow*, singing about troubles melting like lemon drops, stilled me. *Weird.* I'd just been thinking of this tune moments ago, and now here it was. I couldn't believe this was a mere coincidence.

Slumping over the wheel, I sung along to the lyrics, but my shoulders quaked and my voice broke. I leaned to the side and opened the glove compartment, in search of the napkins Dad always stockpiled in there. Sure enough, some spilled onto the floor.

Reaching down to pick them up, I discovered a white envelope with "Olga" written in black ink. I wondered if Dad bought the card for my birthday and then forgot about it. Since the rectangular paper had my name on it, I tore it open. The front had a picture of a lake and birds hovering near a rainbow in the sky. The eerie thing wasn't just that the photo matched the song, but I thought I remembered him getting me this card before.

In red letters it said, "Daughter, This Birthday I Want You to Know What a Special Person You Are." I stared down at the card, déjà vu making it hard to comprehend the words. But I opened it up and read the inside anyway. "You are strong with the strength to carry your dream to completion. You are determined with the desire to meet the world on your own terms, and I never doubt that you will. You are your own person, and you always will be. You are the promise of the future, so precious and rare, and even though you lose faith sometimes, I always believe in you. I love you so much… Happy Birthday, sweetheart. XXOO—Dad."

My heart froze, then pounded, and my face flushed. I turned off the truck and blew my nose into a spare napkin from Jumpin' Java. I *knew* he got me that same exact card for my fourteenth birthday. I never thought a card could stay in circulation that long, but I remembered it well because the words touched me back then as much as they did now. I wondered if Dad recalled buying me the same card and made the purchase on purpose, or if the song and card was just another happy coincidence. Whatever the case, both were just what I needed.

"Olga! Are you out here?"

Disoriented, I glanced at my watch. My friends were picking me up for tonight's celebration, and nobody had a clue as to where I was. I snuck out the side door of the garage and made a loop around the back before coming to the front.

"There you are!" Nic exclaimed.

"Your dad said he left you in the garage, but the door was shut so we were worried. You really should keep your cell with you at all times." Tammy eyeballed me suspiciously as she tossed me my phone.

I guessed they tried to call when I was AWOL and heard it ringing in my room.

"Where were you?"

I wrapped both of my friends in an uncharacteristic hug. "Nowhere. Just went for a walk." I looked at Nate, his head down, standing by the SUV with Kyle and Sean. Pawing a hand through my hair, I tried to think of a way to make up for ignoring Nate for so long. "And now I'm ready to firewalk!"

That statement couldn't have been further from the truth, but hopefully it helped to lighten the mood.

We loaded into Tammy's Lexus and headed for Cedar Springs. As I turned my eyes toward the window, I really did feel like the dark clouds were behind me, that maybe turning eighteen was a new beginning for me.

I sat up front with Tammy; Kyle, Sean, and Nicole were in the back seat, and Nate was shoved in the cargo space. Dressed in the new outfit Nicole gave me, I held the Magic 8-Ball in my lap.

"Remember how you said no to getting tattooed?" Tammy asked.

My body tensed. "Yeah."

"Ask the thingy about it."

I sighed. "Should I get a tattoo?" The liquid sloshed around as I shook. "Ha! My sources say no."

She stuck out her tongue at me. "Ask it if you should go on a date with Nate."

According to the rules of my list, I had to ask, so I did. The radio was cranked loud enough where I didn't think Nate heard our convo anyway. "Ask again later."

"Darn. That thing is on your side."

"Not really. I'm here, aren't I?" I teased, kind of.

Tammy shot me a disappointed look. "I think we should've forced you to 8-ball it all year."

I wrapped my arms around the ball protectively. "Why?"

She shook her head. "Because the whole point of it is to do things you're unprepared for, and a good guy is one of those things. That's what makes them so wonderful. You should give Nate a chance."

Slouching in my seat, I didn't say another word the whole way there. I may have been ready to tackle some new things, but not love.

Before firewalking, we sat around a path of coals, on log benches, listening to a motivational speech from the guy who owned the place.

"Firewalking is a rite of passage. So it's only fitting we have someone here tonight for her eighteenth birthday."

The small crowd cheered as my friends shouted, "Olga Gay Worontzoff," embarrassing me.

"Tonight is a test of your strength, courage, and faith as you try to focus mind over matter. In my life, I've learned to be content, whatever the circumstances, knowing everything happens for a reason. Our destinies aren't thwarted by our failures. We're not bound to our pain. Nobody's perfect, so you just have to trust your gut and follow your heart to live a full life, and that's what this experience is about. Free your mind. Napoleon Hill once said, 'What the mind can conceive, it can achieve.' Let's meditate for a while."

The air was thick with the smell of burning coals as our meditation guy began what he called a five-minute body check-in to create a sense of unity with body, mind, and spirit. Strangely, this technique did force my body to relax.

When we were done, Sean turned to me. "May the force be with you."

I made the sign of the crucifix. "And also with you."

Nate went first since he was the expert. He walked across the hot coals as easily as I imagined Jesus walking across water. Sean ran the length of the firewalk, screaming like a girl the whole way. Nicole swore like a Jersey member of the mafia when it was her turn. Kyle asked us to do a drum roll, so we all banged our hands on our thighs as loud as we could. And of course, Tammy did a cheer:

"The making of a champion"—clap, clap—"Stand up and cheer"—clap, clap—"It's our destiny"—clap, clap—"This will be our year"—clap, clap—"Yay!"

Nate touched my arm. "You're next, birthday girl."

"I don't know if I can do this." I pulled at my ponytail, fighting back tears.

He tapped the side of my head. "You can do anything you set your mind to, remember?"

Tammy began the count down from ten, the small crowd catching on and joining her from eight. "Seven, six, five, four, three, two, one, firewalk."

I stared at Nate, my lips and chin trembling, and he extended his hand. I took hold of it, and with the longest stride I could muster, walked across the coals, gripping his fingers harder with each movement.

Everyone cheered as I traveled my last few steps, but I kept marching because straight ahead, people dipped their bare feet in a small pond.

Adrenaline pumping, I didn't even feel the heat, but that didn't stop me from launching myself up to my thighs before registering the coolness of the water. It reminded me of the night Conner died, how I was so cold I was numb. That made me even colder, but I remained frozen to the spot in the middle of the pond.

"Hey, you okay?" Nate asked.

I just stood there, eyes glazed.

He wrapped his lumberjack styled flannel around me, then guided me to the water's edge. My feet sunk into the grass as we walked through the woods together, the moon, full and yellow, lighting our path. Eventually we were back at the log benches and he sat me down, dried my feet with a towel, then put my socks and shoes back on. He handed me a thermos and ordered me to drink. Thankfully there was coffee inside.

So many thoughts of Conner raced through my head. I wished he was there to celebrate my journey into adulthood. The war within me raged on, wanting to forget, but wanting to hold on. I couldn't make sense of anything, so I turned to Nate, my voice strained, "Tell me a dream."

Before I started ignoring him, our discussions over sudden lucid dreams we had when we 'slept' were my favorite conversations. It seemed like neither one of us had really been able to fully fall asleep since our accidents, and our dreams were always vivid and often involved each other. The whole thing was more creepy than when Luke and Leia kissed in *Star Wars*.

Nate's eyes blazed, but his smile was mischievous. "You were featured in a dream I had last night."

I sucked in a quick breath but kept my eyes on the sky, afraid to look at him, afraid of how hard I could fall if I let Conner go. "Only featured? I should've been the main star! I am the birthday girl after all."

He agreed and went on to tell me such an absurd dream that I was sure he humored me, but I still loved every little detail. I wished I could be surrounded by nothing but nature and the sound of Nate's voice keeping me company forever.

"I got you something for your birthday."

Gesturing to the firewalk with one hand and holding up the Magic 8-Ball with the other, I said, "Did I forget to tell you thanks?"

Without saying a word, he reached into his pocket and retrieved a lavender, jewelry pouch, then handed it to me.

"For me?"

He nodded.

I untied the strings, then turned over the bag and dumped the contents into my open palm. A blue glass pendant on a sterling silver necklace with a diamond in the middle dropped into my hand. "Oh my gosh. It's the necklace I saw at the Coast Guard Festival. How did you know?"

Nate just shrugged, but the words he spoke the night jerkface almost assaulted me echoed faintly in the back of my mind, when Nate told me he always sees me. Not in a creepy stalker way though.

I reached out and wrapped him in a hug. "Thank you so, so, so much. You really shouldn't have done all this. It's way too much." It really was too much. I mean, the necklace must've been on a major sale because I'm pretty sure I remember it costing around five-hundred.

He held me, making me warm again, like a fire burned in my soul a thousand times hotter than the coals I walked over. After a moment, Nate leaned back and took the necklace from me. He fastened the clasp around my neck, and my heart thumped erratically.

A chorus of Happy Birthday interrupted us as the rest of our gang approached, Tammy leading the way with a lit cupcake. I blew out the candle, wishing for success at completing the eight things left on my list before I left for college.

"Did you make a bucket list wish?" Sean asked.

"I can't tell you or it won't come true." My response was muffled, since I'd already shoved half of the pumpkin spice cupcake into my mouth.

He jammed his hands in his pocket. "Well, I think I should be the next student you feature in the *Bucs' Blade*. Ya know, for the bucket list. What do you think?"

I nibbled some frosting off the top of my cupcake. "Sounds craptastic."

"Crap? I'm not the one full of crap!"

With a half-hearted shrug, I shook the 8-Ball for my answer. "Better not tell you now."

"Of course it says that. It hasn't heard my list yet."

Tapping the ball, I said, "Whatever. It's not a living thing, so you have no argument."

"Number one," he listed, ignoring me. "Land a record deal and make it as big as Green Day. I've gotta start making lotsa green for my honey here."

Nicole leaned over, and he kissed her playfully until I made gagging sounds.

"Number two: learn how to yodel. Wouldn't that sound sweet on our album?"

Nicole cupped her hands around her mouth. "No-de-laa-thank-you-hoo. That stuff only flies in the Alps."

Sean smacked his lips. "You don't know what you're talking about, woman. I'm a seventeen-year-old black man from whiteville Grand Haven, telling ya'll that me yodeling on our next album will be off the chain. And now, number three: win a freestyle rap competition. I figured I already conquered the karaoke contest world, so that should be my next thing."

Nate seemed distracted, carving images in the dirt with a stick, but Sean's comment grabbed his attention. "Dude, no offense. You can rock the guitar, you sing good enough backup vocals or karaoke, you can even rap decent, but not freestyle. The last time you tried to drop bombs over the mic in the lunchroom was downright embarrassing."

Sean pulled at a weed, then released it to the wind. "Just chill. I've been practicing."

"Let's hear a freestyle rap for Olga's birthday, then." Nicole's voice sounded doubtful. "If we all think it's good, Olga will put your list in November's paper. Sound fair?"

She raised her eyebrows at me, and I nodded.

Sean stood and mimicked a beat, waving his hand back and forth over his head and dancing. "It's been eighteen years since the planet welcomed Olga Gay/ And she be cool no matter what other people say/ And now she just firewalked as part of her thing/ I just wish this white girl could sing/ We've already taken her to a party and snuck her out/ And that she'll do all her quests, I have no doubt/ And I can't believe that some stupid lightning became our best friend's killer/ When that happened, I thought we'd drown ourselves in Millers/ But instead I hooked up with Olga's best friend, Nic/ The girl from Jersey who be sayin' what the frick/ And for whom this rhyme I just did kick." He pointed toward us, but I wasn't playing any more. "When I say Nic, you say frick. Nic."

"Frick," Nate shouted.

He was the only one.

Clenching my fists, nails bit into my palm. I jumped from my seat, stared Sean in the face for a few seconds, then stomped off to the pond. Silence loomed behind me, so I concentrated on the sound of my feet sliding through the leaves as the wind carried the stink of wood rot. The pond was deserted now, and the only thing keeping me company for a few minutes were the animal eyes gleaming from the surrounding tree trunks.

I skimmed the surface of the pond with my fingers, ripples carrying my touch across the water.

Nate flopped next to me on the bank.

"What about otters?" he yell-whispered, but I ignored him, continuing to dip my fingers in the cool water. He leaned into me. "Seriously, what about otters?"

I suppressed a laugh. The guys took a river kayaking trip this past summer when I was grounded, and while they were planning it one Saturday at breakfast, I mentioned my unnatural deathly fear of otters as being my excuse for never kayaking. "Maybe I deserve to be bitten by an otter."

"If anyone deserves that, it's Sean."

I plucked a dead flower off a nearby branch, then picked at the petals. *Nate loves me; he loves me not. He loves me; he loves me not.*

"He's not the one who killed Conner."

"This again? I thought..." He squinted back toward our friends, then turned and looked ahead, as if gathering his thoughts. "Hey, you wanna do something even more fun than walking over hot coals?" He smiled, and I felt myself smiling with him, despite my sour mood.

"Now, what could be more fun than that?" I mocked, shaking my 8-Ball. "Most likely. What did you have in mind?"

He crooked his finger at me, and I leaned in close as he whispered in my ear. "I've been brainstorming a list of possible perfect pranks for my life list. I came up with one titled 'Nate Barca's and Olga Gay Worontzoff's Operation Rabies Awareness Fun Prank to Ensure the Jedi Order Takes Bites Seriously and Doesn't Get Bit.' And let me tell you, it's really good. Super good. Epic even."

I shook my head and laughed. "What it is, is really long. The title, I mean. Where'd you come up with it?"

"I thought of it after our convo about you being deathly afraid of otters. I watched *The Office* that same night. Do you ever watch that?"

"Of course. It's only like the funniest show ever."

"Word. Well, that one episode was on, where Michael Scott organizes the fun run to raise awareness about rabies after Meredith was bitten. So, the show and your fear inspired me."

"I usually do give new meaning to the word inspired."

"Listen to my idea before you judge. You want to hear the prank plan?"

"Why not," I answered.

He told me, and I must say, the idea was really good. And with Nate's step-by-step instructions, I thought I could pull it off.

We both stood and dusted the moss and dirt off our jeans. Then I held out my hand, and he placed an Alka-Seltzer on my outstretched palm. I laughed at just the idea of pulling off the prank and wished Conner was present to see it. Maybe he was out there, somewhere over the rainbow, and maybe he'd be laughing too. After all, the force was strong with that one.

"Are you ready?" Nate asked, his voice quiet.

I answered quietly in return. "Ready as I'll ever be."

The next second, I screamed, "Otter! An otter bit me! Darn, son of a monkey's uncle!"

Nicole flew off her log seat. "What the frick! Are you okay?"

"Need water." I shook my head kind of twitchy like as she dug inside her tote bag for a bottle of water.

"Rabies," I heard Tammy whisper to Kyle.

He laughed softly as I took a swig of water and then gagged.

Nicole placed a hand on my back. "What's the matter? Are you having trouble breathing? Do you need your inhaler?"

Holding up my hands, one fist tightly clenched to secure the small white tablet, I blocked my face.

She seized my hands and then looked around for help. "Oh my gosh, she's foaming at the mouth!"

As she turned around, I leaned over and tried to bite Sean's arm.

"Sean, watch out!" Nate shouted, playing along.

Nicole dropped my arm and ran screaming with Sean, hiding behind Tammy and Kyle.

Nate exploded into laughter, and I wiped the foam off my mouth onto my shirtsleeve.

Sean said, "Well, the words 'son of a monkey's uncle' should've been our first clue. Nicole, we just got punked."

She stared at me wide-eyed. "I can't believe this crap! There was no rabid otter?"

"Nah," Nate answered through laughter.

I couldn't help but laugh too, even though Nicole continued to stare wide-eyed at me.

"How did you get your mouth to foam then?" she asked.

Sitting back down amongst the log chairs, I neatly folded my hands in my lap. "It was all Nate's idea."

Sean gestured for him to explain as Nate plopped next to me.

"Well, I carry Alka-Seltzer at all times because I used to have irritable bowel syndrome constantly."

Sean threw his hands in the air. "Whoa. TMI, dawg."

"Nicole asked. So, anyway, I got an antacid out of my pocket for Olga, told her to put it in her mouth and scream about otters, get a drink of water in front of everyone, and it worked like a charm. Nicely done, Olga."

Everyone applauded.

"Yeah, I only wish Nicole was acting when she tried to save her sorry butt instead of saving her best friend."

"What's up with that?" Sean asked.

I turned my head and saw Sean looking at me with a half-smile.

"Oh, and I'm sorry about earlier. I'm an idiot. I didn't mean to ruin your birthday."

"You didn't ruin anything. I overreacted." Smiling, I studied Nicole. "Looks like I have that in common with my best friend."

"I have no excuse," she meekly mumbled, a first for her. "I'll make it up to you. One more birthday wish. Anything you want."

I rubbed my hands together. "Let me drive to school on Monday. I need extra practice."

She winced. "Um, let's ask the Magic 8-Ball first. It's the rules, right?"

Looking at my watch, I noted it was almost midnight and gave the ball one last ceremonial shake. After all, I was eighteen now, so I must put childish things behind me. "Without a doubt."

Letting loose an exasperated sigh, Nic said, "And without a doubt, I'll get whiplash. Can I come to church with you tomorrow?"

I pressed my lips together. "*What?* Why?"

She pointed skyward. "I have some sins I need to confess. Ya know, just in case."

I knew she joked, but the thought of possibly causing another accident and losing my other best friend made me grip the 8-Ball harder.

One. Last. Shake.

Should I let go of my guilt?

Yes, definitely.

Focus Question:

Several things on Olga's list caused her emotional pain or to be out of control. How do you identify with those feelings? Do you think it's necessary to lose control or feel pain to eventually find happiness?

Chapter Fourteen

"The difference between a successful person and others
is not a lack of strength,
not a lack of knowledge,
but rather a lack of will."
—Vince Lombardi

I studied the calendar hanging over my bed, the one Nicole created for me as part of last year's Christmas gift. November displayed a picture of the Jedi Order holding up our corn dogs in front of the Pronto Pup hotdog stand.

Chuckling to myself, I crossed off Friday's date with my Sharpie. November eleventh, A.K.A., my final day as a cheerleader. Even though the Grand Haven Bucs' played their last football game of the season tonight, we didn't have school because of Veteran's Day. Sunlight slanted in through my open window, and I knew what item I had to cross of my list next. The Bookman was closed, the weather perfect, and if I waited any longer, it'd be too cold. In fact, this was the last weekend the sailboat rental places in town were open before winter set in. Picking up the phone, I dialed Nate's cell.

"Good morning, sunshine," he answered.

I squinted out the window, light stabbing at my eyes. "Do you want to go sailing with me today?"

Goose bumps popped up on my arm as I waited for his reply.

"I crashed at Sean's house last night. I can come by on my skateboard and pick you up. A half-hour okay?"

"Yep, and thanks."

Thirty minutes later, Nate strolled into the kitchen, pulled out a chair, then took his place at the table with me. "Pumpkin pie and coffee for breakfast again?"

"It's sooo yummy," I said, my mouth half-full. "Lots of sugar in the morning is good for any physical activity."

He laughed. "You're a strange girl. And do you realize how often you talk with your mouth full, Miss Piggy?"

"One of my many endearing qualities. I'm also brilliant and insightful and freakishly good looking. Did you want some?" I held up a forkful toward him.

He muttered something, too low for me to hear, but it sounded inappropriate. Something about wanting to be the pie, but that couldn't be right.

"What's that?" I asked, my eyebrows shooting up.

A smile played at the edges of his mouth as his thumb stroked my bottom lip, brushing away a crumb. His touch was better than the pie and coffee, and I was almost tempted to give him a dose of his own medicine by taking his thumb in my mouth to nibble teasingly.

Almost. It would've been fun to see his reaction.

"Only kids eat pie for breakfast. Besides, Sean's mom already served up a breakfast for champions with toast, scrambled eggs, bacon, and grapefruit."

"Oh, so you're too old to eat pie in the morning but not too old to let someone's mommy fix your breakfast," I mumbled, shoving the last bite into my mouth.

He grunted in agreement.

"Ha! Now who sounds like a pig?"

I watched him bite back a smile. "You done?"

"Yep," I responded as Dad barreled into the kitchen, wearing his sailboat boxer shorts and nothing else. "Dad!" I yelled, mortified.

"Sorry," he apologized in a robotic voice. "Must. Get. Coffee. Hey, Nate."

"Hello, sir. See you at the game tonight?" Nate asked, helping me out of my chair.

Nate attended every football game to watch me cheer and wanted to believe my parent's noticeable absence was because they were letting me get really good before they came.

Dad didn't look up as he poured his coffee. Not a good sign. "Game?"

Nate took a breath and held it in his mouth. He looked like a squirrel hoarding acorns in his cheeks before finally exhaling slowly. "Yeah, it's Olga's last one."

"Oh?" Dad took a hard, obvious swallow of his black coffee. "Did you want me to come?"

I knew he was caught between a rock and a hard place. Mom and I had an understanding. In the last few months, we both struggled to be in as much control of our shared universe as possible. If Dad agreed to attend my game, he'd put himself smack dab in the middle of our fight and upset our perfect, albeit psychotic, balance.

"Nope," I lied. "We're going sailing. See ya later, Dad."

"Wait. Sailing?" Shock rolled over his features like a wave cresting. "Yep."

Running a hand through his gray hair, he seemed to contemplate the right words to say. "Be safe."

While Nate skateboarded, I rode my bike to Grand Haven Beach Rentals. I hadn't been there since the day Conner died, but I tried to keep the thought from reaching my heart.

"Truth or dare?" Nate asked, and I was grateful for the distraction.

Eyes squinting in the sun, I said, "I thought you were too old for kid stuff."

His smile wavered. "Okay, truth it is. Do you want your parents at the game tonight?"

I frowned at him. "Why do you keep harping on this?"

He put his hand on my shoulder. "Number seven on your list is telling people what you really think."

I rolled my eyes. "Have you memorized my list?"

"Call me Rain Man."

I shrugged. "Is that another inside joke with yourself that I don't get?"

"No, I'm referring to the movie with the savant capable of remembering obscure details."

Scanning the street, I checked for traffic before we crossed the intersection. "Hmm, never heard of it."

He jumped off his skateboard, then kicked a rock in an outrage that I'm positive was eighty percent fake because he laughed. "We need to have another movie night. That one should definitely be on your list of top one hundred flicks."

I let my long hair fall over the side of my face to hide my shame. Remembering our last movie night still caused me to cringe. "Yeah, sure. Back to the list though. I'm the list keeper here, not you."

It was true. The *Bucs' Blade* had run two bucket list features now. While waiting for class to start, people came up and talked to me all the time about their lists. And when I walked through the halls, I'd often shout things like, 'Hey, Amy. How's learning to drive a stick shift going?' Or, 'Jack, did you start writing the next great American novel yet?' It was all a bit surreal going from death threats to the school's most popular journalist.

"Chillax. You can keep your title as official list keeper. I'm only interested in two: yours and mine. And as your Mr. Philosophy best friend, my advice for dealing with your mom is to be part of the solution, not the problem. It's time for a candid convo between the two of you. It may not be pleasant but—"

"It definitely won't be pleasant. Nothing with her ever is."

"Right, but it's necessary. If you guys start communicating with each other clearly, you can avoid future misunderstandings, which will help make your senior year the best ever."

"Conner's not here, so it never had the potential to be the best," I retorted, my voice grim.

He sighed loudly. "Are you gonna debate every point I try to make?"

I waved a hand through the air. "Sorry."

"It's okay. You're a journalist; it's what you do. But even if it won't be the best year, it's your last year of high school, and don't you want to leave on good terms with your mom?"

A disheartened shrug was my only agreement. "Listen, if you think telling my mom the truth will help us bond or whatever, you're wrong."

"Well, you love proving people wrong, right? Go home this afternoon and try it. Invite them to the game. I triple dog dare you. And if they say yes, you owe me."

Punching him in the shoulder, I said, "Oh, yeah? What will I owe you?"

He remained quiet for a minute. "I don't know yet. But I'll think of something."

"Well, if I win, I want you to tell me your number one thing."

Everyone in the Jedi Order had completed writing their own '18 Things' list. It seemed my mission not only brought me purpose after Conner's death, but it brought purpose to them as well. Somehow, we ended up turning a very negative into a somewhat positive. But when it came to sharing time, Nate refused to reveal his top thing to anyone.

He shook his head, his dark hair sweeping low on his forehead.

"You are so nosy. No worries though. Your parents will be at the game tonight," he predicted, skating into the parking lot.

Twenty minutes later, sunlight flickered on the lake. I shivered in the shallows, pushing our tiny sailboat further into the water. The cold radiating through my legs made me panicky. I knew it wasn't cold enough for hypothermia to set in, but the expression 'worried to death' came to mind. Once, my sixth grade science teacher told the class this story about a man trapped in an unplugged freezer, imagining himself freezing to the point of actually dying.

Nate shrieked from the cold, snapping me to present, and we both hopped on board. He adjusted the sails, and I was frozen to my spot, my mind calling out 'mayday, mayday.'

Closing my eyes, I inhaled deeply and breathed in the sea air, letting the sun massage its warmth onto my shoulders. A gust of wind swayed the boat, and I wrapped my arms around myself, rocking back and forth with the vessel, trying to fix my eyes on something steady.

"Are you okay?"

Hearing the rush of my heartbeat in my ears, I looked up at Nate for a split second before bending over the ship's side and puking up breakfast.

"Here," Nate said gently, handing me a water bottle.

"Thanks." With trembling fingers, I brought it to my lips, then drank. The thought that I'd just barfed into Conner's remains made me want to vomit again. "I'm never seasick. I don't know what's going on. The water's not even choppy."

Eyebrows drawing together, Nate said, "I don't think it's the rough sea making you sick. Are you sure you're ready for this? We can turn back now if you want."

"No. We each already paid our twenty dollars for the rental."

He wrapped me in a hug, and I squeezed him back.

"I don't care about the money; I only care about you."

His embrace didn't comfort me, and I realized probably nothing could in this moment.

"I know, but I need to do this. Putting it off won't make it easier. Just give me a minute."

Pulling my knees to chest, I curled up in a ball and laid down.

We were silent, watching the seagulls swoop through the sky, breathing in fresh air as I prayed for strength to help me get through my next task, for peace to know why Conner died.

Nate opened a bag of chips and munched, and the sound lulled me to sleep, another strange dream invading my thoughts.

I'm walking home after sailing, everything in black and white. My apartment looks like a haunted house, the interior misty like it's filled with dry ice. Cobwebs are everywhere, and the air smells like Dad neglected to take out the trash for weeks. The faceless, black-shrouded figure is back, standing silently in the hallway. I move past him and enter my parent's room. Mom cries on the bed, flipping through old photo albums from when I was a baby. Reaching out, I touch her shoulder and everything turns Technicolor, bursting with life. I turn around and the hooded figure explodes, turning to dust. The dust changes to fluffy, white clouds and carries me outside, everything black and white again. The clouds come up to my knees, and I imagine this is what being on a rollercoaster is like as I ride the floating vapor all the way to school.

Grand Haven High is covered with dead vines. Dead leaves from dead branches cover the grounds. When I'm at the entrance, I push open the door, and everything turns to vibrant color again. Students fill the hallways, all more beautiful than I've ever seen them before. Sun streams through the glass front doors, and this overwhelming feeling tells me all is as it should be. Someone starts chanting my name, and soon everybody joins in. I feel pure love and acceptance for the first time in my life, and tears roll down my face in gratitude.

I woke up with a start, thickness in my throat.

"Have a nice nap?" Nate asked.

Unable to articulate what just happened, the real tears started.

Nate wrapped me in his arms again and it finally felt right, like my dream of love and acceptance manifested. After a few minutes, he offered me a tissue from my backpack, and for the first time, I looked around. We were out on Lake Michigan now. Unknowingly, Nate had returned us to the exact spot of Conner's death. There was nowhere to run, but I knew this was fate at work. Taking the water bottle Nate handed me earlier, I dumped the last few sips into the lake before searching for my standard pen and paper in my backpack. I scrawled a note to Conner.

Dear Conner,

Thank you for being my best friend for twelve years. I'm sorry I couldn't protect you in the end. I wept for a long time and thought it was the end of me, too. But I know you'd want me to move on. Thinking of your strength and boldness helps me face each new day. I'm never without you, as I feel your presence all around me. I try to enjoy the blessings of life even more now that I realize what a precious gift it is. I'm not gonna lie. Life still has its challenges and difficulties, but my heart is full of wonderful memories with you, and those serve as reminders that life is good. Thank you for the effect you had on my life. I pray your light will always shine through me so I can make it possible people will never forget you. I love you.

Yours Forever,

Olga

I folding up the paper, placed it in the bottle, then laid it ceremoniously in the lake, something Dr. Judy suggested months ago, but I wasn't ready then.

Nate and I watched my message in the bottle bob in the water, and I decided letting go felt like someone stabbing me in the heart.

"With hardly any wind, it'll be hard to keep the boat moving back to shore," I told him lightly, trying to block out the pain.

He nodded. "I know. It's weird; it just died down when I got to this spot. But I'm okay with relaxing for a while if you are."

I almost laughed aloud. Conner would've never let me get away with that. Always the competitive one, he'd want to engage the wind in some fierce battle. "I'm okay."

As I leaned back in the boat, I realized for the first time in a long time I truly meant those last two words. The last time I truly felt okay was the last time I was here with Conner.

Boats raced back and forth across the water, trees waved at me from the shoreline, and the gentle waves lapped against our sailboat, whispering, "Welcome home."

Tonight was the biggest game of the season. If the Bucs pulled off a win, we'd make it to the playoffs. We'd been working on the numbers for weeks now, which involved a medley of all the best parts of the routines we did this year. We ran, skipped, and jumped onto the field, shaking our pom poms above our heads.

The loud music and cool air hit me all at once, motivating to cheer my booty off even more, just to get warm. Everything blurred as we raced into formation. Perfection didn't even come close to describing my arabesque in the pyramid. They tossed me into the air, and I completed a toe touch before returning to the cradle of girls who caught me.

I'd never felt so carefree.

My final move of the night included a round off, back handspring split combo—it still amazed me that I'd somehow perfected that move—and the crowd went wild with their cheers when we finished.

Over five thousand people attended tonight's game, a record, and my parents sat among them. Mom and I had our heart-to-heart when I arrived home from sailing. So Nate won the bet, although I had no idea what he'd claim as his prize.

I spotted him sitting next to Mom and Dad in the stands directly in front of us. My chest filled with warm fuzzies, and I smiled for them alone.

Nate and I watched my message in the bottle bob in the water, and I decided letting go felt like someone stabbing me in the heart.

Chapter Fifteen

"Nurture an appetite for being puzzled,
for being confused, indeed for being openly stupid."
—Lee C. Bollinger, 12th President of UM

University of Michigan
1220 Student Activities Building
550 East Jefferson
Ann Arbor, MI 48109

The Seventeenth of February

Dear Ms. Worontzoff,

Congratulations on your admission to the University of Michigan. It gives me great pleasure to send you this letter, and you have every reason to feel proud of the work leading to this moment.

In evaluating candidates, the Admissions Committee seeks to identify students whose academic achievement, diverse talents, and strength of character will make them feel at home in this remarkable community academically ranked in the top twenty among the world's universities. We look forward to you becoming a vital contributor to the University's mission.

While the final candidate's reply date is May first, we would love to hear from you before then. On April sixteenth, your future classmates will visit UM for Wolverine Campus Day, our program for admitted students, and we hope you join them. To register for this event and to connect with other admitted students, please visit our website at http://www.umich.edu. You can also e-mail us with any questions regarding our school. Welcome to the University of Michigan!

Sincerely,

Spencer Carver
University of Michigan
Dean of Undergraduate Admissions

With my heart pounding so loud my eardrums ached, I sprinted to the front door, waving my letter in the air with the other unopened mail and squealed, "I'm in, I'm in, I'm in!"

Dad paused the last episode of the tv series *LOST* and then wrapped me in a monstrous hug.

"Congratulations!" He cupped my face in his hands. "Of course, there was never any doubt in this old man's mind." He tapped the side of his head. "Especially after your SAT score of 2130; you could've gotten into Harvard." Elbowing me playfully in my side, he said, "Not too late to apply."

I mulled that thought over for a second and then sighed. "My scholarship is contingent upon attending college in-state."

"I know, but we can work out something, hun."

I felt the sincere energy oozing from his words. "It's okay, Dad. This is what we've been working toward my whole life."

Mom entered the living room in her robe, toweling off her wet hair. "What are you two going on about in here?"

I handed over my acceptance letter, and she read it carefully. I expected a formal congratulations. Instead, she clasped her wrinkled hands to her chest as her body shook with happy tears.

"Well done, Olga. I'm so proud of you."

From the time I was a little girl, I'd been waiting to hear those five words from my mother, and I scarcely believed my ears. Yet I had this surreal out-of-body feeling, like I wasn't here at all, so the emotional punch of it didn't reach my core.

"Let's eat my homemade chocolate chip pancakes for breakfast to celebrate and then I'm calling all our friends and family to brag."

Not hearing her talk in her pissed voice after so many months of it felt weird, not that I complained.

In the kitchen my laptop rested on the small table and I took a seat in front of my computer to blog about my acceptance letter. No sooner had I finished my pancakes, Nate called. *Of course*, I thought as looked at the Caller ID. Nate was always the first to read my blog, which boasted over one thousand followers these days. I pushed my chair out and stood by the window overlooking our pond, shaking my head and sighing as he rambled on and on about how he was proud of me.

The feeling was mutual.

After the Cantankerous Monkey Squad won the Battle of the Bands during the Coast Guard Festival in September, they performed a few more gigs where Alan from Mixed Tape Records brought some bigwigs. By the end of November, they'd signed a contract, each member receiving a thousand dollar advance, but they'd just started recording their new album this past week after school. The plan was to have it done by May. Alan was already busy negotiating a tour for them. The band would be a good match as an opening act for several of Mixed Tape's well-known bands, and the tour would most likely last the entire summer.

I knew this meant I should be pulling back. We were both on to bigger and better things. But every time I hung out with him, that became more of a lost cause than ever.

"So there aren't many things left on your list, but I thought going on the biggest rollercoaster in the U.S. would be the perfect way to party," Nate told me.

I cocked my head to the side, studying Mom at the sink, soaping up dishes. "When?"

"Tomorrow. If we leave by six, we'd get there by eleven when they open. They close at eight, so tell your parents we'll be home around one in the morning."

"Okay, hang on a sec." I covered up the receiver with my hand. "Mom, Nate wants to visit Cedar Point tomorrow to celebrate. Can I go?"

"Cedar Point in Ohio?"

It annoyed me when she asked dumb questions like that. What other Cedar Point was there? But I had to watch myself. "Yep. It's number five on my list. Go on the biggest roller coaster."

"Oh my goodness." Mom placed a hand over her heart. "That'd scare the bejesus out of me! What about church?"

I'd never missed church unless throw up was involved. "It's a five-hour drive. I can listen to a sermon on the radio or bring my Bible along and have my own church time."

She brushed a curl out of her face. "Well, I don't think they'll even be open when it's still winter. It's usually in the thirties this time of year."

True, but spring came early for the second year in a row. Grand Haven already made it to sixty degrees, and since we were heading south, logic told me it was warmer there. Echoing my thoughts, Nate interrupted with an announcement on the other end, apparently still able to hear everything even with the receiver covered.

"They decided to open it up for the holiday weekend since the weather is so good." President's Day was on Monday. "The meteorologists are saying it'll be a record, averaging highs in the low seventies."

Repeating the information to Mom, she still seemed hardly convinced of letting me proceed with our travel plans. "Is anyone else going?"

"I didn't ask anyone else yet, but I'll invite Sean and Kyle, and you can call up Nicole and Tammy," Nate said.

"Sean, Kyle, Nicole, and Tammy," I repeated, not mentioning they actually weren't confirmed yet. "Please, please, please, Mom, can I go?"

The sound of the kitchen light buzzed overhead, and I knotted my fingers together, praying she'd say yes.

"Elizabeth, letting go, remember?" Dad said from his Lazy Boy recliner, reminding her of our conversation in November when they agreed they'd accept the decisions I made now as those of a mature adult.

So technically, I didn't need her permission, but internally I did. If that made any sense.

She stepped forward, drying a coffee cup with her towel, then slid a damp hand over my shoulder.

"You're right, John," she called over her shoulder, then turned back to me. "You've worked hard all year and deserve a break. But you should listen to a radio sermon on the way there."

I nodded and uncovered the receiver, not that my hand being there did anything. "You hear?"

"Roger that. You call the girls and see if Tammy can drive. Be here by five forty-five on the dot. I'll have coffee waiting."

I smiled. I wasn't used to getting what I wanted, but I liked the feeling.

"For everything there is a season and a time for every matter under heaven…" Father Jamie read from Ecclesiastes. Mom found a CD in her archives of sermons and gave it to me before we left, said she thought it'd be a good message for me to hear.

"Do we really have to listen to this load of crap?" Tammy asked from next to me as I turned up the volume.

I pressed my finger to my lips.

"The point Solomon is making is God has a plan for all people," Father Jamie continued. "Although we may face numerous problems seeming to contradict God's plan, these shouldn't be barriers but opportunities to turn a negative into a positive. It's up to you to make the best of your time, to live your dreams, to discover your purpose. As we see in these verses, timing is very important. All the experiences listed in these verses are appropriate at certain times. The secret to peace is to accept and appreciate God's perfect timing. So know there is light at the end of every long, dark tunnel. Be strong, and wait for a new morning, where fresh opportunity knocks on every door who seeks it."

I hit the FM button and cranked up the volume, deciding to spare Tammy any more religious jargon since it was, after all, her vehicle. I didn't always agree with Father Jamie's messages, but as I watched the changing landscape while Tammy drove, I must admit I agreed with this one. Ten months ago, I would've felt differently. Back then, I couldn't see the light or even imagine it. As I looked out at the world passing by, it seemed everything in my life was a sunny sky.

Over the next few hours, crisp air better than any air conditioner poured through the open windows and tossed my hair in my face. I don't think I'd smiled that much in a long time.

The first thing we did when the six of us arrived at Cedar Point was make a beeline for Millennium Force, brushing past strangers in the crowded park. Everywhere I looked, I saw another eighteen things for an amusement park bucket list alone: get stuck at the top of a Ferris wheel, spin so fast in the tea cup ride you make yourself sick, swing on a pirate ship so high you'll probably poop your pants, eat only fried donuts and caramel apples for an entire day.

Soon the whoosh of air brakes meant we were next on the longest steel roller coaster Cedar Point had to offer. I thought about the last time I was at an amusement park, our eighth grade trip to Michigan's Adventure. I wouldn't go on the roller coasters with any of my friends, since I was too scared. They all gave me their stuff to hold, but Conner felt bad I'd be waiting alone. So he ran inside a gift shop, then returned with four stuffed animals. The characters—Charlie Brown, Snoopy, Woodstock, and Lucy— all mascots for the park, were to keep me company. He said they represented the personalities in our group. I was Charlie Brown, of course, a loveable determined loser dominated by insecurities. Conner was Snoopy, my sidekick. Nicole was the critical Lucy, and Sean was the resourceful Woodstock. I think that was the first semi-romantic gesture a boy ever showed me.

I smiled, thinking about how Conner would be proud of me right now.

"Here goes nothing," I said to Nate sitting next to me. In my head, I repeated the mantra *everything will be okay* over and over again.

We put our arms in the air, hands linked, as we climbed the sky.

"We're almost there," Nate said excitedly, as if I couldn't see that for myself.

I imagined Conner on my left, holding my other hand, something he always did so well since I was rarely brave enough to do anything on my own.

Then, the rush started. The car whizzed over the track, the sound of our laughter and the roar of the coaster bringing me back to the childhood I never really had. My sunglasses were off because I was scared I'd lose them, so my eyes watered and my hair blew back as we took one deep plunge after another.

I'd never gone so fast, but for once I wasn't scared. I'd been the definition of an emotional roller coaster this past year, but now, everything seemed so amazingly clear, so reachable. The future was full of potential, and I must strive for the peak of the mountaintop.

For the first time, I started to believe what Nate had been telling me these past months. I could do anything I put my mind to. When the ride came to a screaming halt and we unloaded, I bounced on my toes. It all felt like a dream, like I couldn't have possibly just done that and enjoyed it.

"Can we go again, can we, can we?"

While standing in line for the fourth time, I noticed Tammy clutching her sides. "I don't mean to be a party pooper, but I think I'm gonna sit this one out and grab a smoke. Somebody text me when you're done."

She sauntered away in her sleek spandex pants, the words 'Sure' on her left back pocket and 'Thing' embellished on the right back pocket, both in pink rhinestones. Kyle didn't take the slightest notice of her words, and I shook my head as he, Nate, and Sean discussed band business. Their voices were quick and the roller coaster was loud, so I didn't catch any of their convo, but I smiled sadly at their enthusiasm as I felt my one *sure thing* slipping away from me.

I gave a quick wave to Nic before jogging after Tammy, yelling, "Wait up!"

When I reached her at the entrance to the ride, she asked, "You feel queasy too?"

Shrugging, I told the truth. "No, I just didn't want you to be alone."

She lit a cigarette, even though there was a *No Smoking* sign, and I followed her across the park until we were at a railing overlooking Lake Erie. I watched the sun playing peek-a-boo in and out of the clouds, the waves hitting sand, then ash flicking on pavement.

"Why do you smoke so much?"

She swatted away a couple of buzzing flies. "Why do you drink so much coffee?"

I pointed to her as she pulled the thin paper from her lips, blowing rings of smoke. "At least my vice doesn't hurt others."

I shooed the smoke away with my hand.

She shrugged. "Well, I'm selfish."

"I don't believe that." I crossed my arms. "That's a total cop out. If you were really selfish you wouldn't spend so much time investing in people."

"Who do I *invest* in, oh wise one?" Her voice was full of defiance.

Tilting my head toward the rollercoaster behind us, I said, "The Jedi Order, your dad, your neighbor, the cheerleading squad. So tell me honestly, why do you smoke?"

She turned her nose in the air and blew out another puff. "Another model introduced cigarettes to me when I started in the biz at thirteen. It began as a way to stay skinny, keeping my mouth occupied instead of shoving food into it when I got hungry. We didn't have much in my house to eat anyway, since Dad never grocery shops, but cigarettes were plentiful. He was always too drunk to notice some missing. Of course, I'm old enough to find food for myself now, but it helps with the stress. So I'm sorry if my bad habit offends, but *to tell you honestly*, I really don't care how you judge me."

I held up my hands. "I'm not judging, just curious. It's your life, and I respect that." Shaking my head, I continued, "I can't believe I spent most of high school stereotyping you as a simple-minded, snobby, backstabbing cheerleader."

She took one last drag, then stomped out her cigarette on the ground. "Girl, neither can I. I mean I only stole your prom date, threatened to light you on fire, and slapped you in the face."

We laughed until our faces flushed.

"Ah well, everything happens for a reason, right?" she said once we calmed down. "Isn't that what your guru on the CD was saying?"

My ears rung with the sounds of the hustle and bustle of the park as they slowly melted away into the silence of the familiar truth. "Yep." The residual almost hurt my ears because for the first time in my life, I actually did believe everything happens for a reason.

She twirled a piece of her blonde hair. "You really think all the horrible stuff I did has a reason?"

Bumping my hip against hers, I answered, "Well, it's not that cut and dry. I think all the good and not-so-good stuff happens for *many* reasons. There's rarely one single cause for anything."

Gosh, I'm sounding more and more like Nate every day!

Tammy blinked rapidly for a moment, like she was batting back tears. "So what was the reason behind my mom dying after giving birth to me and my dad becoming an alcoholic?"

I placed a steady hand on the railing, not knowing how to respond. The absolute truth I so firmly believed in a moment ago seemed overwhelming now, but I knew I couldn't settle for the half-truths anymore. "I think we find our own meaning from each experience. It may not be something fully revealed for a long time. Life isn't black and white, like our first stereotypes of each other. And the good thing is there's beauty in the shades of gray. You just have to look for them."

"Golly, you are so corny," she teased, poking me in the ribs.

But I grabbed her hand, holding on for a second, letting her know I was there and it was okay to be real with me. Then I shrugged happily. "Yes, well. Like mama used to always say: smile and the world smiles with you."

My phone buzzed in my jeans pocket, and I checked a text. "They're done. They told us to meet them at Mean Streak."

Mean Streak was another one of Cedar Point's most thrilling roller coasters, one of seventeen in the park.

She gave a one-sided smile. "I'd rather let the skirmish settle. Ask if they'd want to ride a more tranquil ride first. Like that antique car ride," she added, pointing.

After sending her request, I got another text from Nate. "He says YOLO. We didn't come to the Rollercoaster Capitol of the World for kiddie rides."

Sucking in a deep breath, she said, "Can't argue with You Only Live Once, can I?"

I pressed my lips together. "I'll text back to meet at the Frontier Trail for the All-You-Can-Eat buffet instead. It is lunch time, and I don't wanna tackle any more roller coasters on an empty stomach anyway."

"What'd he say?" Tammy asked when my phone beeped loudly a few seconds later.

"Yes, of course! Food is always the way to a man's heart."

After we gorged ourselves on fried chicken, potato salad, baked beans, and root beer floats, we square danced to the country tunes blaring on the overhead speakers. I called out various moves to the beat of the music, instructing my friends. The buzz of the rollercoaster rides still hadn't worn off.

"How do you know how to get jiggy with it hoedown style?" Sean asked.

I grasped his left hand and swung him around in a half-circle, then I grabbed hold of Nate.

We pulled away from each other slightly and then came back, chest to chest before he pulled back again, lifting up his arm so I could cross under it. The smell of grease lingered in the air, and I was glad for the chance to work off the meal—and to hold a piece of Nate, if only for a few seconds at a time.

This realization scared me.

I knew it didn't make sense to want him right now. All the insecurities about us moving in different directions after graduation, about not being over Conner, about not being good enough for Nate, nagged at the back of my mind. In spite of all those feelings, I knew I believed in Nate and he believed in me, more than anybody. If nothing else, this *did* make sense to me.

"Eighth grade physical education class," I shouted over the deafening music. "After I got the flu and missed a week of school, my requests for electives were late. All the cool sports were taken. So I learned good ole' American square dancing instead, because middle school wasn't already humiliating enough."

Zigzagging across the floor, I stepped to the music with Kyle as other park guests joined us on the wooden floor. Then, hands on hips, I shimmied back to Sean.

"That's not square dancing proper, is it?" he asked.

Looking over my shoulder as I circled around Nate, I said, "Hey, that's just how I roll! Shakin' it head to toe!"

Soon, we were all free styling, trying to outdo the other. The small crowd of people formed a circle while the six of us each took our fifteen seconds of fame in the middle. Everyone held their own until Kyle took center stage.

"Dude, what do you even call that?" Nicole yelled to him from the outside of the circle.

He shot her a playful grin. "It's called bringing sexy back."

Nicole crossed her arms over her chest. "You're not bringing sexy back! You're the reason sexy left!"

"Oh!" yelled Sean. "She took her shot and killed it!"

"Yeah, she went there, bought the ticket, and loaded the train," Nate added, stretching out his hand to me.

I stuffed my hands in my jeans pocket. "You really didn't expect to get a high five, did you?"

"Access denied!" Tammy said, laughing, and I reached up and gave *her* a high five instead.

"Whatever. You'll be sorry you didn't high five me when I win this thing." He jumped back into the middle of the circle, pointing to us one by one, then gestured for applause.

In the end, Sean received the loudest cheers. I pat his shoulder as we headed back to our table for a refill of our drinks, exhausted.

"Being here on this Frontier Trail, trains going by, square dancing—kind of makes you wish for a simpler time," Nate said to me underneath the shaded pavilion as we sipped our root beers.

"Well, according to you, I'd already match the old-fashioned values that go with it since I'm rooming in an all girls dorm and all," I said, flipping my hair flirtatiously.

Nobody in our gang understood why I didn't want coed dorms, but no matter how tough Mom acted, I knew it was hard for her to let me go. I thought staying in an all girls dorm would help ease her fears, and I didn't need boys distracting from my college education anyway.

"Are you still gonna go to CMU in the fall if your band goes big time after the summer tour?" I asked.

He wrinkled his brow, contemplating. "I'm not sure. That'll depend on a lot of things, I guess."

Central Michigan University was about a two-hour drive to Ann Arbor. I had already looked up the directions online.

Beside us, Kyle burped loudly.

"Excuse me." He patted his stomach. "I ate so much I think I may hurl."

"Well, there's plenty of coasters here that'll help you do that," Nicole said, checking her teeth in a pocket mirror she carried in her purse.

Sean slammed his fist on the picnic table, and we all jumped.

"Oh, yeah. Let's get this party started. Top Thrill's next. Who's with me?"

I whirled around to face him. "I thought Mean Streak was next."

He pointed to Top Thrill, visible from anywhere in the park as the second tallest roller coaster in the country. "We're closer to this one now. Come on, ya'll."

As we waited in line, I felt light-headed just from the rush of screams flying above us.

"It's gonna be fun. I promise," Nate said, squeezing my sweaty hand, which only made my stomach drop more.

"I'll hold you to that." Wheels scraping against metal never sounded so scary as the passengers roared to a stop in front of us. Shuddering, I heard the click of a camera as I securely pulled down the lap bar.

Nicole laughed as she checked out the photo on her tiny LCD screen from the seat in front of me. "You should see your face right now. You're as white as a ghost."

"You laugh now, but we'll probably be ghosts after this ride." I looked at Nate next to me, and he grinned widely.

But his eyes were big and soft, almost sultry as he studied me.

I looked down at my feet.

"What are you doing?" he asked.

"Clicking my heels three times in hopes I'll be whisked away in a whirlwind."

"Oh, you'll be whisked away alright," Kyle said behind me as loud music by Republica blared around us, singing about being ready to go. "This baby goes up to 120 miles per hour in three-point-eight seconds."

I turned to Nate again. "And we're sure people have lived through this to tell the tale, right?"

"All the time. We just saw many of them get off the ride, remember? Let's take a deep, cleansing breath. In, out, in, out. There we go. That's better." He placed his hand on top of mine. "I'll buy you a T-shirt if you can make it through this without puking on me. Deal or no deal?"

"Deal. How tall is this thing exactly?"

"420 feet."

"Keep arms down, head back, and hold on," the automated recording said.

A motor revved, and we were launched into the sky.

I squeezed my eyes shut and counted to ten before we stopped abruptly. "That's it?" I asked, keeping my eyes closed as people screamed. "Why are people screaming if it's over?"

"Uh, stay calm. Don't open your eyes." Nate's voice sounded shaky, so of course I opened my eyes and discovered we were stuck at exactly 420 feet in the sky. "I told you not to open your eyes."

I peered over the side and vaguely registered an elevator coming up, but mostly the thought I was about to die registered. "What the heck!"

Nicole turned around. "You looked down, didn't you?"

Sean angled himself in his seat to face us, too. "Man, I'm gonna crap my pants so many times I could fill my own personal septic tank if they don't get us down in a minute."

Tammy snagged my sleeve from behind. "I hope you wore your good shoes because this could be a long walk down."

Throwing my hands in the air, I figured I was entitled to a meltdown right about now. "I knew this was a bad idea. This is why I don't ride roller coasters. I mean, who in their right mind thinks making a ride this tall is a bright idea? They just want to pat themselves on the back, and who cares if someone is killed in the process? Isn't 420 like the universal sign to get high? That should've been our first clue to stay far away from this thing. Nobody in their right mind would board this crazy train. Usually I'd be the girl at the bottom, taking a video of the stupid morons who decided to ride this thing, not the girl stuck up top because of some life list—"

Nate seized my arm and shouted, "Olga, will you go to prom with me?"

I gaped at him. This was so random. "And why are you asking me now?"

"I was going to ask you soon, since it's only six weeks away, and thought why don't we save ourselves the heartache of finding a date and go as friends?"

The part of just attending as friends felt worse than being stuck up here.

"And of course, in case we die."

I shoved him lightly, afraid if I hit him too hard, he might fall out of the cart. "Not funny."

But somehow, he did make me laugh, even as nervous sweat poured down my forehead. Or maybe the perspiration just came from being this much closer to the sun. I swore I could've reached out and touched its rays. Even the helium balloons from below popped before they made it this far.

The Jedi Order chanting "say yes, say yes, say yes" snapped me into focus. Our fellow thrill seekers joined them. Funny how a situation like this bonded people together so quickly. Before I could answer, a man literally stepped out of an elevator and stood on top of the track, adjusting something. Just seeing that took ten years off my life.

The chanting halted, and Kyle shouted to the worker, "Dude, they probably don't pay you enough to risk your life like this."

He smiled. "Just hold on tight, folks. We'll have you down in a sec."

"What happened?" Tammy asked, clearly annoyed.

He scanned the gages inside a box as he answered. "Well, on rare occasions, a combo of weight distribution, the force of the launch, and the wind can stall the coaster on top of the tower."

I heard Nic suck in her breath. "Define rare."

"I believe this is the third time in the ten years since its opening," he answered, wiping a bead of sweat from his forehead with a gloved hand.

Kyle snorted. "Weight distribution. I knew I shouldn't have eaten so much at lunch."

"Yo, how much longer we stuck up here for? We've been up here at least twenty minutes." Sean's eyes glistened as if he were ready to cry.

The worker chuckled. "It's been about three minutes, and you'll be down in about ten seconds. Hold on tight."

My heart jumped in my chest, and I barely breathed as we nose-dived to the ground. When we came to a screeching halt, I turned to Nate. "Yes."

Everyone cheered. I knew it was because we were all safe, but it felt like I'd just done the scariest thing by agreeing to attend Senior Prom with Nate. The g-force of the roller coasters at Cedar Point had nothing on falling in love.

"I can't believe I spent most of high school stereotyping you as a simple-minded, snobby, backstabbing cheerleader."

Chapter Sixteen

"Following the light of the sun,
we left the old world."
—Chris Columbus

Nicole and I pulled into the senior parking lot at Grand Haven High on Friday, April first, and a large crowd stared at something in the sky. Local news crews gathered everywhere, and Nicole barely squeezed into a parking slot.

"What in the world?" I wondered aloud as Nate opened my door, unusually silent. Upon hopping out of Nicole's Honda, I discovered the nine-foot monkey statue from the entrance of the local Jungle River Mini Golf, standing atop our school's roof. I turned to Nate.

"Oh my gosh! I can't believe you did this. It's so awesome! I thought you said pulling off the perfect practical joke would be too obvious for April Fool's Day?"

"I'm sure I don't know what you're talking about." He leaned toward me, and his eyelashes fluttered against my cheek. "We figured the fact it was so obvious added to its perfection," he whispered in my ear, sending chills up my spine.

We met up with Sean and Kyle in the lobby. I noticed they all dressed alike, even Nate wore his Cantankerous Monkey Squad shirt underneath his heavy checkered flannel. They greeted each other with fist bumps as Nicole, Tammy, and I rolled our eyes.

"So is this the extent of our senior prank, or do ya'll have more plans for the day?" Tammy asked.

"Let's just let this be a wait and see kind of thing," Nate said, divulging nothing.

"Well, I don't know if you fellas know this or not," I scolded in my best redneck voice. "But stealing is in fact a punishable crime in these here parts, and Jungle Golf will be darn tootin' mad when they discover their monkey has been abducted."

"True," Nate said "But no monkeys were harmed during the operation of our prank, and if they don't come for it themselves sometime today, we'll return it to them tonight."

"You morons!" Nicole let out an exaggerated sigh. "Don't you think they'll have a stake-out tonight and wait for something like that so they can arrest you?"

Sean half-shrugged. "You girls worry way too much."

The bell tolled and I waved, hurrying off to class.

A couple hours later, I dropped my book bag on the cafeteria floor with a loud thud. "Is your band's CD playing?"

"Sure sounds oddly familiar," Nate said, offering his arm and ushering me toward the food line.

People around the lunchroom flashed a thumbs-up toward him.

I honed in on his guitar solo as we moved through the line. "Okay, you have to tell me how you guys did this."

He pumped ketchup onto his hamburger. "I'd tell you, but then we'd have to kill you."

"Whatever," I said, adding chocolate milk to the last space on my lunch tray. "I guess nothing says Cantankerous Monkey Squad better than a publicity stunt. Your only problem is the music clearly pins the prank on the three of you."

"Maybe." He stole a fry off my now loaded tray. "Or it could just be a fan, or arch-enemy trying to make it look like us. There's no hard evidence. And maybe I'll get special treatment since my best friend is the probable class valedictorian."

He playfully elbowed me.

There was the dreaded 'friend' word again.

Setting my tray on the lunch table, I cleared my throat. "Don't you dare drag me into this."

He rubbed his goatee. "Hmm, dare? Now that I think of it, I did win a dare when your parents came to your last cheerleading game. I never did cash in."

174

I shifted my legs underneath me in the plastic chair. "You know, dares died out with middle school."

"Poor, Olga," Sean said. "Too chicken to accept the terms of a dare rightly won."

"All right," I agreed, knowing if I didn't, I'd be labeled as a wuss forever. "What are your terms?"

The drama teacher, Ms. Frost, entered the cafeteria with hurried steps, her arms swinging at her sides. We directed our attention to the melodrama unfolding on stage with the rest of fifth period lunch. Our cafeteria also served as our auditorium, and from the look of things, Ms. Frost came to put an end to the boys' prank. The guys must've hooked up their stereo equipment with the CD playing on a loop through the stage's loudspeakers and not the main office, to make it difficult for someone like the lunch duty ladies to locate the source of the prank through all the wires.

Ms. Frost pulled the plug, and then, giving a steady stare at the band, indicated with her index finger that the boys should follow her.

They did, but first Nate turned toward me with a rueful smile. "Aren't you coming?"

"What?" I eyed him nervously.

He swiped his hair to the side of his face and laughed. "You helped us, remember? United we stand, together we fall."

I nodded slowly and stood, understanding these were his terms.

"Wait up!" Nicole and Tammy shouted. "We're coming, too."

Nate put his arm around me as we walked down the hall toward the main office. "I didn't really expect you to follow, but thanks. Lunch just wouldn't be the same without you."

By seventh period, Kyle reported the monkey had left the building, returned to its rightful owner. When interrogated, the boys confessed to nothing but the music. Of course, Principal Matthews didn't buy their omission of truth, but like Nate said, they had no hard proof. So it was lunch detention, as Nate predicted, for the rest of the week for all of us. I just hoped they weren't dumb enough to pull off another stunt before the day's end. But I should've known better. Boys will be boys.

Nate asked to use the facilities during our eighth period Photography II class. After ten minutes, he still hadn't returned.

The bell rung, signaling the end of the school day.

The teacher shot me a puzzled look, but I just shrugged and gathered mine and Nate's things before heading out the door.

Greeted by hundreds of squeals as I exited, it seemed like a million super-sized bouncy balls rebounded off the hard surfaces of the school's tiles and walls. I caught one ball in mid-air and examined it more closely. Inside the glitter, a tiny, brown, angry monkey floated around. Sliding it in my jacket pocket, I laughed my way through the mania.

I passed Principal Matthews in the hall and heard the funniest walkie-talkie conversation ever. "Dean Reynolds and Janitor Michaels, I need help cleaning up immediately! I've never seen so many balls in my life! How are we ever going to get rid of all these monkey balls?"

Nate's hand gripped my shoulder out of nowhere as he leaned down and whispered, "Best senior prank ever," Nate said as he gripped my shoulder from behind and spun me around.

I laughed, hugging his side. "I just hope they still let you graduate high school after all this."

As we made our way outside past the school dumpsters overflowing with boxes from Mario's Pizza, a weekly Friday special, everyone patted Nate on the back while scurrying past us, already making plans for the weekend.

My phone buzzed from the front pocket of my backpack. I kept my gaze straight ahead and met the rest of the Jedi Order by Sean's truck, the phone between my ear and shoulder.

"Hello?" I asked breathlessly, feeling dizzy from all the excitement.

"Olga? You'll never guess what just happened." The familiar voice practically shouted at me in a rushed, excited tone.

"Calm down, Dad, what's up?"

I held the phone to my ear, a wide grin on my face as I listened to Dad and watched Nate chest bump with passerby.

Shutting the phone a few minutes later, I smiled from ear to ear. Practically screaming, the old cheerleader came out of me. "My parents invited all of you to Mackinac Island with us for this weekend. Who's coming?"

"What?" Nate's brows came together. "Are you serious?"

Mackinac was this place Conner visited with his Boy Scout troop for three summers in a row during middle school. His dad was the scout leader and secured a weeklong gig each summer for duty at Fort Mackinac. Ever since Conner told me about it when he returned from the first trip, I wanted to vacation there. I even thought about writing it on the life list, but then everybody made their suggestions and I ran out of room.

I polished my sunglasses on my T-shirt, then slid them on. "Yeah. One of the wealthy dudes my parents do business with at the marina owns a luxury sailing yacht. They were meeting today about something, and when this guy heard about my acceptance to UM and all the stuff that happened this year, he wanted to do something nice, so he told my dad to borrow one of his boats for the weekend. Dad asked him if it'd be okay if we took it to Mackinac, and he said yes. The vessel houses a dozen people, so we can all go."

"I'll come," Tammy said, lighting a cigarette.

Nicole adjusted the wide purse strap over her shoulder. "Count me in."

"For sure, yo!" Sean held out his fist to me for a knuckle bump.

The Volvo next to Kyle whirled to life, and he jumped. The kid honked his horn and screamed praises for the band's prank through the car window.

Nate raised two fingers to his forehead and gave a salute.

"Dude, I'm totally there," Kyle told me.

Sean opened the door to his Toyota Tacoma and then slid his key into the ignition, waiting.

"Sounds sweet," Nate agreed, climbing into the back seat of the truck behind Sean as Kyle took the front passenger spot.

"Great. We leave tomorrow from the marina at 6:00 in the morning, and then we'll arrive back home Sunday around 10:00 at night. Don't be late. You know how my mom is about punctuality." I directed my gaze at Tammy. "You ready to follow the boys?"

She nodded.

We were meeting Conner's family for a small remembrance ceremony by the lake, since today marked the year anniversary of his death. His parents said we'd all release a balloon as a symbol of sending prayers up to heaven and letting go of our grief. Today had been one of those sad happy days. Conner was present in the back of my mind, just like every day, but I was glad the boys went ahead with the prank. It honored Conner more than sitting around and being sad.

Tammy tossed her cigarette on the ground, stomped out the last of the burning ember just before we loaded into her Lexus, then hit the gas with her famous lead foot. I was whiplashed back into the memory of last April Fool's day, the image of her blowing smoke in my face and peeling out of the same parking lot as I waited for Conner to head out for our first spring sail.

The irony sent chills up my spine.

Nate and I explored the entire ship before settling into our favorite spot on the boat, an area in the front where there was a gracious view of both the sparkling lake and the sails dancing in the wind, and plenty of sea spray to cool our faces. Passing by all the gorgeous homes along the shore caused me to fantasize about plans for the future. But my fantasies came to an end when Sean barked at us to join the rest of the Jedi Order in the hot tub.

I nodded in the direction of our friends. "I can't believe there's actually a hot tub built into the back of the boat, because the water we're floating on just isn't enough, apparently."

"Catch up with the times. Hot tubs on boat decks are all the rage now."

Nate stretched his legs out in front of him and I did the same, my bare feet resting on top of his ankles. "Maybe in South Beach, but it seems out of place for Michigan."

He laid a hand across my shin. "Well, it's not really a hot tub. It's a deluxe jetted soaking tub you have to fill up and drain with each use, probably because a hot tub would be too much maintenance for the amount of time these millionaires actually spend on this thing."

Rolling my eyes, I gazed up at him and asked, "Why are you always so correct?"

He lifted his hands in an I-don't-know kind of way, then we helped each other up and hurried below deck to our separate cabins. There were four bedrooms, each with a queen-sized bed, and the extra room served as a study. All three girls shared one room, the three boys in another at the opposite end of the hallway. Mom and Dad's room separated us, as well as Robert and Loria's.

My parents invited Conner's parents because they thought getting out of town on the anniversary weekend of his death would do them some good.

Plus, Mom probably didn't want to be responsible for six teens all by herself.

Searching for my duffel bag in the pile of stuff thrown on the floor, I quickly found it and changed into my yellow and white striped one piece with the fake daisy on the right shoulder strap. I walked barefoot across the hardwood floor with rigid posture, returning to the saloon the same time as Nate. I admired the sight of him shirtless and sporting his black and white checkered swim trunks, then the boat rocked, waves pounding against the low windows. I lost my balance, falling straight into him, just as he also lost his balance. We ended up on the couch together. Warmth I never knew existed assaulted my body. His breath against my throat wreaked havoc on my nervous system as the stubble of his chin tickled me. He tipped my chin, forcing me to meet his eyes.

"Fancy meeting you here." He smiled, holding me, dragging his fingers lightly across my arms.

"Are you guys coming or what?" Nicole called from above.

Biting my lip, I looked at Nate's hair falling in his face, thick and dark, and my cheeks flushed.

"Guess we should head up," he said.

Reluctantly, I flipped over, not wanting to get up and climb the stairs, but I did. When we arrived on deck, everyone was in the water. Most noticeable was Tammy sporting her leopard print halter-top bikini. We passed through a sunken level with chairs just before the Jacuzzi, and above the four seats, a sitcom played on the wall-mounted television.

"Awesome." I slipped into the warm, bubbling froth. "I didn't notice the tv here before."

"Covered up." Kyle held up a large remote with more buttons on it than my laptop computer. "This little wall slides open with this control."

"Cool! Let me see." I snatched the remote and repeatedly opened and shut the secret wall before I noticed their annoyed stares.

Sean whispered loudly to Nicole, "Girl, I hate to tell you this, but your best friend has issues."

Tammy sighed. "I'm gonna be so spoiled by the end of this weekend. You'll have no other choice, honey, than to make tons of money so I can marry rich and live on a cruise ship the rest of my life."

Kyle wrapped her in a hug. "Anything for you."

"Oh, barf," Nicole muttered.

179

"You know, baby, you could try a little more affection," Sean said.

"Enough of the mushy. What cult classic do you all want to watch?" Tammy asked, stepping out of the hot tub, displaying her supermodel legs and dangling belly ring. She held up *The Goonies* and *Bill and Ted's Excellent Adventure*.

"Goonies!" We all shouted in unison, except for Nate.

Nate sighed. "Well, I hate to do this to you kids, but I'm gonna play the patriarch card."

Sean laughed. "Patriarch? What you talking about, dawg?"

"I'm the oldest member of the Jedi Order, which makes me the leader—or patriarch."

"Bill and Ted it is," Tammy said, inserting the DVD.

I moaned. "Where'd you discover these movies, anyway?"

"Ransacked the movie cabinet in the saloon." Tammy hit play. "Get ready for one sweet adventure."

"Most excellent," Nate imitated in Keanu Reeves-like style.

"Most bogus." Nicole disappeared underwater for several seconds. When she surfaced, she spit water into Nate's face.

Nate let out a whoop and plunged under, but he laughed when he finally came back up.

Thirty minutes into the flick, we were bored out of our minds. I studied Nate, thinking of what his punishment should be for picking such a craptastic movie, then dunked him. He emerged with a mouthful of water and squirted it in my face. Retaliating, I snagged some bath beads from a fancy soap dish on the ledge above the imitation hot tub, then crushed them on top of his head. Oil oozed down his forehead.

In one fluid movement, he reached for an unopened bottle of champagne, pumped it in the air with all his might, then uncorked it. Sparkling wine spritzed everyone as they scrambled out of the tub, squealing. Then he shot the beverage at me like a loaded gun.

A box of bath salts sat on the ledge and when Nate tried to jump out of the tub, I dumped the contents down the back of his swimming trunks. Then with one giant swoop of his hand, he grabbed whipped cream off the counter, which was laid out with chocolate covered strawberries by the service crew along with the champagne.

Nate sprayed a massive amount onto his hand in record time, then hurled the creamy topping toward me. I ducked under water, only to be hit square in the face when I came back up for air. Wiping the foam off my cheeks with one hand, I stretched my arm back to wind up for retribution, but he tackled me, bringing me under water again.

When we rose to the surface, we could only laugh hysterically for a few moments, his arms still around me from when he dragged me under. Finally we stopped, breathing heavily. I sucked in a deep breath and then let it out slowly. Still panting, his well-shaped lips were just inches from mine. I felt his hot breath and studied his expression, and I was certain something crossed his face I'd never seen there before. But I knew *the look* well. I'd seen it reflected in the mirror many times.

Longing.

I ached for Conner for so long and missed my chance.

Nate pressed his body against mine, my skin tingling, hoping all the things I'd been denied would be mine. At the same time, I wondered again if this risk was worth it. I was still confused about Nate's feelings for me. Sure, we were attending prom together, but he said as friends. Even if the 'just friends' part were true, I couldn't deny the heat travelling up my body had nothing to do with the hot tub and everything to do with Nate, his moist lips daring me to kiss him.

"Um, hello?" Tammy interrupted my thoughts.

I'd forgotten any of them were even present.

"Like, get a room already."

The breath I'd been holding rose out in front of me, the moment evaporating. Nate scowled, and everyone laughed. By the time Nate and I cleaned up our mess, the boat docked at Mackinac Island, and all my desires swirled down the Jacuzzi drain. Everyone wrapped themselves in towels and enjoyed the sights of the village and harbor.

Nate shifted out of his towel and swept an arm from side to side. "Do you know how long the boat is?"

I shook my head.

"I asked the owner at the marina this morning before we got on. Eighty-eight feet."

I whistled, peering over the side. "Impressive."

He squeezed my shoulder. "Not as impressive as you."

My head snapped up. "Whatever." But oh my gosh! I suddenly wanted to kiss him so badly.

I nodded toward Tammy standing at the other end of the yacht—she was out of earshot and lighting a cigarette. "I just wish I had a body like hers. It's not fair some girls get all the perfect parts."

Nate leaned down and whispered in my ear, his face tight. "You really don't get how beautiful you are. I much prefer the natural, All-American-girl-next-door look."

I eyed Nate as he straightened to full height. "Did you just compliment me by calling me wholesome?"

Breathing out a sigh, he asked, "Is that a bad thing?"

"It's not the best compliment I've ever received, but I guess I'll take what I can get."

Tammy dropped her cigarette into the water below, then sauntered down the steps toward the cabins. My concern for her was like a buzzing in my ear, but I shook the thoughts from my head for now.

After all, I was on vacation.

"Okay, each time we pass a fudge shop, we go in and eat some," I told everyone when off the boat a half-hour later. A fudge shop was the first stop on our island tour. In fact, the whole island carried the thick aroma of the world-famous Mackinac chocolate.

"No way." Mom exhaled loudly. "I already laid down on the bed to zip up these jeans."

Tammy threw her head back in laughter. "I love your mom."

I offered Mom my best puppy dog face. "Come on. Just for a sample at least? We're on vacation! Calories don't count here." I never needed an excuse to indulge in a piece of creamy peanut butter fudge, but I thought my argument was sound.

Mom stared off into the distance and answered in a monotone voice. "Fine."

I linked my arm with hers as we strolled along the shoreline, splitting a slice of peanut butter pecan fudge. Lots of horse-drawn carriages passed by. The island banned motorized vehicles, creating the atmosphere of a simpler time. A few minutes later, we stumbled upon a bike rental shop, providing us with the perfect outlet to explore the island.

Nate's eyes lit up. They were never consistently blue, just like the ocean. Sometimes they sparkled blue-green; other times the irises reflected a very deep blue, black almost.

"Hey, Olga," he shouted. "Check this out! You wanna rent a two-seater?"

I felt a rush of affection for his childlike ways and wanted to reach out and touch him, but I restrained myself.

While everyone picked various bikes according to their liking, Nate and I settled upon ours, then headed toward the high rocky buffs where a colorful forest loomed. The ride felt like a marathon of mountain biking as we zoomed over the gazillion trails throughout the island. Thankfully, the weather was overcast. The sun peeked out from behind the clouds every so often, so I wasn't sweating too profusely when we arrived at the popular Grand Hotel.

"Have you ever seen anything more picturesque in all your life?" Loria asked as we parked our bikes.

The sign read the hotel had the world's longest porch, measuring 660 feet long. Dad and Robert walked inside to inquire about a tour while the rest of us waited on the porch looking over the grounds.

Mom's eyes were wide and shining. "What I would give for a garden blooming with lilacs like this."

"Look." I pointed toward the pool. "It's shaped like a serpent."

Kyle grinned. "And it's about as big as a football field. I hope we can go swimming."

Tammy rubbed her arms as a breeze blew over us. "Only if it's heated like the hot tub."

Loria sauntered over and stood next to me, placing her hand on mine as I leaned over the porch railing. "So, I see you've created quite the movement at Grand Haven High."

I flashed a shaky smile. "What do you mean?"

"Well, as supporting alumni, Robert and I receive the *Bucs' Blade* in the mail every month. We've really enjoyed your bucket list feature." Her eyes widened a bit, and her compliment felt genuine. "And it got us thinking about creating a scholarship there in Conner's honor. And we want to tie it together with your '18 Things' list."

Shuffling a step back in surprise, I said, "Really? How?"

She beamed at me. "You know how the last issue of the paper in May always features a humorous Most or Best whatever list. Like a spoof on those awards for the yearbook, Most Spirited and so on?"

Sweeping my hair back in a ponytail, I entered planning mode as I had a total ESP moment. "Oh, I totally understand where you're going! We could have a writing contest to submit the best item on their list of eighteen things, and then, the newspaper staff and you and Robert could vote on the best picks for like Most Poignant, Most Scary, Most Athletic, Most Humorous, and Most Ambitious."

She nodded. "Exactly. Do you think Mrs. Cleveland would go for something like that instead of her usual list of satire?"

The gray clouds parted and sunlight filled the porch, like something straight out of a movie, a total light bulb moment. "I think so, but she'll need details, and fast, if you're going to pull this off within two months. Do you want to keep it at the five categories I named or just do one best overall?"

"Five sounds perfect." Loria leaned forward, and I peered over the side to view what she might might be looking at.

The view of lovely landscaped grounds, couples leisurely walking along the shoreline, and romantic horse trail rides took my breath away.

After a few minutes, Loria leaned back and smiled at me. "We could do five thousand dollars for each student for the next four years. Does that sound okay?"

A small gasp escaped my lips. "That's twenty-five thousand dollars each year!"

I was sure she'd already calculated the math, but I couldn't help myself from observing the obvious.

Loria shrugged. "We already had more than that set aside for Conner's college education, so it seems fitting for other deserving students to receive those funds, especially members of his graduating class."

Mom leaned in between us and wrapped an arm around each of our shoulders. "This is a wonderful plan the two of you are creating. You and Robert are very generous."

Dad interrupted our moment by returning with a reddened face. "We paid ten dollars a head just for the self tour!"

I choked back a giggle at the contrast of Robert's charitableness and Dad's cheapness.

But the price was money well spent. We visited the horse stables, collected rocks and shells on their private beach, and built a giant sand castle. In the afternoon, the boys played bocce ball in the Tea Garden. The girls enjoyed a spot of tea while cheering them on, in a civilized manner of course. Some guys who looked to be college age drove past on a golf cart at full speed until the driver caught sight of Tammy, and distracted, he swerved to the side, dumping the two riders sitting on the back of the cart onto the dirt.

"Oh!" Sean yelled. "Epic fail!"

I slurped tea from my flowered china, trying not to laugh. I've always thought it was weird how people love to laugh at failure.

But these dudes didn't seem fazed at all. While one of the guys stood and brushed off, he yelled back, "Whatever! That was exactly as fun as it looked!"

The driver laughed and then directed his attention back to Tammy. "Waz up? Did I just die and go to Heaven, because you must be an angel. Why don't we go for a ride? I'll show you how to fly." He winked the creepiest wink in history.

And the amateur comedy show didn't end there.

Tammy shook her head and smirked. "I don't believe in dating college guys who major in idiocracy, so I'm thinking I'll just go."

She turned and marched in the other direction.

I made a quick decision to follow her. Even though the guy was a total show-off, it wasn't normal behavior for Tammy to ignore anyone's advances, even if she did have a boyfriend.

"Good one," I called from behind.

She kept a steady pace, and I half-jogged to catch up.

"Hey, I'm here if you want to talk about it."

Turning around, her eyes grew wide, like I uncovered a secret.

"What?" Her voice didn't sound calm at all.

"Even as a genius with zero common sense I can tell something is up with you," I replied with a shrug.

At those words, she burst into tears. "I wish I had your IQ. Then I wouldn't be flunking out of high school two months before graduation."

Now it was my turn to say, "What?" Her usual brave face was gone and I wrapped her in a hug, her shoulders shaking, and felt myself start to cry, too.

I didn't say anything else while I let her cry it out. After the tears stopped, I reached into my over- the-shoulder bag and then handed her a Kleenex.

"Thanks. And sorry."

"Tammy, don't apologize for crying."

"I haven't cried in ten months, since my dad almost died in the hospital." She wiped the dampness from her face. "So, um, I need to like, keep a two-point-five GPA to retain my cheerleading scholarship. And yesterday afternoon, my guidance counselor called me into the office. As of right now, it's two-point-two." She tucked a piece of hair behind her ear, the row of silver rings on her hand glinting in the sunlight. "My whole life I've been waiting to get outta Grand Haven and my craphole of a life with my dad. I just can't believe I let this happen. I'm so stupid!"

She collapsed on the grass, and I squatted next to her.

"You are *not* stupid." My voice was stiff, reminding me of my own protective mother. "You are smart, confident, and accomplished. You were Prom Princess last year, Homecoming Queen this year, voted Most Involved in our poll for the *Bucs' Blade*, Class President, Head Cheerleader, president of the Booster Club. Plus, you have your modelling job outside of school and take care of your dad. I mean, I don't know how you could even expect to maintain a two-point-five with all the things you do for everyone else."

Flinching, she said, "What are you talking about? I've lived my whole life for myself, made all the decisions according to what I want, and learned not to have expectations. Now I know why. All it gets me is disappointment. At least I'm successful at being a failure, right?"

I pressed my lips together, thinking of how to respond. Once again, I found myself asking, what would Conner do? "Hey, it's not too late to fix this. I can help you study. We'll go to the counselor, see what else we can do to bring up your grades. Maybe there are extra credit projects you can do or something. And it wouldn't hurt to talk to the counselor about how you're feeling, too. What's your Dad say about all this?"

She pulled at the necklace around her neck. "Didn't tell him."

Slowly releasing a deep breath, I gauged how hard I should push. "Why not? I mean, he's been recovering without any relapses, right?"

"Hasn't had one drink in the past ten months—the longest I've ever seen him last. But that's the catch twenty-two, ya know? It's like I keep him at arm's length because I'm scared he'll disappoint me again. And because even though I love him, I don't want to get close now. I want to leave and hold onto that hurt, let it carry me outta here."

"You should tell your dad you love him," I said.

She looked at me with huge eyes. "It's weird you say that because lately he's been telling me he loves me all the time—and how proud he is of me. That's another reason I don't want to tell him about maybe losing my scholarship. What if it makes him drink again?"

The sun was barely visible through the darkening clouds, but at least it was still there.

"Look, you are not responsible for what your dad does. You need to release yourself from that burden. Just like I had to release my guilt over what happened to Conner. And you need to let people love you. You deserve love. But you need to give in order to receive, too."

She crossed her ankles and leaned back on her elbows as thunder rolled in the distance. "He knows I love him though. Nobody could love that man *but* me."

I pointed at her. "See? That's the hurt coming back, mad at him for not being there, and you need to let the pain go, too, because it'll hold you back. We all fail at one time or another. One day, maybe twenty or thirty years from now, you'll probably do something hurtful to your kid and need to ask for forgiveness, and you'll look back on this time in your life, glad you forgave your dad."

Sitting up, Tammy wrapped her arms around her waist. "But I don't know if I can get out those words, and yeah I know nobody's perfect or whatever, but some are more perfect than others. And my dad was an 'other.' I feel like I should punish him for making me miss my childhood. Like if I actually say I love you to him, it'll excuse everything he did."

I nodded, plotting out what to say next. "Well, the Tammy I know does *not* have a problem with communication. We hear you loud and clear all over school."

She laughed.

"Telling him I love you back doesn't excuse his behavior, but it will free you. Believe me, I was locked away in an emotional cage not telling someone I love them for way too long. I felt like I was losing my mind. So this is more for your sanity, not his. Get it off your chest. Go home and tell him you love him, and give him a hug. And as for your lost childhood, I have just the cure for that, too."

She pulled some grass up with one hand and then released the blades to the wind. "What?"

"Your own list of eighteen things. Eighteen things you missed while growing up, one for each year of your childhood. We'll complete them together while the boys are away this summer, before *we* go to college. Deal or no deal?"

"Deal," she answered as rain came in the form of a gentle sprinkle.

By the time we returned our bikes, I felt the first pangs of hunger as dinnertime approached. We retreated to the yacht to shower and change. I decided on a navy pencil skirt and white tank top with a classic red knit blazer and five-inch cherry-red heels. Looking at myself in the full-length mirror on the back of the cabin door, I let out a laugh.

"What's so funny?" Nicole asked as she brushed on some lip color.

"I just can't stop thinking about how everything keeps coming around full circle," I explained, fluffing my curls. "Like this time last year. A prank, a boating trip, a rainstorm—one bringing death and the other life, a feud beginning and a feud ending, back then wanting to rid myself of my All-American girl next door persona, and now returning to it."

I spun, showing off my preppy outfit to demonstrate.

She shook her head. "Gosh, you're right. It doesn't seem too long ago when all of that stuff happened. How can that be?"

"Life goes on, and we have no control over it." I embraced the concept more each day.

At dinner, I asked for coffee as soon as the waitress approached the table. Everyone bent over their menus, deciding what was good. Nate ordered the Yankee Rebel Tavern's Prime Rib and consumed all fourteen ounces, and even sampled a bit of my pot roast. He looked handsome in his pair of khaki pants and long sleeved buttoned down white shirt, topped with his favorite Star Wars necktie.

After our meal, we separated from the parentals right away, excitement for a night on the island by ourselves becoming contagious.

"Any ideas on what you guys want to do?" Nicole asked, her black hair in playful Princess Leia buns. The shimmering gold sweater she wore even reminded me of Leia's golden metal bikini from the *Return of the Jedi* movie. It was almost like her and Nate planned their outfits, which was comical since they couldn't have been more different.

Pointing to him, I said, "You're always the man with a plan. You decide."

His face settled into a puzzled look with the cutest frown ever. "It's vacation. There is no plan. Let's just walk around and see what we find."

We meandered back toward Main Street and while passing the Mission Point Resort, noticed a wedding reception in one of the flower gardens.

"I know what we're doing! We're crossing number eighteen off your list tonight." Nate's voice edged with excitement and everyone got jacked up to crash a wedding.

"I don't know." I felt like a dork because only I hesitated and this was my list. "What if we're caught?"

"Come on. We just pretend we're long lost relatives if questioned." As if Nicole was an expert on the subject.

Sean nodded. "Yeah, girl. Besides, the band is already playing, so all the formal stuff is over, and servers are passing out drinks like hot cakes. Nobody will notice us. We even dressed up tonight, so we'll blend right in."

"Fine." I plucked a piece of lint from my blazer. "I guess if Keanu Reeves can act, I can pull this off."

Nate offered me his arm while holding his other arm over his chest, pretending my Keanu jab wounded his heart, and we slinked across the freshly mowed grass, Earth's homemade dance floor.

Strings of clear mini-globe lights zigzagged between trellises, and votives glowed from surrounding tables, providing a low light idyllic for hiding. The band played everything from rock to traditional bluegrass to country. I watched the bride and groom with jealous eyes as Nate and I swayed to the music.

Looking up, I caught Nate studying the happy couple, too. "Hey, try not to act like a creepy stalker. We're in hiding, remember?"

He touched his forehead to mine. "Guess I'll just stare at you then. You look really good tonight, by the way."

His compliment made my breath catch, and before I could respond with a compliment of my own, the band announced the cutting of the cake.

The crowd cleared, and we headed to the dessert table so we could have our cake and eat it too, so to speak. There was a cool island display consisting of a pineapple tree stuck with watermelon, cantaloupe, and strawberry kabobs. A chocolate fondue fountain stood adjacent to the tree, along with many glasses of champagne. We loaded up plates with fruit, and everyone grabbed a flute except me. We ate off to the side in the dark shade of oak trees to avoid the crowd.

After downing her drink, Nicole announced in a happy voice, "Olga, I've gotta pee. You wanna help me locate the bathroom?"

She already looked disheveled, her face red and pupils dilated.

I guess she's definitely a one drink limit girl. "Um, sure."

When we returned a few minutes later, the guys finished their second glass.

Again, I needed to be the responsible one. "Hey, take it easy. The little bubbles cause the alcohol to get absorbed faster in your stomach and into your bloodstream, so you get drunk faster."

Nicole totally ignored me, grabbing another flute. "How would you possibly know all that?"

I blushed. "I remember a *Today Show* wedding segment, and they mentioned how people need to go easy on the champagne because the hangovers are worse."

Tammy raised her already empty glass in a toast to me. "Cheers to our resident goody-two-shoes."

"Cheers," Nicole shouted. "I've got nuttin' but love for ya, honey."

"Thanks," I murmured as she held her arms out for a hug.

I extended my arms to oblige when out of nowhere, a pile of red and white roses landed there instead. The wedding guests applauded. Apparently, I'd just caught the bouquet. As the band announced the garter toss, the boys rushed to the dance area.

Much to my chagrin, the groom performed a sexy dance up to the bride and stuck his head up her dress, pulling the garter off with his teeth, egged on by lots of laughs and whistles from Nate, Kyle, and Sean. I knew the winner would earn the right to slip the garter on my leg afterwards. Cold sweat trickled down my sides as I scanned the small crowd of single men, praying for Nate to catch the stupid thing.

A little girl skipping across the makeshift dance floor interrupted my thoughts. She flung her arms around the bride while jumping in her lap, oblivious to this evening's concluding event.

God bless her, I thought, as she inspired an idea.

About to toss the bouquet off to another girl and bolt in the name of self-preservation, my wallflower instincts weren't needed this time. Nate shoved his way to the front of the line just in time to catch the garter. I felt my cheeks grow hot when he turned toward me and bowed slightly. He walked over and held out his arm formally and I put my arm through his. I studied the surrounding tables to see many sour faces from all the girls under twenty-five, and I could only guess they were jealous because the hottest guy at the wedding belonged to me, for the moment.

Still, I thought Nate pushed our inconspicuousness when he paraded me along the perimeter of the dance floor before finally leading me to the waiting chair in the middle of the dance area.

The band played *Real Good Man* by Tim McGraw, and the lyrics went on about loving with velvet hands just as Nate slipped the garter underneath my skirt, stopping just above my right knee, always the perfect gentleman. Yet I still managed to quiver with delight.

He stood and offered his hand, pulling me up with him. "Would thou carest to dance, m'lady?"

Oh great. If he's resorting to Shakespeare impressions, he must be buzzed. "I guess so, but then we leave."

"What? Why?" His voice cracked, reaching the eighth octave like a thirteen-year-old boy's entering puberty.

I ran my finger over his knuckles and couldn't help smiling. "Because the guy I hired to kill you for turning me into a wedding crasher should be here any minute now."

He faked like he was shot as we headed hand in hand onto the dance floor. A bridesmaid and groomsman danced our way, and I figured explanations were in order soon.

"So how do you know Risa and Simon?"

I assumed they referred to the newlyweds.

Nate didn't miss a beat. "Second cousin thrice removed on the groom's uncle's side. We're from Detroit. It's a shame we haven't kept in touch, been far too long really. Though from what I hear, I'm surprised the bride is wearing white, if you know what I mean."

He waggled his eyebrows as their mouths stood agape.

I intervened quickly. "Um, well, it's been a wonderful night. They're such a cute couple. But we really should get going. Nice meeting you."

Dragging a chuckling Nate, I left him alone for a second to gather the rest of our gang, only to discover him downing another glass of champagne when I returned.

"Are you insane?" I yell-whispered.

"Nope." He belched loudly. "Well, maybe."

As we toddled down Main Street, I formulated a plan. "Okay, there's still an hour until curfew. I'm going to buy a twelve pack—of water," I clarified when excitement spread across Sean's face. "Then you guys can hydrate yourselves as you walk off your buzz. Now, stay until I return."

Kyle barked in obedience, and I entered the store, rolling my eyes.

Five minutes later, I marched out holding plenty of water, aspirin, and breath mints for everyone.

Nate raced down the street. "Nanny nanny boo boo, you can't catch me."

"You've got to be kidding me," I mumbled, squaring my shoulders and studying my five-inch heels. "Well, these hurt something fierce anyway." I slipped them off my feet. "Tammy, distribute the goods among yourselves while I drag a naughty Nate back to the boat. I'll meet you back there in an hour. Don't be late."

She nodded and slurred, "Yesss."

I sprinted ahead, shoes in one hand and bottled water, a mint, and two aspirins in the other.

When halfway caught up to him, he turned around, ran to me, slapping my shoulder, and yelling, "Tag! You're it!"

He veered east of Main Street into Marquette Park, and I faked tiredness. "Please, stop. You know I'm not as fast as you."

Standing at the edge of the island's harbor, he pumped his arms in the air. "Victory is mine!"

I acted like I'd push him into the water, but instead handed him his water.

"No, thanks. I'm good."

His voice was loud.

"Um, no, you're not. Sip and take these." I forced the two Aspirin in his other hand, and for whatever reason, he listened.

He lifted me in a bear hug, then plopped me down on the bench behind us.

"What was that for?"

He slapped me hard on the back, then laid his head down in my lap and closed his eyes. "You wanna know my number one thing?"

The thought made me itch.

"Sure." I swallowed hard, my throat tight.

"Drum roll, please." He pounded his hands on top of his khakis with charismatic flair. "Tell Olga I'm in love her. I mean, with her."

My heart jumped, and dizziness washed over me. I focused on breathing in and out, the scent of lilac bushes filling my nostrils.

Before I could respond, light snoring escaped his lips.

Unbelievable! Perfect timing again!

A lump rose in my throat, and I tossed his mint in my mouth, sucking on the peppermint thoughtfully. Now I *knew* he loved me, although a drunken confession wasn't exactly an ideal circumstance for bearing one's soul. Still, why didn't he just say it before and ask me to be his girlfriend? Looking around Fort Mackinac, adjacent to the park, I discovered my answer.

I'd built a metaphorical wall around myself, extending far beyond just this past year since Conner's accident. It had always been difficult for me to tell the people I cared about that I loved them. Thinking back to my and Tammy's convo earlier, I pondered the emotional cage I referred to. At the time, I thought I was only talking about Conner, but now I realized it was more.

If I was honest with myself, over the last few months I'd driven myself crazy with not telling Nate how I really felt about him. Every day, I made a pro and con list in my head. Was the risk of loving someone again worth the pain or not? Of course, I pushed Nate away many times. No wonder he kept his number one a secret. He was probably scared I'd run away, like I often did to prevent potential disaster.

But wasn't that what caused my great regret? I had my chance to tell Conner I loved him, and I let it slip away. The statue of Father Jacques Marquette, for whom the park was named after, stood on his high pedestal, judging me. I made the sign of the cross and vowed not to make the same mistake twice.

———◆———

"Like, get a room already.' The breath I'd been holding rose out in front of me, the moment evaporating."

———◆———

Chapter Seventeen

"Through love to light! Oh wonderful is the way,
that leads from darkness to the perfect day!"
—*Richard Watson Gidler*

I stepped into elegance as I slipped on my prom dress. The ivory gown featured a swooping neckline, the top half-embellished with fancy beadwork tight on my tone figure, and a flowing hemline ending just above my ankles. I accentuated the dress with the diamond necklace Nate gave me for my birthday. My hands shook way too much, so Nicole applied my makeup and fixed my curls and even tied in some blue strands of hair bling.

"Okay, you look hot." She grabbed my hand and twirled me around. "Don't worry about a thing. I'll make sure it's perfect before you guys get there."

I nodded, hugging her before I perched myself on the bed to slip on my strappy high heels. Then, I headed down the hallway to sit in the living room by myself and wait for Nate's arrival. Mom and Dad already left. I'd have to lie and tell Nate they got called into work for a boat emergency, because he'd think it was suspicious they weren't here to take pictures.

He was already confused when our Jedi Order told him we didn't want to get together for a pre-prom dinner. We told him a lame excuse. We'd be at a restaurant afterwards until five in the morning anyway.

These past few months, Tammy helped organize some post-prom activities with the local hot spots. Grand Haven Trolley agreed to connect all of the festivities for free, running from midnight to five. Students could bowl at Starlite Lanes, where they were turning down the lights and turning up the music for Midnight bowling. Meijer's provided free prom photo sessions at their store. DeeLite Restaurant offered free pancake and sausage breakfasts and their mic for karaoke. Diary Treat served free ice cream cones and hosted a Banana Split Eating Contest. Nate would love to get in on that action, but he was already scheduled to play with Cantankerous Monkey Squad at Jumpin' Java Coffee Shop. With their free hot coffees, hot chocolates, and sodas, I thought they got the best spot for a gig.

A tap on our front door pulled me out of my reverie. I rushed to the doorway, taking a step back to drink in Nate. In an effort to match me tonight, he dressed in a white jacket with navy colored pinstripes, a white vest, and a blue tie. His pants were solid white, and when my gaze met the floor, I laughed. He sported orange Skywalker Pilot shoes.

"You know me, I had to be a little rock n' roll." He shrugged.

I wanted to kiss him so badly, but I bit my lip, forcing myself to wait. "I wouldn't have it any other way."

"What do you think of my suit?"

Okay, I wasn't a vain person, but Nic put a lot of effort into making me look good. The fact that Nate didn't comment on my appearance took my self-esteem down a few notches and caused me to rethink my plan for tonight.

Tugging at my dress, I said, "Um, it's cool. You look great."

He pointed at his watch. "Thanks. You got your Mom's car all ready to go? We should hurry before we're stuck here taking pictures."

Opening my mouth to set him straight, I stopped short when Nate snorted with laughter.

"You should've seen your face! I got you good, girl!"

I shoved him playfully, knocking him into the door. A witty comeback on my part would've been nice, but all I could do was join him in his outburst of laughter.

"Seriously, it should be against the law to look this good," he said, flashing me a wide-eyed look that made me giggle again. "If looks could kill, I'd be a dead man."

Grabbing his vest, I pulled him inside. "Your compliments are a bit cliché, but I'll take them."

He scanned our tiny apartment. "Where are your folks?"

I explained quickly about the emergency at the marina and he seemed convinced, slipping the blue corsage on my wrist and snapping some photos with his camera. "If I would've known your parents weren't home, I would've invited Mom and Dad in to take some pictures for us."

They'd dropped him off since he still had his license revoked. I, on the other hand, finally obtained my driver's license this past week and planned on driving him to the convention center in Mom's Camaro.

"It's okay; we'll get plenty of pics at the dance tonight." I pinned a rose to his tuxedo jacket, then shut the front door on our way out, knowing as I did, the chapter in my life as Nate's good friend was closing, too.

We pulled into the packed parking lot of the Harborside Convention Center.

"Wow. And it's only 8:00. Is it normal for everyone to be so on time for prom?" Nate asked as I killed the engine.

Of course, this was a valid question since he'd never been to prom, but then again, neither had I.

"Yep," I lied again as my heart hammered against my chest. In hindsight, I wished I hadn't brewed so many cups of coffee. This morning I thought I needed all that energy to organize what we were about to walk into, something I'd planned all week with the help of our friends and family. But now I paid a price more jacked up than the ones at Starbucks, my insides a nervous wreck.

He opened my door for me and said, "Oh, well, hope we didn't miss anything. Ready?"

Ready to stop pretending something more doesn't exist between us? Absolutely. "Ready."

I took one deep breath to calm myself and stepped out of the car. Nate slipped his arm around my waist, which was a very good thing since I felt dizzy. I just prayed all that caffeine I drank earlier contained a swig of courage.

He opened the door into an empty foyer, and I listened carefully, basking in the quiet. Nate's wristwatch beeped steadily, and it comforted me, Time an old friend I welcomed back as I finally prepared to move on. My pulse slowed. I *was* ready for this. Nate anchored me to this world, helping me navigate the choppy waves of life this past year.

He looked extremely confused though, running a hand over his face. "This is eerie. It doesn't even sound like anyone's here, but the lot is packed."

A flutter ran through my stomach, and my eyes widened in anticipation as he opened the next door.

Time of Your Life by Green Day began playing, cueing the start of our four minute world record breaking Flash-Freeze.

Thousands froze into position: sipping drinks, embracing, sharing a secret, bending down to tie a shoelace, fixing a friend's hairdo, stabbing a piece of gum into their mouth, poised with a camera or video recorder, in the midst of a high five or fist bump. People came up with so many different creative ways to freeze. Tammy and Kyle locked lips at the front of the crowd. They stood next to my parents, who held a sign that read: "Don't just stand there. Walk to the center of the room for a special message."

My eyes burned, and I tried not to cry. I didn't want to mess up Nicole's makeup job. Conner's parents were next to mine, pointing the way.

"What is this?" Nate asked, his voice light and totally surprised.

We navigated through the crowd.

"Did you do this? Is this for your life list, break a world record? Are we breaking the record for world's largest Flash-Freeze Mob right now?"

My fingers hovered over his for a second before fully taking hold of his hand.

"Yep," I replied, stone faced, forcing myself not to smile and give something away. "Only one more to cross off." Okay, I couldn't help but smile now. "Come on. Let's go see about the mysterious message."

Time in slow motion, tile seemed to stretch on forever as my heels clicked against the surface of the dance floor, leading Nate to our fate. My breathing echoed loud in my ears, overpowering the words of the song singing about the end of a relationship, a turning point, something unpredictable but in the end right, reminding me whatever happened was meant to be.

We reached the center of the room, and I stepped backwards, letting Nate read the sign I painted for him two days ago. Nicole and Sean stretched the banner in front of them, faces frozen with a smile. The song faded, and amidst the silence of over three thousand people standing still, Nate read my words aloud to himself.

"Nate, I'm in love with you. You've been one of my best friends through the last grueling year of high school. I was kinda hoping you'd be my boyfriend for, I don't know, forever maybe. Yours Truly, Olga."

I forgot to breathe as he repeated the words I've wanted to tell him for months, but then he turned slightly and took my other hand in his, and the warmth of his skin calmed me again. On the verge of tears, I tried hard not to shed them out of habit, but at least these were happy tears.

He reached up and brushed them away with the back of his hand, then leaned in, his breath against my breath. The kiss was tentative at first, then grew bolder, the confidence of our love taking over. I couldn't believe how good it felt, my heart crashing into my sides, my breathing fast.

Cheers and applause reminded us we were not alone and we opened our eyes, smiling widely at each other.

He rested his head on my shoulder, curling his arms around my back, and whispered. "I love you, Olga."

They were the words I'd longed to hear, completing my list ahead of schedule.

"I've always been in love with you, from the first time I saw you. I love every little thing about you. That was my number one," he confessed, not remembering his drunken tell-all, and I knew I'd need to come clean later. "I can't believe you beat me to the punch! I was gonna see how tonight went and then maybe ask you to be my girl."

I nodded. "Why didn't you tell me before if you've been in love with me this whole time?"

He let out a long breath. "Well, for one thing, I didn't know if you loved me back. You've been on the rebound from Conner and vulnerable. I wanted to wait until you were over the guilt of Conner's death because I thought it'd be incredibly selfish to throw one more ball at you to juggle. Then, there was also the issue of waiting for the perfect time and place. I didn't want to just blurt it out in conversation. That's why tonight seemed like maybe it would work, but I was also scared if I told you I love you on our first date that you might run away."

I thought of the night of the meteorite shower and shuddered. "I think I've been in love with you for a while now too, but I didn't want to admit my feelings. I was all too content to hide behind them, or rather from them, but then I realized it was more important to reveal my feelings instead of living a lie."

I Don't Want to Miss a Thing by Aerosmith blared over the loudspeakers, and everyone unfrozen and dancing, gave us our time alone. The disco ball rotated steadily, illuminating the room as Nate's reasons illuminated the situation we'd been in, caught in spin cycle, for the past couple of months. Just like the surface of the crystal ball above us consisted of thousands of facets to produce its complex display, my and Nate's relationship contained thousands of complex moments leading to this final reflection of the heart.

I scooted closer, my body pressing against his. "Tell me again."

"I love you, Olga," he said with all the confidence of leading me toward my future.

On May twenty-seventh, promptly at 7:00 p.m., the commencement ceremonies began at Harborside Convention Center. A flurry of nervous energy in a sea of burgundy colored gowns overtook the foyer. There were plenty of hugs, kisses, and post party talks until Principal Matthews shushed and commanded us to take our spots.

The school band played *Pomp and Circumstance,* and I was at the tail end in the processional of students pouring into the main hall. Our class vice president approached the stage to deliver the invocation, and then, a well-groomed German exchange student who served as our treasurer, lead us in the Pledge of Allegiance.

Afterward, Nate sang the national anthem. Our class secretary gave a greeting, and our class advisor, Mrs. Cleveland, stepped up to the podium for a special presentation.

"Good evening to all our special guests, most of all our graduates. In a few moments, we'll hear from your valedictorian, Olga Worontzoff. Even though I'm proud of her accomplishment of earning the highest grades over the past four years, they're just a cluster of the letter 'A' on a piece of paper helping to secure her place at college. Down the road of life, the grades you earn in high school don't really mean anything. You've lived to learn your whole lives, and now, you must learn to live. Along those lines, Olga did something more important this past year than just earn good grades. She helped spark a movement after her best friend, Conner Anderson, died in a terrible accident last April. As a writer for our student publication, *Bucs' Blade,* she headed up a monthly bucket list feature this year after creating her own, titled 18 Things. Her list got students thinking about their own life goals and eventually led to a writing contest with a scholarship opportunity, thanks to Conner's parents, Robert and Loria Anderson.

"For the past month, many of you sitting here today submitted your number one item on the to-do list for your life. Our staffers at the *Bucs' Blade*, who judged the submissions, chuckled as we read many creative ideas. The catch was you already had to complete the item submitted, and have proof, which most did in the form of a photo. Some of the ones we enjoyed the most were hiking to the bottom of the Grand Canyon."

A picture flashed up on the super-sized white screen behind her, and I could honestly attest the brochures for this tourist destination did not do it justice.

"Lose seventy-five pounds," Mrs. Cleveland said as the slide show continued, showing a girl holding up her old fat jeans, the slogan "no pain, no gain" written in black sharpie across the butt.

"Drive Route 66 during senior spring break, attend Mardi Gras, go skydiving, go on a meditation retreat, tour Michigan in an RV, ride the human hamster wheel at the circus, skinny dip in Lake Michigan."

Mrs. Cleveland paused as the student body laughed at the picture. "Thankfully, this student thought to blur some parts of his photo before submitting. As you can guess, picking the five winners to receive a total of twenty-thousand dollars each, over the course of four years, was not an easy task. The recipients will be acknowledged in our last edition of this year's newspaper when it comes out in two days."

The underclassman still had two weeks left in school.

Ha, ha, suckers!

"But tonight I have the honor of announcing our winners to the graduating class. When I call your name, please make your way to the stage. For Most Poignant—witnessing a baby being born from Cindy Boren."

I was worried this one might be controversial since the baby was hers, but she was in the top ten percent of our class and definitely needed the financial help to make it to college now. People didn't let me down though; Robert and Loria handed her a ceremonial super-sized check on stage while the local newspaper reporter snapped some photos, and everyone applauded and cheered.

"For Most Scary—kayaking next to blue whales off the Gulf of Mexico from Ashley Reynolds. For Most Athletic—running a marathon to raise money for his cousin who has leukemia from Blake Hulliberger. For Most Humorous—living like a primitive native for two weeks from William Saidi."

The snapshot for this one showed Will squatting in the entrance to a teepee created from tree branches, a cooking pot on his head, and raccoon furs tied to his feet while he munched on a handful of raspberries, a fire burning brightly in front of him. In a world driven so much by technology, we really did get a kick out of this one.

"And I saved the best for last. This person didn't even enter the contest, but all of us unanimously agreed when Olga suggested her."

Tammy directed her questioning eyes at me on the stage, but all I gave her was a wave.

"For Most Ambitious—making your school a better place, Tammy Fitzgerald."

Her reaction was in slow motion, seeming unable to process the information. After figuring out how to make her body unfreeze, she walked trance-like up to the podium. She posed for photographs, and I smiled, looking down at my Morticia Addams ring, thankful Conner's legacy didn't die with him.

I still didn't quite know what to make of everything, but I had to find my voice soon because as class president, Tammy introduced the students giving the salutatory and valedictory addresses next. I never really set out to be valedictorian, and if I were really smart, I would've calculated things to stay at a steady third place in the academic race at GHHS.

Third place didn't have to make a speech.

After the salutatorian spoke, Tammy delivered an anecdote about me as I tried not to hyperventilate, giving me a few moments to compose myself.

"Our next speaker, Olga Gay Worontzoff, really needs no introduction."

Of course, she had to use my full name!

"Cheerleader, writer, sailor, wedding crasher, world record breaker, and Nate Barca's girlfriend. All in that order." The crowd laughed. "Some people from high school come into our lives and go quickly. Others stay awhile and leave footprints on our hearts and we are never, ever the same. Olga is the latter. Please, help me in welcoming the most intelligent, fearless, ambitious, and *sneaky* person I know."

The crowd applauded, and I looked out at my friends shouting, my family nodding, and a thousand faces smiling.

I approached the microphone, my hands shaking uncontrollably, and tried to summon Conner's spirit to help me. "I'd like to thank everyone for being here tonight—my mom and dad for supporting me in my endeavors, Mr. and Mrs. Anderson for standing by me and creating the Journey Scholarship, my friends whom Conner endearingly called the Jedi Order, my *boyfriend*, my teachers, the Cantankerous Monkey Squad." I paused until the cheers died down. "And before I begin, I'd also like to thank Conner Anderson and Mr. George Lucas for inspiration and pray there are no sticklers for copyright laws present tonight."

While the crowd laughed at my joke, I peered at my notes on the podium.

"A long time ago, in a galaxy far, far away, the leaders of Grand Haven brought forth this great school, and 140 years later, conceived by our parents, our graduating class was brought forth into a world where all men and women are created equal. Well, *were* equal until the introduction of the Jedi showed us some are more equal than others.

"The force is what gives a Jedi his power. It's an energy field created by all living things, surrounding and penetrating us, binding the galaxy together. I dedicate this night to those Jedi's here with me, who have endured thirteen grueling years of school. In fact, can there truly be any experience binding us together more closely than high school? It is all together fitting and proper we should do this together tonight, but in a larger sense, we cannot truly express the suffering and pain through which each of us has gone. The brave Jedi graduating before us who struggled through it understand words can do little to add or detract from it. From the first formative years of finger painting and nap times, from progressing to learning about the three R's, and then lo and behold, being introduced to such foreign concepts such as biology, physics, calculus, and sex education."

My heart fluttered, making me dizzy. I knew my parents weren't joining in the laughter over the last joke, but this wasn't about them.

"The galaxy will little note what we say here tonight. It would be wise for us to remember the famous quote from *Star Wars*, 'Obi-Wan Kenobi? Obi-Wan... now that's a name I haven't heard in a long time... a long time.' We can make it possible to never let them forget us. It's up to us, the graduating class, to be dedicated to the challenges that lie before us in the real world. Our lives stretch out from this point. Do not graduate in vain. Yes, this is the end, the last part of something real and significant in our lives. But it's also just the beginning. We have a new birth of freedom from parents, from high school, and from any Darth Vader-like force that has tried to strike us down these past four years. For me, during this past year at least, it has been dealing with grief and depression after Conner was taken from us. But just as Obi-Wan said to Darth, I say to any dark force, if you strike me down, I shall become more powerful than you could ever possibly imagine."

I rapidly blinked back a rush of tears as everyone stood and cheered.

"I now look back on the day of the lightning strike not as the day I almost died, but the day I finally started to live the life I was created for. I read a quote the other day by Teddy Roosevelt, a man I'm certain could've served on the Jedi High Council. He said, 'Far better it is to dare mighty things, to win glorious triumphs, even though checkered by failure, than to take rank with those poor spirits who neither enjoy much nor suffer much because they live in the gray twilight that knows neither victory nor defeat.' So let's meet the future with Yoda-like wisdom, knowing we can succeed, so this great class shall not perish from the galaxy unknown. We're entering life. Sometimes it will be painful. We all have our, 'Luke, I am your Father,' moments, some more than others."

I looked up from my notes and raised my hand.

"Maybe to the point that some people have nicknamed you the Death Star, but don't take the path of least resistance to the Dark Side. Sure, they may have cookies, but one thing death and life have taught me is life is short and it's worth the pain. Make your life count. I'm not afraid to use Jedi mind tricks either to make you listen."

I waved my hand in the air, eliciting more giggles.

"Leave your mark on this world while you can. And remember our destinies aren't thwarted by failure. George Lucas said, 'Even when Anakin became Darth Vader, he was still the chosen one.' Many times we can turn around our failures for victories. In fact, it's impossible to be victorious without failing first. I wish you all the best of luck, and may the force be with you."

Nate pulled a lightsaber from underneath his graduation gown, wielding it in the air while standing on his chair. Before the ceremony, I handed one to him, Nicole, Tammy, Sean, and Kyle and told them they'd know when to use them. The rest of the Jedi Order mimicked his movements, and the crowd erupted with thunderous applause and wild cheering, a total standing ovation.

The minutes ticked by like hours during the presentation of diplomas, the tassel ceremony, and benediction. When it was time for the recessional march, I moved quicker than anyone out into the foyer to find Nate, a mob already surrounding him, giving their congratulations for the best moment in GHHS graduation ever.

Throwing my arms around his neck, I pulled him close and planted a full kiss on his lips. Renewed applause was awarded. I wasn't sure if they cheered for his performance or mine, but I think it was because of both.

Focus Question:

Assess what you would do if you were Olga.
Would you open up your heart to love again?
Provide reasons to support your decision.

Chapter Eighteen

"For my thoughts are not your thoughts,
nor are your ways my ways, says the Lord.
For as the heavens are higher than the earth,
so are my ways higher than your ways..."
—Isaiah 55: 8-9

H ow's your ice cream?" Nate asked.

"Perfect."

He laughed as I licked the chocolate-coated sprinkles dripping along the side of my cone. "You look a mess."

I grabbed a napkin to wipe my mouth, but before I could, he said, "Let me take care of that."

He drew my lips to his and slid his arms around my waist, holding me close.

I pulled away after a minute, but only slightly. "Another thing I love about you. You're always full of surprises."

"Life is full of surprises," he said, releasing me and gazing out toward the Grand River channel leading out to Lake Michigan, the lighthouse and pier looming in the distance.

All around us, couples and families relaxed on their blankets stretching out across the grassy knolls along the boardwalk, enjoying a perfect day. It was Memorial Day weekend. I would've never guessed a year ago I could feel this happy. Back then it felt like there'd never be anything important in my life again, only the accident and dealing with the accident. But this was the weekend last year when everything changed for me, when I was introduced to Nate at the counselor's office. It seemed like just yesterday we met but also a million years ago.

We were about to head to the hospital for our last therapy session. Dr. Judy asked us to come in together today.

Nate ran a lanky hand through his hair longer than ever.

"I have one more surprise for you before we head to the hospital." He reached for his case.

"I was wondering why you brought Breedlove with you." I nodded toward his guitar and then he strummed some chords.

"I wrote a song called *Summertime* for you. Wanna hear it?"

I smiled. "The blue sky and the warm sun are nice, but there's nothing I love more than you singing a song. Of course I do!"

He looked into my eyes as he sang, and I swore I could get lost and found in him at the same time, if that made any sense.

"While I sit here eating apples/ your love for me baffles/ my mind/ like I should push away so you can find someone refined/ But then lightning strikes/ and eighteen things change our lives/ as love rocks me like a baby/ I know that this sounds crazy/ but I wake up to birds on my window sill/ and they sing to me that this is for real/ So under the Michigan sun/ my life with you has finally begun/ even though I met you a year ago/ It took me a while to say I love you so/ But now it's summertime/ and I'm gonna make you all mine/ we'll carve our initials in the sand/ and I'll brag about you to the guys in the band/ Let's drift away out to the sea/ Cause baby you are all that I need/ in summertime."

Tears fell from my eyes. "That was really beautiful. Thank you."

He handed me a napkin, and I dried my face.

"You're beautiful, and you're very welcome. You ready?"

Standing, he held out his hand and I grabbed it, letting him pull me up.

It's funny how I actually felt like I was going to miss high school and being at home. I never thought I would, but this past year somehow connected me to this place in a lasting way. Still, as the sun beat down upon us in a summer scorching way, comfortingly familiar and helping us keep track of time, I knew the brightest days were ahead.

The timer went off in Dr. Judy's office, signaling the end of a session. When the door opened, I was surprised to see my parents walking out.

"Mom? Dad? What are you guys doing here?"

To my dismay, they ignored me and exited the waiting room, heading down the hospital corridor, Dad's arm draped around Mom's sagging shoulders.

"They can't hear you now," Dr. Judy said, standing in the doorframe. "Please, come in, both of you."

My sneakers squeaked against the tile as I walked past her with wobbly legs. We took our seats in front of her desk, and she closed the door behind us.

My breathing came rapidly.

Nate placed his hand on my back, rubbing circles there, trying in vain to comfort me.

"What's going on?" I asked Dr. Judy as she sat in the leather chair behind her desk.

She scooted forward, hands folded neatly on the flat mahogany surface. "Well, you two have a lot to digest during your last session today, but it's time you learned the truth. I've been keeping a secret from you. A big secret."

Nate's brows drew together as he looked at me and then back to Dr. Judy and said, "I'm guessing this secret isn't a good thing?"

She nodded. "Nate, you died in that car crash a year ago."

My breath caught as he squeezed my hand.

"You're crazy. If I'm dead, then how is she here? How are you here?"

Leaning across the table toward me, eyes intense, she asked, "I bet Olga can answer that question. How are you here?"

For a brief moment, I thought, *leave it to a psychiatrist to answer a question with a question.* But then, I got it, and I hugged myself with shaking arms, squeezing Nate's hand harder than ever as I sobbed.

"What? What is it?" he asked, wrapping me in a hug.

"I never told you this." It was difficult to get the words out even now. "I took some, some pills. Twenty of them. They were pain meds after the boating trip, after Conner died. It was an accident. I didn't mean to die, to commit suicide or whatever."

He didn't say anything for a few minutes, but I finally got the courage to look him in the eye.

"You mean, you're dead, too?" he asked with a trembling lip.

Dr. Judy gave another quick nod. "Yes."

"Then who are you?" he asked the doctor. "You're dead? I don't get it. What is all this about? How have we been living our lives the past year if we're dead?"

She offered a sad smile. "I am your guiding spirit through the after-death purification process."

He rubbed a hand over his face.

I still couldn't stop crying.

"The what?"

I was just as confused as Nate. Maybe *this* was all a dream.

I lost my grip on reality after Conner's death. Maybe I never got it back. Maybe this was all in my head. But somehow, I knew she told the truth.

Nate, however, still seemed skeptical as he bit his fingernails. I didn't blame him. I was just numb. I was so happy not even ten minutes ago, and now, I just didn't know how to feel.

Staring at the picture of Grand Haven Pier behind Dr. Judy's desk, I found myself wishing I could click my heels three times and be whisked away to a boat and sail far, far away from here. Maybe I could, if this was Heaven. But I didn't think it was.

Dr. Judy ran a hand through her butterscotch hair. "You both died accidentally but through your own bad choices. Olga wasn't attempting suicide outright, but a little part of her knew she was risking death when she took those pills. No, she wasn't actually trying to die, rather just trying to escape her pain, just like you when you decided to street race your car at one hundred miles per hour. Since you were both children of God, and because you both had people interceding for your souls on Earth, God did not want to condemn you to everlasting separation between you and Him, the Creator of all things. But because you died without receiving God's grace, love, and healing, you were not pure enough to enter Heaven."

Nate and I looked at each other, his mouth falling open. Tilting his head, he asked, "So, this has been purgatory? It's real? I thought it was all just folklore."

Dr. Judy raised her hands in front of her and gestured around the room. "More like a form of limbo. You're on a spiritual plane where you created your own reality, your own timeline."

Nate pursed his lips for a moment. "So, nothing that happened during the past year was real? It was like one big dream?"

"Whatever happened was real to you and Olga, and that's all that matters. You see, prayers were sent up to Heaven when both of you died. People wished you could've gotten to live your lives because you died so young." She trained her eyes on only me now. "You never got your driver's license, never went on a date and had your first kiss, never graduated high school or got your hard-earned acceptance letter to college. My suggestion of a life list was an effort to take you through those experiences, and even though you and Nate were separate projects assigned to me, I was delighted when you started to work together on your healing." She smiled, light seeming to radiate from her, as though Nate and I had made her extremely proud. "In the process, you both found love, you both received love, and finally found a way to love yourselves. You had things to work out, so you had to stay here for a while, but now you can move on. That's what today's session is about."

My shoulders slumped. Even though I should've been happy at this thought, something still bothered me. "What about everyone else we left behind? I mean, yay for me, I'm healed. But I was my parent's only daughter. Do they get to *move on?*"

Eyes narrowing, she said, "They'll move on with time. They have to work out their own healing, but I'll help them, too."

She twiddled her thumbs, like she was trying to figure out how best to explain things.

I rubbed my arms. "Yeah. How does that work? You said they can't hear me now? But they're not in this spirit realm, right?"

For a second, I had the sickening thought they were dead too.

"No. For this appointment only, I let you cross over to Earth, in case you didn't believe me... so you could see for yourselves."

Weaving my hands into my hair, I pulled it back into a ponytail. "So, they still look that sad, a year later?"

She nodded, an encouraging smile on her face. "Yes, but they are getting better. You may think right now the last year was all for nothing, but you couldn't be further from the truth. Just as their prayers affected your afterlife, your actions during the purification process affected them too, helping them go on with their lives. Even when you were alive on Earth, there was always a spirit realm at work; you were just unaware of it then."

Turning away, I glanced out the window. "I want a do-over."

She crossed her arms over her chest. "There are no do-overs in life once you're dead. All your friends have that YOLO saying backwards. It should be YODO because really, you live every day, but... You Only *Die* Once."

I looked at Nate. A grim expression twisted his mouth and I wondered if he was thinking what I thought. Where's the candid camera, because this had to be a joke.

Dr. Judy wrung her hands. "So sorry, but no do-overs. And there are no shortcuts in the after-death purification process. There are things each person must accomplish here before they can move on, and you have. Congratulations."

I watched Nate's gaze travel around the room, to the couch against the wall, to the shelves filled with books and puzzles, finally to the chairs we sat in. "But why not just tell us from the start this was all fake? I mean, no one likes to feel duped, you know? Why not just tell us the situation we were in from the first time we met here?"

Dr. Judy smiled at Nate, and Nate stared at her.

"Those are the rules of this realm. I don't make them, but I play by them. My guess is many wouldn't care about their success if they knew they were dead. Just like you two at the start of this process. Many wouldn't care about their soul at first and the risk of truly dying as a consequence of not completing their mission. Think back to the beginning—you were both very depressed spirits."

We all sat in silence while Dr. Judy let us digest her info dump. I clock-watched for the next five minutes, then become restless and tapped my fingers on the arm of my chair.

"I have another question," I told her. "When I first met Nate in the waiting room, my attraction to him was so strong, physically and emotionally. I'd been in a fog for months, which was my new normal after Conner died. I was stricken by guilt and grief, and then Nate made me wake up, so to speak. Were those really my feelings, or were you able to manipulate those feelings?"

Rising from her chair, she almost floated to her door. "Those feelings were your own. The reason you felt them so strongly, though, is because of the realm you're in. Now, a part of your soul is attached to his and vice versa. If one would've failed to accomplish their mission of love and healing during the completion of the life list, then the other would've failed by default. I didn't plan it that way, but you unknowingly took that sacrifice upon yourselves when you fell in love. In my experience of being a guiding spirit, I've never once had this happen between two of my subjects, but my boss, who happens to be a certified angel, informed me of this. He said your two-fold connection wrapped your destinies together, like a real cosmic Romeo and Juliet love story."

She smiled kindly and opened the door. There was no waiting room, only a bright light.

"Is Conner in there?" I asked, looking toward Nate, giving him an 'I need to know' type look—I wasn't sure if he was the jealous type.

Dr. Judy gave a small, pleased smile. "I knew you'd ask me that, but I'm afraid I cannot answer your question, my dear child. Conner was not my mission."

Nate and I sat in silence for a long time again. Well, who knows how long or short. It got very hard for me to be sure of time here, or anything else for that matter. I studied Nate in his khaki shorts and navy blue T-shirt with the picture of the cantankerous monkey I made for the band last summer. Taking hold of his hand, I marveled at how it was clean and unscarred like the rest of his body, even after flying through the windshield of his car.

Standing, I moved blindly, without thinking, toward the light, pulling him with me. The warmth radiating from the light was so inviting.

"Hold on. Wait a second." Nate tugged my hand and looked at Dr. Judy. "You say we're ready to move on, but what if I don't feel ready?"

Dr. Judy closed the door and then opened it again, everything happening in slow motion. The waiting room was back. "Your time in the in-between is done. Well, unless you want to become spiritual guides yourselves. Although we've never hired teens since they aren't usually mature enough for what the job requires, so I'd probably have to take you in as interns or something." She gave a light chuckle. "Anyway, I wouldn't bother with that route. But you are free to roam the Earth until midnight, saying your final goodbyes. I'll be here when you're ready."

"Where should I go first?" I asked in a rush. "I mean, how do I even say goodbye to everyone I ever cared about?"

Dr. Judy shrugged. "I have no idea. This is your process, not mine."

I glared at her. For someone who was supposed to be in charge of this whole after-death purification process, she was infuriatingly vague.

Nate advanced toward the door, took my hand, then we shuffled past another patient in the room. She didn't seem to notice us. Once we were outside, I couldn't find our reflections in the store windows.

My tears were real though, and I wiped them from my face before speaking. "You know what? There were clues."

Nate rolled his eyes at me, a first for him. "Clues for what? That we're really dead? You can't be serious."

I closed my eyes and nodded. "No, listen. My asthma is gone, I don't need glasses to see well, and I didn't feel any pain when I got cut by that knife in your kitchen or when I ran into the slider at Kyle's house. Even though we weren't in Heaven, things must operate differently in the spiritual realm. Makes sense since our bodies aren't real. You mentioned not having IBS anymore, remember?"

My tone was bitter, but I couldn't help my annoyance at the whole situation. I waited a few minutes for him to answer, and when he didn't, I prompted him. "Remember?"

He nodded. His eyes focused on the pavement as if he couldn't meet mine, or didn't want to.

"Yeah, things are starting to make sense now." His voice was faint, the usual confidence gone. "I mean, it was kinda too convenient how I showed up just when the Cantankerous Monkey Squad needed a singer. I was an exact fit. And how my parents just forked over five hundred dollars for your birthday necklace when I only asked as a joke. I never had any scratches after my accident, and when I floated above my body, I must've already been dead."

I paused near the discount cart outside The Bookman and spotted Nic through the window, leaning over the counter and smiling at Sean on the other side. "Yeah, I had a floating experience after I swallowed those twenty pills. I chalked it up to being high when I thought about it afterwards."

Still gazing into the bookstore, I watched Tammy walk toward Nic and Sean, sucking a frozen coffee drink through a straw and holding Kyle's hand. I drew a deep breath. Tammy and I never becoming good friends was one of the hardest truths about this whole mess. It all seemed so real to me. I wondered if she and Nic became friends because of what Nate and I did in the spiritual realm or if they would've become close on their own.

"You know what? I didn't need coffee any more to stay awake this past year. I mean I still drank it because I liked it, but I didn't rely on it like I used to. Heck, I don't think we even need to sleep! That's why we were such insomniacs and had all those weird dreams. *And,*" I added, drawing out the word and plopping down on the sidewalk curb. "Cheerleading and all those gymnastic tricks came way too easily for me. Yep, we're definitely dead."

I stated the truth boldly, coldly. My voice came out bare, nothing to hide anymore.

Nate fell down next to me then pulled me toward him, kissing my lips.

I closed my eyes, breathing in his scent.

After a few minutes, he stopped and gazed into my eyes. "But this, me and you, are real."

"Totally." I gazed over his shoulder, into the distance, for a long time. "What do you think Dr. Judy meant about becoming spirit guides?"

A heaviness rested in his limbs, making him look older. "I'm not sure. You don't want to move on?"

I paused, leaning back against the discount cart. It was on wheels, so my weight should've moved it, but it didn't budge an inch.

Interesting. "Um, I just…" *Am worried about Conner,* but I couldn't tell Nate that. Not now.

He sighed before looking me directly in the eyes. "I don't know either. I feel like the white rabbit just ran by, I chased him, fell down a hole, and ended up some place where nothing makes sense."

After giving a little gasp, he started to cry. I hugged him tightly and cried more earnestly than I ever had before, even more so than when Conner died.

Nate regained his composure. "I need to go back to my hometown, see my grave. Does that sound narcissistic?"

I shook my head.

"Plus, this whole time I thought the other kid from the accident was okay. Now, I think he's probably dead. It's probably part of the reason for why I needed to go through the after-death purification process, right?"

His eyes were blank, devoid of all hope, and I felt his heaviness on my shoulders.

"Why didn't you ask Dr. Judy?"

"I was scared." He took a deep breath, then dug into the skin around his thumbnail. "And I just need to go see for myself."

"I'll come with you."

Nate smiled. "I knew you would, but I think it's something I need to do myself this time. Do you understand that?"

My mind wandered to the image of my parents walking out of Dr. Judy's office. I nodded, looking down at my lap where our hands intertwined. Tears lingered on my nose and dripped onto my finger. After another moment of silence, I asked, "When do you want to meet back up?"

Nate wiped the tears from around my eyes. The breeze swirled around us, bringing the fresh scent of bread from Camburn's Bakery, and I wondered briefly what Heaven smelled like.

"I'm not sure," he said, pausing briefly. "My old town is three hours away. I mean, what happens if I don't make it back in time?"

I shrugged. "Maybe you just get caught up in a whirlwind to Heaven? I remember reading about Elijah going that way in the Bible."

"I wonder if…" He closed his eyes, hands clasped in prayer. "I wish to go home."

He disappeared.

"That's *very* cool, God," I said, looking up at the sky. The purity of blue and warm sunlight made me forget my worries, if only for a moment.

I stood and peered into The Bookman a while longer, studying my friends. Deciding this wasn't a great way to say goodbye, I decided to muster some courage and attempt to walk through the solid surface. Aside from a case of vertigo akin to a long elevator ride, there was nothing to it.

Tammy and Nic fanned through the pages of a magazine together while Kyle and Sean talked animatedly.

"Sometimes I feel like a geek for all the Star Wars stuff Conner brainwashed us with through the years," Kyle said. "But then the universe drops this dude on the trolley today, going on and on about Dungeons and Dragons spells, like resurrection and mind control. And about sacrificing their mind controlled subjects for greater power. I felt like one of the cool kids."

"You mean you felt like me," Tammy said, a wide, face-splitting smile on her face.

"Ha ha ha," Kyle faux-laughed, grabbing her frozen coffee off the counter and sucking down a huge gulp.

"Oh my gosh! You know I hate it when people steal my caffeine."

Kyle held his head in his hands. "Ah, brain freeze!"

"Serves you right," Nic mumbled, stashing the magazine under the counter as a customer walked in.

The group dispersed throughout the store so Nic could help the tourist locate a book. Well, I wasn't positive the man was a tourist, but with his Grand Haven baseball cap, camera strapped around his neck, and fanny pack secure on his waist, I'd bet my life if I still had one. Anyway, I took his appearance as an opportunity to peruse The Bookman one last time, a staple of my childhood.

Surprisingly, I discovered a mini-section on bucket list type books that I'd never seen here before. When Dr. Judy first informed me I was a dead girl, I was upset the eighteen things didn't really happen. Like I was caught in one of the many books I'd read while working here with a really bad ending. The ones I read and thought, *really? That's how it ends? Because honestly, a fourth grader could've written a better conclusion than that!* But when I thought about each item on the list now, I realized they really were about me and nobody else. And like Judy said, they were real to Nate and me, so I guess that was purpose enough.

Still, I wondered about the Cantankerous Monkey Squad. Did they ever find Conner's replacement? I wished I could use some Jedi mind trick on Sean and Kyle to find out. I sighed, deciding these questions and answers didn't really matter. Whatever happened was meant to be and all that. Maybe they're supposed to go to college instead of touring the country playing music. Then I thought about college and the scholarships.

Tears filled my eyes again. I really wanted that part to be true. As I reached into my purse for a Kleenex, the bookstore's newspaper rack caught my eye. The Grand Haven Tribune's front page featured a story about last night's graduation ceremony and the five recipients of the Journey Scholarship, sponsored by Mr. and Mrs. Anderson.

I breathed in a sigh of relief and wondered if Dr. Judy had anything to do with suggesting the idea to them. The only thing left to do now was visit my parents. I took one last look at my friends, blinking my watery eyes until my vision cleared. The Jedi Order looked more beautiful and somehow more real than ever. I knew they had a bright future ahead of them.

On my walk home, I took in every sight, every smell, and every sound... the sailboats in the water, the trees swaying in the wind, fresh mowed lawns and hot dogs on the grill, birds chirping and babies laughing, wondering if I'd miss it once I got to Heaven. Maybe Heaven had all those things, too.

When I passed my church, I decided to stop at the cemetery behind it. Trying not to shake, I wondered if I really wanted to see my grave. About halfway across the cemetery, my knees locked and I dropped to the ground, wishing I had a friend here to hold my hand. But I knew I didn't deserve that since I took myself from them.

Forcing myself to get back up, my legs tightened as I practically ran to the edge of the cemetery. Beneath the shadow of trees where birds sang, I found it. I stooped to study the spotless gray granite, and my heart nearly exploded. Words were etched on its surface: Our Precious Angel. Then a short way below was my name, Olga Gay Worontzoff, and below that the dates of birth and death, October 31, 1994-April 9, 2012. Sunlight highlighted a picture of an angel with wings and a halo sleeping on a fluffy cloud underneath the date.

If they only knew.

The quote below the image read: "You saw how the Lord your God carried you, just as one carries a child, all the way that you traveled until you reached this place."—Deuteronomy 1:31.

I read the words slowly, wondering how my parents picked out this particular Bible verse to rest here for all eternity. Pressing my arms hard against my chest, I thought of the *Footprints in the Sand* poem hanging on the wall in my room. I should've let the Lord carry me through my suffering, but I didn't. And now look where it got me, a skeleton lying in a coffin six feet under, all the people I cared about oblivious to the fact of where I actually was.

Nothing could've prepared me for the awfulness of seeing my own grave. I took in deep, sharp gulps of fresh air, trying to steady myself, gripping the grass so hard my knuckles turned white. Or maybe they were white because I was a ghost.

I couldn't shake the feeling that Dr. Judy should've told Nate and me about already being dead as we completed the list, so this wouldn't have been such a complete shock, no matter how many 'clues' popped up along the way. I lingered on the grass and imagined my parents and friends coming here to visit me. All the wreaths of flowers made me want to puke. I stood, frowning and trying not to cry again, wishing I never came to the cemetery.

Next to my headstone stood the faded graves of my maternal grandparents. The plot on the other side was empty, and I guessed it was most likely reserved for my parents. Most certainly, they'd go straight to Heaven.

If I stayed in the in-between, would I ever see them again? I turned around, feeling as if something heavy pressed on my chest, the same sensation I felt after Conner died, a grief that had actually weighed so much on my heart it broke. I didn't think I could stand another moment here.

My whole body was stiff as I ran back through the cemetery, down the sidewalks of town, my breathing shallow and beads of sweat dripping down my face. But I didn't stop, and I never looked back.

When I finally reached my apartment building, I was shocked to find the front door locked. In all my eighteen—well, I guess seventeen and a half—years on Earth, I didn't recall my parents ever locking the door.

I walked around the back and found Dad grilling on the porch, his garden full of tomatoes and corn plants. I pat the wet soil, admiring Dad's work. I'd never know if I inherited Dad's green thumb or not.

Sitting on the metal chair, I was relieved I didn't fall through it.

"Daddy," I said aloud, even though I knew he couldn't hear me. But if what I did on the spirit plane affected things here, then maybe my words now could somehow get through to him. I prayed they did. "I know I hurt you badly. I should have gone to you and Mom and God with my problems, but instead I made a stupid decision in the moment. I hope you know I didn't take my life on purpose. I would never do that to you, but somehow I did. I pray you can forgive me. I pray you find the strength and courage to keep moving on with your lives. I'll miss you, Daddy."

I stood, then kissed him on the cheek.

He brushed the side of his face as if he felt my touch, then raised his hand toward the sky and looked up. "I miss my baby girl, God."

A single tear fell. He wiped the side of his face again, opened the grill, flipped the steaks, then headed inside.

Fresh pain washed over me as I followed him, and after he slumped down in his reclining chair in the living room, I searched for Mom. In my room, she sorted my things into boxes. One was labeled trash, another one donations, and a third one storage. She was on the carpet next to the storage box, flipping through the scrapbook Nic helped me make the week after Conner died, the one Mr. and Mrs. Anderson set out at his funeral.

Lots of tears flowed freely from Mom's eyes.

I squatted next to her, laid a hand on her shoulder, and did the only thing I could at this point. "Lord, give her your peace that transcends all understanding. Help her to let go of any guilt she may be holding onto about what she could have or should have done. Help her to rest in the knowledge you are God. Reveal to her the possibilities of lists for her own life, and help her accomplish things I'll never be able to."

I watched her trace over the words of a quote by Victor Hugo I wrote in the scrapbook. "*Have courage for the great sorrows of life and patience for the small ones; and when you have laboriously accomplished your daily task, go to sleep in peace. God is awake.*"

Dad came in and knelt down beside her, then they embraced.

"Steaks are ready."

They both laughed, maybe at the absurdity of how life goes on.

Out of nowhere, Nate appeared by my side.

I smiled for him, even though I wanted to curl up on the floor and cry with my parents. "How'd you get in here?"

He shrugged. "I thought it, and it happened." He took in the scene. "Everything okay here?"

I hesitated as I looked around one more time to the worn-out carpet I played on, the desk and swivel chair I spent so much time studying in, the shelves crammed with old books that beckoned to me on rainy and snowy days. "No, but it will be. I don't belong here anymore though."

After giving my parents one last hug, I grabbed hold of Nate's hand and led him to the living room. "So how do we get out of here? Walk through doors or just wish to go to Dr. Judy's office?"

Nate was unnaturally still and not answering my question.

I chewed on my lip. The realization of what Nate probably discovered on his trip gradually settled over me. "Hey, are you okay? Did—"

"You want to know how I am?" His eyes widened with terror. "I am horrible. I am ripped apart. I'm broken. And not because of me. Not because I'm dead. But because I killed someone else." He took a deep, pained breath. "And I know I've spent the past year telling you to let go of your guilt, but that's different. Your actions really didn't cause the death of another human being, mine did."

Tugging him, I forced him to sit on our lumpy couch. "No, you didn't. You didn't force that kid to race you. You both played an equal part."

He yanked away from me. "Then why isn't he going through the after-death purification process?"

Silence. I stared out the window toward the pond, the ducks coming in for a landing. "Maybe he is somewhere else. Everyone has different realities. I think the number one lesson we learned from today is we really don't know anything."

Nate squirmed in his spot then stood up again, choking back tears. "Well, it doesn't matter. I've made up my mind. I'm not ready to move on. I want to help others through the after-death purification process. I don't want this to be for nothing, for this past year to be a waste of time. If I can help someone else, I have to do it. But I'll understand if you want to move on with Conner instead of staying with me."

I nodded and sighed, because I wasn't even sure if Conner 'moved on.' And I wasn't sure how I felt about being a 'waste of time' either, so I logged the statement away to argue about later, on a day when Nate and I weren't just handed the biggest plot twist since the final episode of *LOST*.

Mom and Dad walked toward the kitchen for dinner, shattering any pity party I thought about having for myself.

God, I'll miss them so much.

I looked for a long moment into Nate's eyes, and he returned my stare. "Will you come with me to one more spot before we see Dr. Judy?"

He grabbed my hand and I closed my eyes, then muttered a prayer.

A second later, we stood atop one of the sand dunes, overlooking Lake Michigan. Since Conner was never buried, this was as close to his graveyard as I'd ever get. It seemed fitting this is where he died, since he was always at peace on the lake, as if God had displayed his splendor out on the water in a show just for us.

I watched kids splash and shriek in the water, and I smiled, remembering my and Conner's childhood together. He'd already moved on in his own way, and now I would, too. But I felt something more than nostalgia when I thought of him in my moment of silence. My breath caught unexpectedly as the sun glowed brightly against the blue waves crashing in, and I pressed my hands over my heart.

Somehow I had this sixth sense my journey with Conner wasn't over. I'd discover what happened to him after he died, even if it took all eternity.

"Are *you* okay?" Nate frowned and curved his arm around my shoulders. "What are we doing here?"

"Saying goodbye."

Leaving this place would be hard. Not taking the easy route to Heaven would be difficult, too. I knew there was only peace and life there, and who knew what kind of pain, fear, and loss we might be helping people through if we became spirit guides. But I knew Conner's death would help me relate to the pain of others. And I knew nothing could be nearly as hard as losing Conner, or if I were to leave Nate.

I turned my body toward his and kissed him on the lips. Even if I was dead, I felt fully alive around him.

The truth was though, I had no idea what I was getting myself into. There were only three things I was certain of. One, if I got to pick my forever, I chose Nate. Two, I'd already lost Conner once, and if I found him again, I wouldn't want to lose him twice. And three, I'd risk my own soul for either one of them.

This probably wasn't a good thing.

The theme of religion pervades the story. What do
you think the author's attitude is toward God?

Prepare for a preview of Jamie Ayres' next book,

With the lessons the 18 Things life list taught her engraved on her heart, Olga embarks on a new adventure as a spirit guide.

But Nate wants nothing to do with the startling 18 Truths she's discovering along the way.

He leaves her no choice but to break every rule in the book and attempt a dangerous journey on her own.

*"For, after a certain distance, every step we take in life
we find the ice growing thinner below our feet
and all around us and behind us
we see our contemporaries going through."*
—*Robert Louis Stevenson*

Truth: Every morning when I woke up, the biggest truth I've ever faced landed like a grenade in my heart. I never said this when I had the chance: I loved Olga Gay Worontzoff with all my heart, soul, mind, and body.

Okay, maybe not body because we never touched outside of platonic handholding and hugs, and usually because there were tears involved on her behalf, not in an "I want you" kind of way at all. But I digress, which happened a lot lately since there wasn't much to do here other than have silly conversations with myself.

Now, where was I?

Oh, false: It's better to keep your feelings to yourself so you don't ruin your friendship. What a bunch of crap. I couldn't believe for twelve years I freakin' ate a pile of that sh—

Um, I mean, crap. That was one of Olga's favorite words, a word I used a lot these days as I worked on my language..

It was all I thought about in Juvie. No, not sh—crap. Although maybe if I had said a few less 'bad' words, then maybe I wouldn't have ended up here. But I seriously didn't think the Big Man Upstairs cared so much about that stuff as He did people. Otherwise, He would've sent me straight to Hell like I probably deserved.

But, like I was saying, every morning I woke up after another weird dream that usually involved me yelling at Olga to hurry, like I was the white rabbit and she was Alice, and then it hit me again like a ton of bricks. I was dead, and I never once told Olga I loved her, was *in* love with her.

And now? Too late.

I didn't know if she survived the freak boating accident on Lake Michigan that involved lightning and hypothermia and took my life, but even if she didn't, she was in Heaven. I knew this because she was an angel even on Earth. But me? I was stuck in Juvie, one of the four realms of the Underworld. Juvie was reserved for teenagers like me who were undecided about the whole God thing at the time of their unfortunate demise.

I squeezed my eyes closed, trying to shut out my agony. Here was another truth: there were tears after death, at least where I resided. My homies Sean and Kyle would probably revoke my Man Card for admitting I cried, but I figured I had nothing to lose at this point. Okay, that was only half-true. I could still lose my soul.

Even if this part of the Underworld was temporary until Judgment Day or whatever, there was a terrifying finality to it. I tried to focus on Godly things to get me through, but Olga filled my thoughts instead. Not always the PG version either.

I climbed off my cot in the darkness and stood. It was always dark here, with very little light. I paced around, going stir crazy once again.

I can't take this anymore.

My roommate yawned luxuriously, and I was thankful for the sound of something real. I threw my pillow at him.

"Wake up, Sunshine!" His real name was Brad, a seventeen-year-old like me. He died in a car crash, so cliché.

Brad reciprocated my gesture, and a pillow fight ensued. "I was having a *really* good dream, Conner."

Truth: all good things must come to an end.

"Sorry, but breakfast waits for no man."

The Underworld would be unbearable if I didn't have some friends here, but one thing I had always been good at was making people love me. I just sucked at loving them back. Loving someone required faith, something I obviously never had; otherwise, I wouldn't be in this predicament right now. But I did have faith in Olga. Her friendship was like a good rock ballad, something I used to sing myself to sleep with to keep the nightmares away.

Brad and I headed outside. I never imagined the Underworld while I walked among the living, but even if I did, it wouldn't have come close to this. Juvie kinda felt like I'd been shipped to a boarding school for rednecks. You might be a redneck if… your parents send you to a boarding school where you live in tents. Yep, there were a bunch of tents for us to stay in. When I had first arrived and met Brad, I observed, "Man, this place is intense."

Hahaha! In tents=intense. Well anyway, he laughed and that pretty much sealed the deal on our bromance.

Everybody had a roommate in Juvie, an accountability partner as Leo stated. Leo was our angel headmaster, in charge of the two thousand teens housed in Camp Fusion. Juvie was divided into many camps with one angel in charge of each. My home at Juvie was just one small fraction of this plane. And if you thought two thousand teens were a lot to handle for one angel, then you hadn't met Leo. Besides, there was a lot less opportunity for sinning here, so two thousand thirteen-to-nineteen-year-olds camping together wasn't such a big deal. Since we were still fully human, with um, human desires. Leo said the same commandments we should've followed on Earth applied here.

There wasn't much else Leo explained to us though, only we weren't fit for Heaven or Hell, so we were in a holding cell of sorts. We'd forever remain the age we were when we died, had daily assigned chores, and still attended school. Although, there wasn't much separation of church and state here. In fact, most of our studies focused around religion.

Brad and I made our way past the community bathrooms to our left, the red barn with animals in it to the right, and headed down the path lined with fields of wild flowers. The actual school sat across from a lake that was always the perfect temperature for swimming despite the absence of the sun to warm it. Old trees and manicured hedges lined the sidewalk leading up to the school's front entrance. Just inside to the left of the foyer was the cafeteria.

I opened the glass door and called, "Honey, I'm home," like I owned the place, because that was how I rolled. A year ago, when I stepped into Camp Fusion High for the first time, my arms and legs felt like Jell-O. I was terrified at the uncertainty of what might go down in a place like this. Plenty of time had passed since then, and I'd regained my title as Most Popular. Oh sure, I had gone through all the phases before acclimating myself to this new environment—shock, disbelief, bargaining, guilt, acceptance. Waking up in a place like this had been a complete mindfreak, and there were still days when I expected a call from Criss Angel telling me this was all an illusion. I still hadn't made it around to the hope phase yet. Hope would be seeing Olga again, and that was never going to happen. I'd heard of heartbreak, but I never knew your heart could literally break into a tiny million pieces, repeatedly with each remembrance that the one thing you lived for was gone forever.

Dang, this sucked. I just couldn't believe I had never told her. I thought about that lame question teachers used to ask us as an icebreaker on the first day of school: "If you only had one day to live, what would you do?" I'd always come up with some bullsh—crap answer. Seriously, Leo should create some sort of shock collar for me to break my cursing habit. Must be the sailor in me.

If I could have one more chance, I knew exactly what I would do: tell Olga I was in love with her. Hell, if she walked through the cafeteria doors right now. I'd probably drop down on my knees and ask her to marry me. Forget about the no marriages rule in Juvie.

I wondered if she had a man now, if she survived. She had to survive though, right? We should've had on lifejackets. I remembered bits and pieces of that day. Maybe my submission to all things reckless had angered God and that was why I died. Olga tried to save me. She probably thought she failed, but then again, if I would've died a few years later, I wouldn't have been a teenager anymore and would've been sent straight to Hell so in a twisted way, she *did* save me. I still wasn't very comfortable with this God stuff, but Brad told me that was okay. He said if we could just trust we were all here for a moment and that was real and something had to cause all that—then that made a great first step.

I had a while to figure it out, I supposed. I sought out God in my studies—though we didn't have teachers here; class was more like homeschooling ourselves. There were plenty of books… Olga would've been happy to know that. I was pretty sure her idea of Heaven included an unlimited supply of books and coffee.

So, I tried to figure out the God stuff. I mean, yeah, He was real, obviously. But Leo told me my job now was to get to know Him, and I had no idea how to do that. I mean, the Dude didn't even visit! I just wished I would've had my, "Luke, I am your Father," moment a little sooner in life. Then, if Olga was in Heaven, I would've been with her. Pretty much, before I died, the only religion I knew had been Star Wars. I didn't claim to be an expert on much, but nobody could deny my status as a Jedi Master when it came to all things created by George Lucas.

I figured if Darth Vader could overthrow the emperor at the last second and still be saved, then maybe that was what Juvie was all about. God wasn't through with us yet. We all had a little bit of Luke and Vader in us; we just had to choose which one we were going to listen to the most.

Brad took a seat at the picnic table and poured himself a bowl of cereal. "What's eating your brain? You've been quiet since we stepped in here."

"Star Wars," I answered through a mouthful of chocolate chip pancakes. Piles of food mysteriously appeared on the tables at mealtimes, but then they also magically disappeared after an hour, so you had to be quick.

"Dude, that horse is dead. Time to put the stick down."

The orange juice I sipped squirted out of my nose a little as I let loose a laugh. "Look around my friend. Reality has absolutely no place in my world."

I got sidetracked by the sight of Julia eyeballing me from across the table with those big baby blues of hers. She had the look of a girl who knew she was exceptionally beautiful and knew that you knew it, too.

"What?" I mumbled.

"You have bed head."

Julia reached over and smoothed down my hair. We'd been going steady for four weeks now, my new record. Our courting was proof we weren't trying to create a Utopian Society here by any means. So far, our relationship had been filled with happiness and disappointment, confusion and clarity, and all the other things, good and bad, that made dating interesting.

She leaned away from me, shaking her blonde-streaked brown hair as she plopped back down on the bench. Her yellow sundress gave her an angelic glow, but this one was no angel.

"You sleep well, handsome?" Waggling eyebrows seemed to suggest to everyone else at the table that we fooled around last night before our midnight curfew.

"Sure," I agreed, but my tone conveyed otherwise. Last night was the first time we advanced past kissing and rounded second base, so I should've had sweet dreams and all that. I didn't know why, but I felt so guilty afterward. Okay, so I lived in the Underworld and was much more aware of sinning or whatever. But that wasn't really what bothered me. It felt like I cheated on Olga, which sounded crazy since I was never gonna be with her.

"Aw, what's wrong?" Julia asked in her annoying, puppy dog voice.

"I dunno," I answered, bringing my best analysis of the situation I was in to the table.

Julia shot me a dirty look, but Brad intervened and started telling her about the weird dream he had last night. We all had weird dreams here, and we told them in detail, almost like ghost stories around a campfire.

I got so lost in deep thought about my Olga dreams that my brain had to travel a few dimensions back to present when the food disappeared and Julia called my name.

She stood behind me now, wrapping me in a hug. It didn't even come close to emitting the warmth Olga's arms had once held for me, but it was the best substitute I could find here.

Stretching my arms above my head like a cat, I stood and faced her. "You're hot," I said ruefully.

She laughed. She had a nice laugh.

"How do you view our relationship?" she asked.

The weight of our four-week courtship settled upon me at last. Here was Julia. In an otherwise miserable existence, she'd brought a little light to my life of late. But she wasn't Olga. She was a carefree indulgence on my part. Did I hope my attraction would bloom into something more like love at some point? Sure, but I wasn't holding my breath.

"I'm crushing on you, girl. You know this."

My answer possessed a nugget of truth, but her eyes flashed for a second and I was pretty sure I pissed her off. Clearly, she viewed me as more already.

"It's just that, like, it feels like there's this invisible wall between us. Can we talk about the accident?"

"No," I deadpanned.

"Conner, please. You've never opened up to me about it, and I think it would help us grow closer. I told you my death story."

She talked about dying a lot. She was an artist and into painting all these watercolors depicting her drug overdose. In truth, I'd experience never-ending shame if I died from swallowing too many pills. What a stupid way to die.

"What's there to dissect? I took my annual first spring sail on Lake Michigan with my best friend. Lightning struck me. I wasn't wearing a life jacket, and the voltage and hypothermia formed a deadly combo, inducing cardiac arrest."

Truth: just the thought of that day made my throat close up. I now knew how wide, high, and deep this galaxy was, but this conversation had a way of making me feel claustrophobic.

Julia eyeballed me again, probably trying to gauge my mood to see if she could push me, but all I gave her in return was a glassy stare.

"Why does it take so much effort to even make cracks in you? Why do you act this way? We're here to heal. You can't do that by bottling everything up."

I felt my body bending away from her without actually moving. "Ugh, Julia. I don't know. Maybe I can't let myself move on because I don't know what happened to Olga. Did she die too? Is she in Heaven? Did she survive the accident? Is she happy if I'm gone? Because honestly, even though people here constantly surround me, I feel alone and I don't know why that is other than my best friend isn't here with me. And that's what keeps me up at night, all the dreams about her. But there's also not a dang thing I can do about it, is there? Because nobody likes to give us real answers around here."

There was a gleam in her eyes, like she understood. "Thank you. I just wanted you to acknowledge the elephant in the room. You've put Olga on this pedestal, and I'm never gonna live up to your hero. I'm tired of competing. You can't date a memory, but you can date me."

I couldn't help myself. This was my Achilles' heel—I couldn't stand to have anyone angry with me, so I leaned forward and kissed her forehead. "You're right. And I want to date you, okay?"

On her tiptoes, she pressed her forehead into mine and we saw eye to eye, literally and figuratively. I'd become that good at lying—able to look someone in the eye and still bear false testimony. Our lips touched briefly, and as we hugged, I promised myself I'd truly focus on Julia. I'd focused all my thoughts on Olga, and it was time to get them back... because she wasn't coming back.

I dropped my hands from around Julia and turned around, ready to head to class.

And suddenly, she's there.

"Olga?" I whispered, my mind spinning. I didn't know if she was just another lucid hallucination or reality..

My first impulse wasn't to drop down to my knees and propose. Instead, I wanted to touch her. I wanted to make sure she was real.

"Olga!" I shouted, running toward her.

Truth: *God, if this is a dream, I don't want to wake up.*

Acknowledgements

I'd like to thank:

First and foremost, Jesus, my Savior, for his boundless love, amazing grace, and perfect timing. My whole family for your zany sense of humor and forcing me to not take myself too seriously. Dan the Man, the offer you made me fifteen years ago to marry you is still & always will be the best offer I ever accepted. It's because of you that I can't seem to stop myself from constantly reading and writing love stories. Kaylee, for harnessing your formidable intelligence and passion into making me a better person. I know we're just a pit stop on your path to world domination. Ashley, for your random insights that make me laugh and your extra hugs that warm me from the inside. Where my heart is, you three will always be.

My A*W*E*S*O*M*E friends for their enduring prayers and much-needed support, including: my Sisterhood of the Traveling Journal (what God brought together nothing can separate! Our friendship is so special because it's centered around our love for Jesus and it's the reason we've been together as long as my marriage—I love you all so dearly), all my blogging buddies (who I cannot possibly all name, but you know who you are, and especially The Bookshelf Muse blog for being such a wonderful resource with their dazzling know-how),my SWFRW group (an extra heartfelt thanks to Marisa Cleveland, who read so many versions of this story she got whiplash, and for Jaime Rush for being a "bad writer" but good friend when she basically told me to rewrite my whole story after reading my three page synopsis, and for the gracious Nicole Resciniti for all her sound advice and for 1,432 hits on my little ole blog in one day), my Vineyard peeps (of whom there is no EGR cases except for Pastor Jamie Stilson—thank you for showing me the power of ugly), my LCPS Family (who inspires me to be the best version of myself every day), my GNO crew (special shout out to Amy Carver for inviting me to the first MOOK's club and getting me reading again—saved me "the trip" of dropping kid #2 off at the fire station at the time), my Homie for cheering me on and chasing shiny objects with me (Ooooh Squirrel!), Blake for inspiring this novel in its beginning stages (so glad you kicked cancer's butt and I hope you complete all the items on your life list someday), my new extended family who I will never dump, the Heidi's (when the zombie apocalypse arrives, I promise to share ammo and Bennett's coffee and donuts with you), and John Breedlove.

There is a quote by Emerson that states, "Every man I meet is my superior in some way. In that, I learn from him." To name every person I've learned from during my thirty-three years would prove an impossible task, but please know that your spirit lives in the voices in my head and in this book—so a special thanks to you, too.

Several people at Curiosity Quills came together in a rather short amount of time to make *18 Things* possible. It started with Sharon Bayliss, who hosted the contest that led Krystal Wade to my novel. Publishing a book was one of those dreams I only dreamed about, and you, Krystal, turned them into reality. Thank you for keeping insane working hours and always answering every little email in record time. I'm convinced you figured out how to clone yourself, or you really are Super Woman. You are for sure the BEE this side of the galaxy! And muchos gracias to *everyone* at Curiosity Quills. Our FB chats are something I look forward to each day, mostly for your rollicking and sinister humor!

My parents—Julie Myers and Jeff Reynolds—my steadfast fans. I hope you celebrate my successes as if they were your own, because none of it would be possible without you. Dad, I'm sure you will hand-sell my books to half the population of the United States at truck stops and Mom, your clients will no doubt roll their eyes after you ask them for the third time if they knew your daughter has a book published. Also, to my sisters, Dawn and Misty, for the pictures and putting up with me and offering support because you love imaginary worlds and fiction as much as I do. And for the real Olga Worontzoff (GG), some day I hope to be just like you, a youthful ninety-five-year-old doing the Kalinka at The Fiddlin' Pig.

Sincere appreciation also goes to the wonderful community of Grand Haven, for providing me with the setting that served as so much inspiration for this book. If any of my readers have never visited this town during the summer, add it to your bucket list!

Finally, my deepest thanks to all my teachers throughout the years. You introduced me to books and together, made me believe in a world where I could go anywhere and be anything I wanted to be when I grew up. And the person I most wanted to be like was you. And to all my past, present, and future students: you can go anywhere and be anything you want to be, and you will. Also, you are alllllllllll my favorites and thank you to every single young adult (or wannabe YA) out there who read this book.

About the Author

Jamie Ayres writes young adult paranormal love stories by night and teaches young adults as a public school teacher by day.

When not at home on her laptop or at school, she can often be found at a local book store grabbing random children and reading to them. So far, she has not been arrested for this.

She lives in southwest Florida with her prince charming, two children (sometimes three based on how Mr. Ayres is acting), and a basset hound. She spent her youthful summers in Grand Haven, Michigan and this setting provided the inspiration for her debut novel, 18 Things.

She really does have grandmothers named Olga and Gay but unlike her heroine, she's thankfully not named after either one of them. She loves lazy pajama days, the first page of a good book, stupid funny movies, and sharing stories with fantastic people like you.

Visit her website at: www.jamieayres.com

Literature Circle Questions for 18 Things

1. Compare and contract Olga to another character in the novel.

2. Imagine you are Nate. Create mottos or bumper stickers that reflect your philosophy of life.

3. How do the quotes at the beginning of each chapter apply to the story at the time?

4. How do you think a person can learn to accept, not resent, pain and even find a bit of good in the long-term from their unfortunate circumstance?

5. At the beginning of the story, Olga is scared to say the words *I love you.* Why? How do Olga's feelings about those words change during the course of the story?

6. Describe the incident when Olga attends her first 'real' party at Kyle's house where Cantankerous Monkey Squad performs and its effect on Olga and Nate's relastionship.

7. What are some of the clues you can indicate after reading the book that hint at the paranormal twist at the end? How does seeing the truth of the story at the end change your understanding of it?

8. Name an internal and external conflict for our protagonists Olga and Nate. What are some internal and external conflicts in your own life?

9. What character traits of Olga and Nate's personalities make them compelling protagonists in this story?

10. Do you believe in angels and spirit guides? Why or why not?

11. Even though the Limbo realm wasn't real, how did Dr. Judy explain that Olga and Nate's actions still affected real life for their loved ones? How can believing in something help it come true?

12. Which item on the list do you think transformed Olga the most? Make a life list of your own 18 things you want to do by the year of your 18th birthday.

13. Olga tells the story in her own first-person voice. How might the book differ if it had been told in Nate's voice? Or in a dual narrative? Or in the voice of an omniscient narrator?

14. Has this novel changed the way you regard human suffering and death? Why or why not?

15. Consider the title of the novel. Are each of Olga's 18 things of equal importance? Which one did you find to be the most unexpected? Most scary? Most humorous? Most Poignant?

16. Describe the events that led Olga to swallow a bottle of pain pills. If you were a character in the story, what would you say to Olga to stop her?

17. Describe one of Olga's memories of Conner. Do you have childhood memories with a friend that is similar to Olga's? How do you think your memories would change if they were inextricably linked to feelings of guilt?

18. How is Tammy a stereotype in some parts of the story? How is she different from other cheerleaders portrayed in young adult novels?

19. Describe Olga and Tammy's relationship and the role that jealousy plays in their friendship. Are you ever jealous of your friends? What effect does that have on your behavior or your feelings for them?

20. Some of the items on Olga's list of 18 Things cause her to rebel against her parents beliefs. Knowing the consequences, would you still try to rebel against your parents to accomplish things on your life list? What would be the pros and cons?

Thank You For Reading

Curiosity Quills Press
http://curiosityquills.com

Please visit http://curiosityquills.com/reader-survey/ to share your reading experience with the author of this book!

Buried, by Gerilyn Marin

Fane's Cove isn't the average coastal town- not with wandering apparitions, disembodied voices and poltergeist activity occurring on a regular basis- but the residents are used to it. As far as they know, it's simply always been that way.

Somehow, Cadence McKenna can't shake the feeling that the seemingly-normal new resident, Gray Addison, is hiding something stranger than all of the town's odd happenings combined and she's determined to find out what that is – by any means necessary.

The Gathering Darkness, by Lisa Collicutt

They say: "the third time's the charm" and for sixteen-year-old Brooke Day, they had better be right. She doesn't know it yet but she's been here before—twice in fact. Though, she's never lived past the age of sixteen.

Now in her third lifetime, Brooke must stay alive until the equinox, when she will be gifted with a limited-time use of ancient power. Only then will she be able to defeat the evil that has plagued her for centuries.

Echoes of Dark and Light, by Chris Shanley-Dillman

Seventeen-year-old Bobby Rivers disguises herself as a young man in order to fight in the Civil War. She dares this mission for two reasons: first to fight for the country she loves, and second to find her older brother who came up missing in the Battle of Gettysburg.

Bobby joins up with the 27th Infantry of Michigan Volunteers, and the story follows their real life time line though many battles including The Crater and The Wilderness. On her quest, Bobby finds herself also battling issues within herself, like fear, trust, strength, morality, and falling in love.

Scrapbook of My Revolution, by Amy Lynn Spitzley

I may as well say it up front. I'm Malian. Yeah, one of the freaks.

I've got gold skin and the ability to read emotions. It's great fun, too, believe me. Right… Anger. Frustration. Desire. Try reading those all day!

But I'm not the only one who's frustrated. We're all mixed-up and sick of the bad press and attacks from Regulars. Things are changing, though. I'm getting other Malians at school together. We might be able to show people that we're just as human as they are…

…unless one of my best supporters is really public enemy number one.

Zarconian Island, by Aja Hannah

Alexandra "Attie" Hotep is no virgin to attacks. Her ancestors, the Zarconians, were hunted to near-extinction, leaving the existence of their home, Atlantis, and their people little more than myth.

When a class trip turns deadly, Attie and her friends become stranded in the middle of the Pacific, and Attie finds herself targeted once more.

Enter Doug Hutchinson – the school's soccer star with his own secrets. Attie and Doug soon realize the uncharted island's wild animals aren't the only threats. There is a traitor amidst the group, one that plans to turn all Zarconians into permanent myths. And Attie is next.

Fade, by A.K. Morgen

When Arionna Jacobs meets Dace Matthews, everything she thought she knew about herself and the world around them begins to fall apart.

Neither of them understands what is happening to them, or why, and they're running out of time to figure it out.

An ancient Norse prophesy of destruction has been set into motion, and what destiny has in store for them is bigger than either could have ever imagined.

CPSIA information can be obtained at www.ICGtesting.com
Printed in the USA
LVOW08s2239070114

368544LV00005B/339/P

9 781620 071519